Praise for t

BE MINE

New York Times Bestselling Author
Jennifer Crusie

"Crusie has a gift for concocting nutty scenarios and witty one-liners... Genuine laughs."
—*People*

"Few popular writers handle light romantic comedy as deftly as Jennifer Crusie."
—*Boston Globe* on *Bet Me*

"Crusie seems incapable of writing a boring page, or one that's not aglow."
—*Kirkus Reviews* on *What the Lady Wants*

***USA TODAY* Bestselling Author**
Victoria Dahl

"This is one hot romance."
—*RT Book Reviews* on *Good Girls Don't*

"Sassy and smokingly sexy, *Talk Me Down* is one delicious joyride of a book."
—*New York Times* bestselling author Connie Brockway

"[A] hands-down winner, a sensual story filled with memorable characters."
—*Booklist* on *Start Me Up*

New York Times Bestselling Author
Shannon Stacey

"Books like this are why I read romance."
—*Smart Bitches, Trashy Books* on *Exclusively Yours*

"Shannon Stacey's books deliver exactly what we need in contemporary romances.... I feel safe that every time I pick up a Stacey book I'm going to read something funny, sexy and loving."
—Jane Litte of *Dear Author* on *All He Ever Needed*

"I'm madly in love with the Kowalskis!"
—*New York Times* bestselling author Nalini Singh

Jennifer Crusie

BE MINE

Victoria Dahl & Shannon Stacey

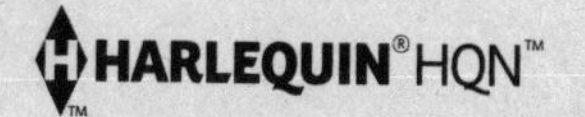

ISBN-13: 978-0-373-77706-8

Recycling programs for this product may not exist in your area.

BE MINE

This edition published by arrangement with Harlequin Books S.A.

For questions and comments about the quality of this book, please contact us at CustomerService@Harlequin.com.

Printed in U.S.A.

CONTENTS

SIZZLE

For Mary Beth Pringle,
who once told me that if I tried, I could write anything.
So I did.

CHAPTER ONE

"BUT, I DON'T WANT A partner," Emily Tate said through her teeth. "I like working alone." She clenched her fists to pound them on the desk in front of her and then unclenched them and smoothed down the jacket of her business suit, instead. "I don't need a partner, George."

Her boss looked exasperated, and she automatically put her hand to her hair to make sure every strand was in place, that no dark curls had escaped from her tight French twist. Be cool, calm and detached, she told herself. *I want to kill him for this.*

"Look, Em." George tossed a folder across the table to her. "Those are the cost estimates from your Paradise project and the final costs after you brought the project in."

Emily winced and clasped her hands in front of her. "I know. I went way over. But we still showed a mammoth profit. In fact, Paradise was the biggest money-maker Evadne Inc. has ever had. The bottom line, George, is that we made money for the company." I *made money for the company,* she thought, *but I can't say that. Be modest and cooperative, Emily.*

"Yeah, we did." George Bartlett leaned back in his chair, looking up at her.

I hate it when he does that, Emily thought. *He's short, fat and balding, and he doesn't have a quarter of my brains, but he's the one leaning back in the chair while I stand at attention. I want to be the one leaning back in the chair. Except I wouldn't. It would be rude.* She sighed.

"Listen to me, Emily," George said. "You almost lost your job over this last project."

"You got a promotion because of this last project," Emily said.

"Yeah, because of the profit. If it hadn't made a profit, we'd have both been canned. Henry wasn't happy."

Henry Evadne was never happy, Emily thought. It didn't have anything to do with her.

George leaned forward. "I don't want to lose you, Emily. You're smart, and you have a sixth sense about marketing that I'd kill to have. But you screw up the financial side on this next deal, and no profit is going to save you, no matter how big."

Emily swallowed. "I'll bring it in under budget."

"You're damn right you will, because you'll be working with Richard Parker."

"Who is Richard Parker?"

"He's a whiz kid from the Coast," George said.

"He did an analysis of the Paradise project. It's in the folder, too. You ought to read it. He wasn't too complimentary."

"George, how much have we made on Paradise?" Emily demanded.

George looked smug. "Close to four million as of last month."

"Then why am I getting whiz kids from the Coast and nasty reviews in my project folders? Where's the champagne?"

George shook his head. "You could have flopped."

"I never flop."

"Well, someday you will," George said philosophically. "And when you do, you better flop under budget. Which is exactly what Richard Parker is here to guarantee. You're meeting him at eleven in his office."

"His office?"

"Next floor up," George said with a grin. "Two doors from the president. Nice view from up there, I'm told."

"Why not my office?"

"Emily, please."

"Is he in charge of this project? Because if so, I quit."

"No, no." George waved his hands at her. "Just the financial end. And you're not the only one he's working with. He's financial adviser for all our projects. It's still your baby, Em. He just watches the spending." He looked at her closely. She'd made her face a blank, but she knew the anger was still in her eyes. "Emily, please cooperate."

"His office at eleven," she said, clamping down on her rage.

"That's it," George said, relieved.

EMILY SLAMMED HER OFFICE door and slumped into her rolling desk chair. Jane, her secretary, followed her in more sedately and sat in the chair across from her. She broke a frozen almond Hershey bar in half and tossed the larger piece to her boss.

"I keep this in the coffee-room freezer for emergencies," she said. "And I've given you the biggest half. Greater love hath no friend."

"How do you keep people from stealing it?" Emily asked, pulling off the foil.

"They know I work for you," Jane said. "They know I could send you after them."

"No, really, how do you do it?"

"I keep it in a freezer container marked 'Asparagus,'" Jane said, sucking on the chocolate.

"And nobody asks what you're doing with asparagus at work?" Emily broke off a small piece of the chocolate and put it on her tongue. The richness spread through her mouth, and she sighed and sat back in her chair.

"They probably figure I keep it for you—you're

the type who looks like you only put fruits and vegetables in your body." Jane studied her. "How come you never gain weight? We eat the same stuff, but I'm fighting ten extra pounds while you look like you're losing. And you've got nothing to lose."

"Frustration," Emily said, breaking off another tiny piece. "I'm working for narrow-minded patriarchal creeps."

"In the plural?" Jane finished her half and checked the foil for crumbs. "Did George clone himself?"

"Evidently," Emily said. "I now have a budget adviser to answer to. Some suit named Richard Parker."

"Oooh," Jane said. "Him I've seen. Things are looking up."

"Not a suit?"

"Oh, yeah, but what a suit. Too bad I'm happily married." Jane sighed. "Tall. Dark. Handsome. Cheekbones. Chiseled lips. Blue eyes to die for. Never smiles. The secretaries are lining up to be seduced and so are the female junior execs, but it's not happening."

"No?" Emily broke off another piece of chocolate.

"He's a workhorse. All he thinks about is finance. Karen says he's always still here working when she leaves."

"Karen?"

"That tiny little blonde on the twelfth floor. She's his secretary now."

"Make good friends with Karen. We need a spy in the enemy camp."

"No problem," Jane said, licking her fingers to get the last of her chocolate. "She loooves to talk about the boss."

"Good, good," Emily said. "He could be a real problem for us."

"How so?"

"He's controlling the money."

"And we're not good with money." Jane nodded wisely. "Good thing Paradise took off like it did. It's been fun rising to the top with you, but I wasn't looking forward to hitting the bottom together when we went sailing over the budget."

"You wouldn't have hit bottom," Emily said. "George isn't dumb. He'd steal you as his own secretary."

"I'm not dumb, either," Jane said. "You and I stay together. I knew when I met you in high school that you were going places and taking me with you. President and secretary of the senior class. President and secretary of student council. President and secretary of our sorority in college. I'm hanging around until you make president of this dump." She threw her foil away and smiled smugly. "I've already made secretary."

"You're every bit as smart as I am," Emily said. "Why don't you let me get you into an executive-training program?"

"Because I'm smarter than you are," Jane said. "I'm making more than most executives here right now, and I don't have to kiss up to the boss. Are you going to eat the rest of that chocolate?"

"Yes," Emily said.

"So I gather you slammed the door in honor of Richard Parker?"

"Yes."

"I know how you can handle Richard Parker."

"How?" Emily broke off another piece of chocolate. She wasn't interested in handling Richard Parker. She wanted, in fact, to eliminate him, but she was always interested in Jane. She didn't insist that the company pay Jane a lavish salary just because they were friends; she insisted because Jane had a lot of ideas and none of them were dumb. If Emily did get to be president, it would be due as much to Jane's brains as to Emily's.

"I think you should seduce him," Jane said.

Emily reconsidered her thoughts about Jane not having dumb ideas. This seemed to be one.

"Why?"

"Because you need to get out more. You live in the office. You only stop by your apartment to shower and change. You don't even have a pet, for crying out loud. I'm your only companionship."

"I like it that way."

"Well, it's not natural. And it sounds like Parker is the same way. You could save each other. He'll be grateful and fall in love with you, you'll get married, and I'll get to buy baby gifts, instead of accepting them from you. You're not going to eat that chocolate, are you?"

"Yes," Emily said, breaking off another piece. "How will marrying Richard Parker help me?"

"Sex always helps," Jane said. "It's like chocolate."

"I need help at the office," Emily said. "This guy is going to tie my hands."

"Kinky."

"Be nice to Karen," Emily said. "This could get very dirty. Now go get Parker on the phone. I have an eleven-o'clock meeting with him, and I want to hear what he sounds like first."

"A meeting, huh? Why don't you change your look? Let that long dark hair down. Take off your suit jacket. Especially take off your glasses. You look like a bug."

"I want to look like a bug. I have a hard enough time getting respect around here looking like a bug. If I start taking off my clothes, no one will pay attention."

"Want to bet?" Jane looked at her boss. "If I had your body, I'd take off my clothes all the time."

"You do take off your clothes all the time,"

Emily pointed out. "Has Ben ever seen you clothed?"

"Certainly," Jane said. "I was dressed for my wedding. You were there. You slapped the best man at the reception."

"You never forget, do you?"

Jane got up and headed for the door. "I'll get Parker. Don't slap him. I'll make friends with Karen, but we'll get further if you seduce the guy."

"Feel free to sacrifice my body for your ambitions," Emily said as Jane went through the door.

"Our ambitions," Jane said. "And I've seen him. It would be no sacrifice."

"MR. PARKER ON LINE TWO," Jane said in her secretary voice.

Emily picked up the phone. "Mr. Parker?"

"Yes?"

"This is Emily Tate. I understand we have a meeting at eleven."

"Yes, Ms. Tate, we do." He sounded bored but patient. She'd been expecting the high tight tones of a monomaniac; his voice was deep with a little bit of New York rhythm in it.

"Is there anything you'd like me to bring to the meeting?"

"No, Ms. Tate, I have everything I need. Is there anything else?"

Sorry, Emily thought. *Taking up your time, am I?* "No, Mr. Parker, there's nothing else."

"Eleven, then," he said, and hung up.

Not good, Emily thought. Efficient and not impressed with her in spite of her terrific track record. Which must mean he was still hung up on the budget overruns.

Jane poked her head in. "Okay, so he's not a charmer. But I still say go for it. Maybe he loosens up in bed."

"Not a chance." Emily hung up the phone. "He probably doesn't go to bed. He probably sleeps standing up in a corner of his office."

"Do you need me in the meeting to take notes?"

"No. Do you want to take notes?"

"Yes."

"Then come along, sweetie, and we'll have lunch at the Celestial afterward. We can discuss the situation."

"Good idea."

"And, Jane, try to pretend you're really a secretary in there. He doesn't need to know you're the brains of our outfit."

"I'll stick a pencil through my bun and borrow your glasses," Jane said.

"What bun?"

"I'll have one by eleven."

"This I've got to see."

WHEN EMILY LEFT THE OFFICE at five to eleven, Jane really had pulled her hair into a bun. It was a terrible bun, with wisps of hair escaping and two pencils jabbed through it, but it was indisputably a bun.

"That's really disgusting," Emily said as they waited for the elevator.

"Wait." Jane lifted Emily's glasses off her nose and put them on. "How do I look?"

"You look like a bug with a very bad hairdo," Emily said. "You look like Norman Bates's mother as a young mental patient. You look like—"

The elevator doors opened, and they got on with several other executives. Emily glanced sideways at Jane and tried not to laugh. If things got really bad, she'd just look at Jane and feel better.

"It's a good thing there's only going to be the three of us in this meeting," Emily whispered. "Anybody else would know you were up to something."

Jane pushed the glasses up the bridge of her nose, sniffed and said loudly and nasally, "I just want you to know, Ms. Tate, that it is an honor and a privilege to work for you, and I really mean that from the bottom of my heart."

"Thank you, Mrs. Frobish," Emily said. "Your loyalty is heartwarming."

"Do you have any of your chocolate left?"

"No."

Jane sniffed.

The conference room was across from the elevator. Once inside, Emily realized she'd made a mistake. It wasn't going to be just the three of them. There were six other executives in there, four of whom had brought their secretaries.

"What is this?" Emily whispered to Jane, frowning.

"I don't know," Jane whispered, "but I'm glad I'm here."

"I am, too," Emily whispered. "Guard my back."

The door at the other end of the conference room opened, and Richard Parker came in, tall, dark and serious. And indisputably the best-looking man Emily had ever seen. Distinguished. Beautifully dressed. Powerful. And sexy, Emily thought. Definitely sexy. Every executive there except Emily stiffened in his or her seat. Every secretary there except Jane smiled warmly. For everyone there, Richard Parker radiated power and authority. For the secretaries and female execs, he also radiated sex appeal. The power and the authority were conscious, Emily decided; the sex appeal wasn't.

He really is extraordinarily good-looking, Emily thought. *Except for his height and that jaw, he's almost pretty. Those electric blue eyes and long dark lashes. Not businesslike. How can*

I make that work against him? If he was female, it'd work against him.

His eyes swept the room and caught hers. She was the only one not looking at him with fear or lust. She met his eyes coolly and stared back at him, calculating. He was the enemy.

He raised his eyebrows at her and moved his gaze on. Jane made a note. Emily looked at her pad. "He's not stupid," Jane had written, "but you can take him."

Emily shook her head. Jane's one weakness was overestimating her.

George leaned over to Emily. "What's wrong with Jane? She looks funny."

"PMS," Emily whispered back, and George nodded solemnly.

Richard Parker looked up and frowned at them.

George blushed.

Emily raised her eyebrows at Parker.

He looked startled, and then his lips twitched.

Almost smiled there, didn't we? Emily thought. *You're not so tough. Maybe I* can *take you.*

"I've asked you to meet with me today to discuss your past performance in budgeting your marketing campaigns," Parker began. "It's abysmal."

Several of the executives tittered and then fell silent. A few colored and looked away. Emily yawned and checked her watch.

"Am I boring you, Ms. Tate?" Parker asked.

"Not at all." Emily smiled back politely. "I'm sure you'll make your point soon."

George closed his eyes.

"The point, Ms. Tate," Parker said without raising his voice, "is that you all regularly exceed your budgets, thereby cutting into the profits this company could be making. You alone went over your budget on the Paradise account by almost thirty percent. That's a lot of money, Ms. Tate. You may have thought there was no price too great to pay for Paradise, but I don't agree. You could have cost this company a fortune."

Emily smiled at him again.

"I could have, but I didn't, Mr. Parker," Emily said. "I made four million dollars for this company by having the guts to go thirty percent over budget."

"That doesn't take guts, Ms. Tate. That just takes lack of control. That's where I come in. I'm your control." Parker's eyes swept the room. "From now on all budgets go through me. So do all purchase orders, all payments. I'm the money pipeline. I'll make sure you get the money you need for your projects. And I'll make certain you stay within your budgets. Now, I'm sure you have questions about how this new procedure will operate, so let's get started."

He sat down and leaned back in his chair while the others began a process of hemming and hawing and assuring Parker that they appreciated his help and were anxious to work with him.

Jane wrote on her pad, "Don't antagonize him."

Emily fumed, although she kept her face a mask. No price too great to pay for Paradise. *Don't get snide with me, buddy,* she thought. *I didn't get where I am today taking that from anybody.*

And then she thought, *yes, I did. I'm modest, co-operative and polite, and I regularly back down. I back down in front of George, who is an idiot, all the time. Then Jane and I sneak around behind his back and get things done the way we want. What am I doing confronting this guy?*

She watched him listening to Croswell from Research and Development. He was listening politely and nodding, and she wanted to throw something.

He patronized me, she thought. *He assumed he was right, and he didn't listen, and he patronized me. He thinks I'm insignificant.*

Boy, is he going to pay for that.

I don't care how good-looking he is.

Without realizing it, she'd let her eyes narrow as she looked at him, so that when he gazed idly around while he listened to Croswell's drivel, he saw her look of undiluted antagonism. His eyes widened slightly, and then he grinned at her as if he was seeing her for the first time, a real smile that accepted her challenge and recognized her as an equal, sharing the absurdity of the moment and of his own new-kid-on-the-block power play.

It was a killer smile.

Emily narrowed her eyes even more. *It's going to take more than a smile, buddy boy. Hit me with another line like "no price too great for Paradise," and I'll wipe that smile off your face so fast you won't know what hit you.*

Jane nudged her and she looked down at the pad. It said, "Why is he smiling?"

Emily took the pad languidly and wrote, "Because he knows I'm angry, and he thinks it's amusing."

Jane took the pad back and wrote, "Then he's not as smart as I thought."

Emily nodded and turned her attention politely back to the group.

"Any other questions?" Parker surveyed the table before turning to Emily. "Ms. Tate, you've been very quiet. Do you have any questions?"

"No, I've found out all I need to know," she said calmly.

"Good. Do you have time to meet with me now?"

"Now?" Emily raised her eyebrows. "I have a lunch meeting. I could possibly meet with you at two."

"Let me check my appointments," he said. "I'll

have my secretary call yours." He looked at Jane for the first time and stopped.

What is she doing? Emily thought, not daring to look. She's probably blacked out a couple of teeth and is now grinning maniacally at him.

"Fine." Emily stood so that she blocked Jane. "Anything else?"

He stayed seated, watching her. "No. There's nothing else."

"Thank you," Emily said, and left with Jane clumping in her wake.

When the door closed behind them, Jane stopped clumping and took off her glasses. "That was dumb," she said flatly. "We get nothing by antagonizing him. What's wrong with you?"

"He's arrogant," Emily said, punching the elevator button.

"Everybody in that room's arrogant," Jane said. "The only difference is that he has reason to be."

"What? You've fallen for that 'hello, I'm God' presentation he just did?"

"He's right," Jane said. "We were over budget. We could have done the campaign for less. He could help you here."

"Whose side are you on?"

"Ours," Jane said. "First, last and always. I'm just not sure he's not on our side, too."

They got on the elevator, and Jane handed the glasses back to Emily. "He likes you."

"Please."

"He likes you. I saw his eyes. Which are incredible, by the way. He likes watching you. He thought you were cute."

"Cute!" Emily exploded. "Cute!"

"Make it work for you," Jane said.

"The hell I will. I'll give him cute." Emily stormed off the elevator and down the hall to her office, slamming the door behind her. A minute later, Jane came in with her coat.

"Your lunch meeting is here," she said. "You promised me Chinese."

"YOU'D HAVE TO DO THE new campaign for less, anyway," Jane said later over potstickers and sizzling rice soup. "The new stuff's not as expensive as Paradise. Your profit margin's lower."

"Not necessarily." Emily spooned the hot soup carefully into her mouth. "We'll sell more—to the younger woman who uses perfume more frequently. We'll be fine. *If* I'm not forced to under budget."

"Give him a chance," Jane said. "There's no point in firing the first shot."

"I haven't," Emily said. "I've just made it clear that I'll return fire."

Jane gave up for the time being. "Garlic chicken?"

"Not if I'm meeting with Attila the Budget Hun this afternoon. Did Karen call?"

"Yep. Two o'clock. His office."

"Of course." Emily sighed. "I'd prefer neutral ground. From now on let's make it the conference room. On our floor, not his."

"I'll try," Jane said. "Prawns?"

"Yes," Emily said. "I'm in the mood to crunch little backbones."

"Then we'll go shopping," Jane said. "I found this incredible pink lace bra and bikini—" She stopped and looked past Emily.

"Ladies."

It was the Hun with George in tow. George *would* bring him here, Emily thought. Showing the new boss the best place to eat. I'll bet he offers to pick up his dry cleaning later. She looked up and smiled tightly. "Mr. Parker. How nice to see you."

"George assures me this is an excellent place to have a lunch meeting." He looked at Jane.

"It is." Emily turned her back and began spooning soup again.

Jane grinned at him. "Lovely meeting you again."

"Oh, yes. You're Ms. Tate's secretary. Mrs. Frobish, isn't it? I didn't recognize you at first."

"Well, that's the lot of the secretary," Jane said cheerfully. "Unrecognized, unrewarded, underpaid..."

"Hardly underpaid," Parker said. "Your salary is part of the budget, you know. It's very generous."

"Actually," Emily said, staring straight ahead, "she is underpaid. And I shall fight tooth and nail to stop any attempt to reduce her salary or to curtail her future raises." She raised her eyes to Parker's, and the steel in her voice was also in her eyes.

"I have no intention of interfering with Mrs. Frobish's salary," Parker said, calmly. "A good secretary is worth her weight in gold."

"Good idea," Jane said. "I'll take that as a basis for my next raise. Let's have two orders of prawns now that I have a reason to gain weight."

Emily thought about stabbing Parker with her fork but decided it would be too overt. Subtlety is the key here, she thought.

"I'll see you at two, Ms. Tate," Parker said, and moved on to the table the waiter was patiently holding for him, George toddling along in his wake.

"I thought you were going to stab him with your fork," Jane said. "Bad move, careerwise, although as your friend I would have been touched."

"I've got to stop hating him." Emily stabbed an egg roll instead. "I've got to work with this overbearing, egotistical control freak."

"See?" Jane said. "Already you're speaking of him with warmth."

THE UNDERWEAR WAS made of hot-pink lace embroidered with silver thread, and Jane bought it. The bra was just two large pink lace roses stitched into demi-cups, held in place with tiny pink satin ribbons, and the bikini was a strip of the same roses and ribbons. It was silly and luxurious and sexy and fun.

"Ben is going to love this," Jane said. "Why don't you get some and try it on Richard?"

"Richard who?"

"Parker," Jane said patiently.

"He'd never go for it." Emily looked at the price tag. "It's not cost-effective. There are small countries that don't spend this much for defense."

"Defense is not what I have in mind." Jane looked at herself in the mirror. "I'm planning on surrendering almost immediately and being invaded shortly thereafter."

Emily sighed. "Sounds like fun."

Jane pounced. "You buy some, too."

"Why? There's no one interested in invading."

"Wrong. Croswell down in R & D still speaks of you with passion."

"Croswell was a mistake." Emily picked up a pink-and-silver lace bra and looked at it longingly. "If he tries to invade, I'm defending."

"Then go back to plan A. Richard."

Emily looked at the pink-and-silver lace and thought of Richard Parker. *If he'd just keep his mouth shut,* she thought, *I could stand it. In fact, I'd be very interested. That long lovely body.*

Those crazy blue eyes. That classic, chiseled, supple mouth.

That mouth. The one that kept opening and accepting his expensively shod foot. "No price too great to pay for Paradise."

"Hardly underpaid."

"Not even if he was unconscious." Emily put the underwear back. "Let's go. I have a meeting at two."

"I'VE LOOKED AT YOUR preliminary ideas," Richard the Hun said. "You're not being cost-effective."

"Already?" Emily tried to stay calm. "I've barely started."

"Rubies." He tossed a folder across the table to her.

"Look, we marketed Paradise with diamonds. Very classy stone. But this new stuff is for a younger hotter market. So rubies. Still classy, but hotter."

"Fine." He shrugged. "Use paste."

"This is for photographs." Emily folded her hands calmly and clenched them until her knuckles went white. "We're not studding the bottles with them."

"Can you rent them?"

"Loose stones? I don't know." Emily tried to consider it, but she was against it. "We might be able to buy and resell. I don't know much about gemstones."

"Well, I know a little, and what you're suggesting would tie up half your budget."

"Gems are a good investment." Emily deliberately unclenched her hands. "We wouldn't lose money."

He shook his head. "We're not in the gem-investment business. Rent them."

Emily shook her head. "We might need the same stones back again for later pictures. We couldn't be sure we'd get them. Plus, we often use them in special displays at openings and benefits. We did this with Paradise, and it was very successful."

He leaned back in his desk chair and looked at her steadily.

"Are you really serious about this, or is this just something you're going to fight me on?"

Hasn't he been listening to me? Emily thought. *Do I sound like I'm playing games?* "I'm serious. And I never fight just for the sake of fighting."

"That was a business lunch today?"

"Jane knows more about this company than you or I do." Emily clenched her hands again. "When you've been here a little longer, you'll know that. I consult with her often, and I value her opinions highly. So, yes, that really was a business lunch."

"Pink lace underwear?" He smiled at her dryly.

He would overhear that comment, she thought.

Emily smiled back sweetly. "I told her you wouldn't think it was cost-effective."

"I don't look at everything in terms of cost, Ms. Tate." His eyes dropped almost involuntarily to the open collar of her blouse.

Emily raised her eyebrows at him, and he flushed. He looked good flushed. *What do you know,* she thought. *He's human. There may be hope.* "I'm sure you don't, Mr. Parker. And I'm hoping you'll see that in the case of the rubies, cost-effectiveness simply doesn't apply. We're selling emotions here, the sizzle not the steak." She leaned across the desk to him, suddenly earnest, trying to convince him. "You can't sizzle with paste, Richard. You need the real thing."

His eyes had widened a little at her use of his name.

"All right." He cleared his throat. "I'll take it under consideration. Now, the next item…"

Emily worked with him for another hour, politely agreeing on a few things she didn't care about, anyway, leaving the others open for further discussion, trying to build a foundation of compromise so that when she came back for real money, for rubies and whatever else she wanted, he'd be used to negotiating with her, not flatly dismissing her. From the look in his eyes, he had a fairly good idea of what she was doing, but he was patient with her. Toward the end, Emily realized her plan wasn't working; any compromising had been done by her, not him. Richard liked saying no or yes and moving on.

When she stood up to go, Richard pushed back his chair and stood, too. "We'll have to meet again. We haven't accomplished much."

"I wouldn't say that." Emily tried to smile warmly but her lips were tight. "I think we've established a very creditable working relationship." She held out her hand. "Please call Jane if you need any information. She knows exactly what's going on."

He took her hand and held it for a moment, and she tried to ignore the warmth he generated there. "I'd rather talk to you. I like to go straight to the person in charge."

"Then definitely talk to Jane." Emily pulled her hand away. "She's been running my life since high school."

"I thought I sensed a lot more there than just boss-and-secretary." He came around the desk and walked her to the door.

"We're partners."

"I envy you. I've always worked alone." He stopped by the door. "Would you consider having dinner with me tonight? To go over some of these points again? Maybe in a…warmer atmosphere, we could get closer on some of these disagreements."

He smiled down at her, and Emily was caught

off guard, her knees going to jelly while she frantically tried to gather her thoughts under the wattage of that suddenly sweet, boyishly endearing, sexy smile.

He's a Hun, she told herself. *Unless you want to be invaded, turn back now.*

"Sorry," she croaked. "I have a dinner engagement."

"Jane again?"

"Oh, no. Jane goes home to a husband and three lovely children."

"And you?"

"I go home to cost-effectiveness reports." Emily opened the door. "I have a very tough budget adviser."

She didn't turn around as she walked down the hall, but she could feel him watching her all the way to the elevator.

"How did it go?" Jane asked, following her into the office.

"Not well, but not badly, either." Emily kicked off her shoes. "I really hate panty hose. They itch."

"Back to Richard," Jane said firmly. "What happened?"

"I tried to compromise. He told me what to do. He likes telling people what to do. He listened part of the time. At one point, he looked down my blouse and blushed. He asked me to dinner."

"Wear something sexy."

"I'm not going. I told him I had a previous engagement. He thought it was with you, but I told him you were happily married. That's about it."

"Go out with him." Jane sat down and folded her arms on Emily's desk. "Sleep with him."

"Sell my body for a perfume campaign?" Emily shook her head. "Not likely."

"No." Jane leaned back, disgusted with her. "The hell with the perfume campaign. Share your body for a wonderful experience. He looks like a wonderful experience. Did you see his hands?"

Emily frowned. "I must have, but I didn't pay attention."

"He has great hands. And he's really very charming. He's a little obsessive about getting his own way, but he's not a Hun."

"No."

"Listen, Em." Jane leaned over the desk again and caught Emily's hand. "I'm worried about you. You haven't had a serious relationship since you dumped that fool Croswell in R & D. That was two years ago. You're not getting any younger. You're obsessive about your work, and that's not going to change. You've just met a truly beautiful man who is also obsessive about his work, but who has focused his eyes on you long enough to ask you to dinner. You could build a life as obsessive executives together. You could have great obsessive sex together. You could have little obsessive children in suits together. This is the man for you. Go buy that pink lace bra and seduce this guy before you're too old to wear pink lace."

"I will never be too old to wear pink lace," Emily said.

"Are you wearing any now?"

"What do you mean?"

"Do you have anything sexy or fun in your whole wardrobe?"

"I have some white lace. Sort of."

"You may already be too old to wear pink lace. Mentally you're already in gray flannel long johns."

Emily sighed and thought about what Jane was saying because she always thought about what Jane was saying. Then she shook her head. "I could never be serious about somebody who told me what to do all the time. Telling people what to do is this guy's reason for living."

"So change him." Jane leaned back again. "He has one tiny fault and the rest of him is perfect. Teach him not to boss you around."

"Maybe." Emily thought about it.

"That's a start." Jane got up to go. "Keep an open mind. I bet he can make love like crazy."

Change him, Emily thought. *No, better yet, change me. I'm in this position because I'm modest, cooperative and polite. Because I'm modest, cooperative and polite, I'm working for a vain, ob-*

structive, rude man like George. And as if George wasn't enough, now I have Richard Parker, the Budget Hun.

A Hun who can make my knees go weak when he smiles, dammit.

Well, no more of that, she told herself. *I'm tired of being told what to do. Starting tomorrow, Richard Parker treats me like a partner, not a slave. Starting tomorrow, I am going to make that man listen to me.*

And starting tomorrow, my knees are going to stiffen up, too.

CHAPTER TWO

"THAT MAN IS GOING to listen to me," Emily told Jane the next morning. "I am going to be courteous and cooperative, but still forceful and demanding."

"This should be interesting." Jane looked skeptical.

"I will stun him with my competence." Emily stuck out her chin. "I will keep an open mind."

And during the week that followed, Emily did her best, but she was doomed. Richard kept ordering her to send him files, ordering her to meet him for meetings and ordering her to arrange conferences until she was ready to throw the whole campaign in his face. When she came into the office on Friday morning and Jane told her that Richard wanted her in the conference room, she broke.

"Too damn bad!" She slammed her briefcase down on her desk. "I have things to do."

"Courteous and cooperative." Jane handed her a folder. "Here's his cost estimates. You won't like them. I think it's showdown time. Be nice to him, but let him know he can't dictate to you. You know, forceful and demanding."

"What happened to marry him and be obsessive together?"

"You can do both. Hey, I did the same thing with Ben. I was nice to him, but I let him know he couldn't dictate to me."

"Ben never dictates to you."

"See?" Jane grinned at her. "It works."

EMILY WAS RUNNING DOWN his cost estimates when Richard met her in the conference room.

"Here." He tossed a small black bottle at her. "Put some of this on."

She caught it and glared at him.

"It's the product." He dropped some folders onto the table and sat down, opening one. "Let's see what it smells like."

The hell with you, Emily thought. *She held it out to him.* "You put it on. We'll see what it smells like on you."

"I tried it last night." He sorted through the folder without looking at her. "It took me two showers to get it all off before I came to work."

"Then you know what it smells like." She put the bottle on the table and returned her attention to the estimates.

"Put it on." He pulled a legal pad for notes out of his briefcase. "See what you think." He looked over at her for the first time and waited for her reaction.

Courteous and cooperative.

Emily sighed and pulled the stopper out of the bottle, putting her fingers over the opening and flipping the bottle over to release a few drops. She tapped the drops behind her ears and on her wrists, then replaced the stopper. "It's nice." She picked up the estimate report again.

"Just nice?" he asked.

"I'm not much for perfume," she said, and he laughed.

"You're responsible for selling four million dollars' worth of perfume. I should think you'd be interested."

"Look." Emily dropped the report, exasperated. "If you got a job selling tampons tomorrow, you'd work hard so you'd be successful, right? Even though you personally aren't much interested in tampons?"

Richard lost his smile, taken aback by her intensity. "Well, yes. Why are you so angry?"

"Because you're treating me as if I were an amusing child." Emily folded her hands in front of her, clenching them to keep her temper. "An amusing *female* child. That crack you made at the meeting, about 'no price too great to pay for Paradise' being my motto was insulting. You would never have made it to a male executive. And now telling me to wear the perfume. Would you ask George to wear it?"

"That's different."

"No, it's not. He's never smelled it, either."

Richard looked uncomfortable. "George isn't part of our team."

"Throwing a bottle of perfume at someone and ordering her to wear it is not teamwork!" Emily snapped. "It's not a team. It's a boss and a flunky, and I am nobody's flunky. I told you I wouldn't put on that perfume, and you simply ordered me to put it on again. You give me orders, and you never listen to me. This is not a partnership. This is not teamwork. I don't need this." She slammed her portfolio closed and stood up.

"You're right," Richard said.

She stopped and glared at him, and he rubbed his hand over the back of his head and smiled at her ruefully. At that moment, he looked more like a boy than a man, sheepish and apologetic. It was devastatingly effective.

"I'm used to being the boss." His eyes pleaded with her. "I'm sorry."

Emily sat down again. *It would be a whole lot easier to stay mad at him if he wasn't so damn charming,* she told herself. *That smile must get him a lot.* She opened her portfolio. "All right, then, *listen.* Our main problem with this product is that we have to distinguish it from Paradise. And that's going to take more than a different name. More than just switching from diamonds to rubies. And it's so important that anything we can do to make the difference clear to the consumer will be worth extra money in the long run."

Richard pulled the cap from his pen, prepared to listen so hard he'd take notes. "All right, how is it different?"

"It's cheaper. But it would be suicide to market it that way."

"Granted." He was still trying to cooperate. "Does it smell different from Paradise?"

"Of course." She unstoppered the bottle again. "It's spicier, sharper. Paradise was heavier, fruitier. We marketed Paradise as a slow, languid, sexy scent." Emily waved the stopper in front of her to smell the scent in the air. "This stuff has more of an edge. We could try for a more exciting approach, I suppose."

She touched the stopper to the back of her hand and sniffed. "It definitely has an edge." She frowned as she replaced the stopper in the bottle and flipped the bottle upside down to moisten it. Then she absentmindedly touched the stopper to the hollow at the base of her throat. "It's just as sexy as Paradise, really. Just different." She moved the stopper down into the V of her blouse, stroking it between her breasts.

Richard watched her, fascinated.

"It will be a while before the scent is true," she told him. "It needs to be warmed by my skin."

"Oh." He swallowed. "Fine."

"It doesn't matter if you don't know much about perfume," she said to reassure him. "We just sell the sizzle, not the steak, remember?"

"Right." Richard cleared his throat. "Does this perfume have sizzle?"

Emily rubbed the silk of her blouse against the skin between her breasts to release more scent and wriggled her nose as it floated up to her. "Yes. Actually, this is pretty good stuff."

He cleared his throat again. "So, uh, how would you base the campaign?"

"Well," she said slowly, "we marketed Paradise as sex—you know, the heavy, filled feeling you get when—"

"Right." He nodded. "I know."

"This stuff is more like…foreplay. You know, exciting and edgy."

"Foreplay."

"I wonder if this stuff builds the longer it's on. We could tie that to sexual excitement. Then we could direct this to a younger, faster customer. If Paradise was classy sex, this stuff could be kinky sex." She saw his eyebrows go up. "Well, not whips and chains, but still…sizzle. I wonder…"

She unstoppered the bottle and slid the black crystal stopper into the V of her blouse again.

He turned away. “Will you stop that?”

“Sorry. I know. Too much perfume can make you gag. I just had an idea…”

“What?”

She leaned forward across the table, and she saw his eyes drop to the V of her blouse. “I’m sorry about the perfume. I’ll wash it off, but listen. Suppose we put something in this stuff to make it *really* sizzle?”

“Sizzle?”

“You know.” She frowned in frustration. “Tingle. Only with heat. A woman wears perfume on the warmest parts of her body—the pulse points. Suppose when she touched the perfume to those places she felt a subtle heat and tingle. It would make her feel excited. Exciting. It would feel like…”

“Foreplay.” Richard grinned, taking Emily’s breath away for a moment. “Well, you’ve got my attention.”

She smiled back, taken with her new idea. “We could call it Sizzle. We’ll get it a product placement in the next really hot movie, something with an electric sex scene. We can package samples with other sexy products for women…”

“Such as?”

“Seamed hose, lace garter belts…” She broke off when she saw him laughing. She sat back and gritted her teeth. “You don’t like the idea?”

"No, no. It's great. It's just you. You're so intense, talking about lace underwear."

"My intensity is what makes me a success," she said evenly. "*You'd* take this perfume, call it 'Night in the Boardroom' and sell three bottles of it."

"Probably," Richard agreed.

"So don't patronize me." Emily looked him straight in the eye. "I don't deserve it."

"I apologize again." He leaned toward her, sincerely sorry. "I really do. Listen, let me make it up to you. Let me take you to dinner tonight." He smiled, and she lost her breath again.

"Come on, Emily." Richard coaxed her with his eyes. He had amazing eyes. "You've got all that perfume on—you really should go somewhere in it."

He has eyes like the sky, she thought. *I love the way he says my name.* And then she thought, *no. I don't need this. I don't even like him.*

"Please." He smiled that earnest killer smile at her.

Don't do that, she thought.

"Strictly business. We can talk about the account. About seven?"

I really don't like him, smile or no smile, but I bet he has a great body under that suit. Not that it matters. "All right." Emily took a deep breath. "If it's all right with you, I'll send a memo to the lab and to the advertising people on this."

"Fine." Richard sat back and picked up his notes, obviously pleased she'd agreed, the human in him fast receding behind the businessman. "Although we'll probably have to scale down some of your ideas."

"Which ones?" Emily asked coldly.

He was back into his reports and he didn't hear the chill. "Well, the product placement will be a fortune. We'll reach more people with print."

"But not the same way." Emily leaned forward. "In a movie, they'll see someone beautiful stroke herself with the perfume, use the stuff against her skin and then go out and have incredible sex with some gorgeous guy. If we get really lucky," she added thoughtfully, "it will be a very explicit scene, and the audience will get another look at all the places she put the perfume."

"And if the movie flops?"

"It flops." She shrugged. "Life's a gamble."

"Not with company funds." Richard shook his pencil at her. "You'll stay inside the budget this time."

She ignored the pencil. "If we get this stuff placed in the right movie, it could be bigger than Paradise."

"And if we get it placed in the wrong movie, we'll go to executive hell." He turned back to his papers.

She took a deep breath. *Calm. Courteous and*

cooperative. "I'm still going to suggest it in the memo."

He didn't look up. "Just as long as you realize I'm probably still going to reject it in the budget."

"Fine," she said, and slammed her portfolio shut.

"Fine," he said, and looked up and smiled. "See you at seven."

"I've got a dinner date with the executive Hun," Emily said to Jane as she passed her desk. Jane rose and followed her into the office.

"Tell me everything."

"It's a toss-up." Emily slumped into her chair. "His face is still beautiful, but he also still has a narrow, little cost-effective mind."

"Which means he disagreed with you."

"Oh, please."

"So where are you going?"

"I have no idea. He, of course, will decide." Emily frowned. "What do you want to bet he orders for me?"

"Why do you care? You can sit and look at him all night."

"A pretty face isn't everything," Emily told her primly.

"Forget the face." Jane sank into her chair. "The body is to die for."

"How can you tell? The man is always in a suit. I bet he sleeps in a tie."

"Karen went in to give him some papers, and he was changing his shirt. He'd spilled coffee on it, and he keeps a spare for emergencies."

"He would."

"She saw him with his shirt off."

"And?"

"She's still speechless."

"I doubt he'll take his shirt off at dinner."

"No, but if you play your cards right…"

"Don't you ever think of anything but sex?"

"Frequently. But let's face it, here. You're not going to dinner to work on Perfume X. You're attracted to him."

"Sizzle."

"Pardon?"

"Perfume X is now Sizzle."

"And does it?"

"It will. I'm on my way to R & D."

"Well, this should be an interesting campaign. What are you going to wear?"

"For what?"

"For dinner, dummy. I suggest you wear something sexy. Drive him wild."

"The only thing I do that drives Richard Parker wild is spend company money. Which reminds me, will you get me Laura in Los Angeles? We need a product placement."

"Big bucks. Did we get the Hun's okay to spend the money?"

"No, we're going to surprise him." Emily smiled evilly. "That man positively needs more surprises in his life."

"HEY, EM. WHAT'S NEW?" Laura said when Emily was put through to her.

"Perfume. A hot new perfume called Sizzle. We need a product placement. Something very sexy."

"Is this the next Paradise?"

"If I have anything to say about it, it will be."

"Then it will be." Laura laughed. "You *always* have something to say about it. I'll get right on it."

"Thanks. How's Gary?"

"Gone," Laura said cheerfully.

"Good. I never liked him."

"He never liked you, either. Thought you were a suit."

"He was right. You don't sound too unhappy about this."

"Oh, he was always just a filler. Only a desperate woman would take Gary seriously."

"Only a desperate woman would take *any* man seriously."

"And you're the woman marketing Sizzle?"

"I said 'seriously.' I've decided you don't have to take a man seriously to have sex." Emily visualized Richard as a cheap pickup to be thrown away like a worn-out glove after a meaningless but passionate fling.

It was a new approach for her, but she liked the idea.

"My sentiments exactly about Gary," Laura said. "I'll get back with you ASAP."

After she hung up, Emily thought about Richard. Sex with Richard. Meaningless though it might be, it would probably be great because he was gorgeous. And intelligent. And he did have a body to die for.

And I'm having dinner with him tonight.

Maybe Jane's right, she thought.

Jane buzzed her. "You told me to remind you about R & D."

"On my way." Emily hesitated. "Hey, while I'm gone, I need you to run an errand."

"Anything, my leader."

"I need some black lace underwear."

"Now you're talking. I won't fail you."

RESEARCH AND DEVELOPMENT always worried Emily. There seemed to be a lot of activity going on and a lot of people in white lab coats, but no one ever seemed to be in charge. After she'd dated the head of that department, Chris Croswell, for a while, she'd worried even more. Chris had the concentration of a fruit fly and the morals of a mink. It seemed such a bad personality profile for the head of a department with so many bubbling beakers. No wonder it looked as if no one was in charge.

"Hello, beautiful," he said when he saw her. "Let's have dinner."

"Sorry, I'm busy." She held out the bottle. "About this perfume—"

"Busy? Who with?"

"None of your business. About this perfume—"

"The new guy on twelfth. I thought he'd spot you."

"Chris, the perfume needs work."

"So does our relationship."

"We don't have a relationship," she told him. "We haven't had a relationship for two years. You've been married and divorced since then. Now about the perfume—"

"Which only goes to show how much work our relationship needs."

She took his hand and put the bottle in it. "We want it to sizzle."

"Sizzle?"

"Tingle a little on the skin. Heat up a little. Can you do it?"

"Sure." He shrugged. "When do you need it?"

"Yesterday." Emily began to back toward the door. "As soon as possible."

"You got it. Now about dinner…"

"You cannot possibly take me to dinner. You've got to put some sizzle in that bottle."

"I'd rather put some sizzle in you."

"Thank you, Chris." Emily backed out the door. "Let me know when it's done."

One thing you can say for Richard, she told herself as she escaped. *He's never that asinine.*

She was actually beginning to look forward to dinner.

THE EVENING STARTED well. Emily brushed her hair in a cloud around her shoulders and wore her new black lace underwear, one of two sets Jane had splurged on with her money.

"Always have a backup set," Jane had told her. "You never know, he may rip this stuff off you with his teeth in the throes of passion."

Emily visualized it. "Sounds good."

She topped the underwear with her best short black dress, dabbed on some nonheating Sizzle, and was just congratulating herself on how sophisticated and adult she looked when the doorbell rang and she went cold with nerves.

This is just dinner, she told herself. *He's a Hun. You don't care. This is meaningless.*

It didn't work.

As much as she hated to admit it, the anticipation she'd felt earlier had grown the more she'd thought about Richard. For the first time in a long time, she was really looking forward to an evening with a man. "So much for a meaningless fling," she told herself, and fought down another little spurt of panic as the doorbell rang again.

Her panic subsided when she answered the door and saw him there, solid and familiar. He stood still for a moment when she opened the door, and then he swallowed and said, "You're beautiful." He brought her gardenias. He handed her into the cab as if she were made of porcelain.

This is good, Emily thought. *He looks like a god, and he treats me like a goddess. This could work.*

He took her to the Celestial for dinner.

"George said this was your favorite restaurant," Richard told her as they sat down.

Emily clamped her lips together. *You could have asked* me *where I wanted to eat,* she thought, and then sighed. *Be nice, Emily. He's being nice. And you need him on your side. And he's paying; he has a right to choose the restaurant. Besides, it* is *your favorite. Besides, he's gorgeous.*

"I'm starving." He motioned to the waiter. "Let's skip drinks and go right to dinner."

"I wouldn't mind a glass of wine," Emily said, but Richard was already ordering.

"Sweet and sour soup. Mongolian beef."

"I don't care for Mongolian beef," Emily said politely.

"Mu-shu pork."

"I like garlic chicken."

"Su-san shan."

"I really hate su-san shan."

"Princess prawns." He beamed at her. "How does that sound?"

"Have you had your hearing checked lately?"

Richard was already handing the menus to the waiter. "That'll be fine."

"Plum sauce on mu-shu pork?" the waiter asked.

"No," Richard said.

"I like plum sauce," Emily said, and the waiter smiled at her and nodded.

Thank God, she thought. *I was afraid I'd suddenly gone mute.*

"We needed to get away from the office." Richard smiled at her. "Too many aggravations there."

The only aggravation there just ordered dinner for me here, Emily thought.

"Your hair looks wonderful." He looked at her, his eyes shining, and then smiled that sexy boyish grin that made her breathing quit every time. "You're lovely in the office, but tonight you're absolutely gorgeous."

He's not that aggravating, Emily thought, remembering to inhale. *He has potential. Be nice, Em.* "This is really nice of you." She leaned forward. "It really shows me how much you want our *partnership* to work. And I'm glad you're concerned about our working relationship, because I think we can do much better."

"Absolutely." Richard took her hand. "I agree with you absolutely."

His touch startled her. He had nice hands. Nice warm hands with tapered fingers. His nails were beautifully manicured, she noted, trying to concentrate on details so she could ignore the warmth spreading into her from his fingers. She breathed a little harder and met his eyes. He was looking at her with naked adoration. He really was sweet.

Do not become emotionally attached to the Hun, she told herself. *Simply use his body mercilessly and then fling him aside.*

"Tell me about yourself." His hand tightened on hers. "I want to know everything."

Emily blinked. "Why?"

He seemed taken aback. "Don't you think it's important for people who, uh, work together to get to know each other?"

"I guess so." Emily thought about it. She and George had worked together for eight years, and he'd never even asked her where she lived, let alone gotten to know her. This was an interesting side of Richard. "All right."

She answered his questions through the soup and the pork. By the time she was finished, she knew why Richard was so successful. He asked the right questions and, this time, listened to the answers. Midway through her life story, she realized he was piecing together the things that made her the person she was; he was doing in-depth research on his latest project—her. It was intensely flattering and not a little disconcerting.

But at least he was listening.

He was also charming, intelligent and polite. Emily relaxed and enjoyed herself with him, and the more she relaxed the more he opened up, so that by the time the pork was gone, there was a vulnerability in him she hadn't seen before. It was devastating. Emily found herself fighting against falling in love with him. And losing.

Don't be a fool, she said, and then she looked into his incredible blue eyes, eyes so plainly adoring her, and fell some more.

"Mongolian beef, princess prawns, su-san shan," the waiter said, putting the dishes on the table.

"Great." Richard ladled Mongolian beef onto her rice.

Emily looked at the stuff. She didn't care for beef in general, and she hated beef cooked in oil. The onions looked like worms. Richard added several spoonfuls of vegetables, also glistening with oil. Then he served her prawns, and she began to eat, carefully avoiding the beef and vegetables.

"You're not eating your beef." Richard frowned. "Is there something wrong? Should I send it back?"

"I don't like Mongolian beef."

"Why didn't you say so?"

"I did. You didn't listen."

He looked at her plate. "Su-san shan, too?"

"Yes. The waiter heard me. That's why I got plum sauce on my mu-shu pork."

"You like plum sauce?"

"Yes." Emily sighed, patient to the end. "I mentioned it."

"I don't listen." He looked at her with eyes like a scolded puppy's.

"No, you don't." She couldn't bear to see him so unhappy so she smiled at him. "Work on that."

"I will," he promised.

"Good. Now it's your turn. Tell me about you."

He hesitated, but she was a good researcher, too, and by the time the fortune cookies arrived, Emily knew everything about his past. They had a lot in common. They both agreed, for instance, that Walt Disney should have been shot, instead of Old Yeller, because they'd both been traumatized by the movie. They'd both been president of their senior class in high school. They'd both been at the head of their classes at business school. They both truly enjoyed their jobs. They'd both had disastrous relationships in the past. They were both determined to have a better one, perhaps a permanent one, in their future.

Emily forgot his high-handedness and was happy again. He was so sweet, so bright, so kind, so vulnerable, so obviously dazzled by her. So sexy, she thought.

So right for me.

So when he took her home, she invited him in.

She closed the door behind them and turned, and he kissed her. He moved slow enough to give her time to say no if she wanted to, fast enough to give her the feeling of being swept off her feet.

Nice timing, she thought as his lips touched hers. Then she stopped thinking.

He hadn't spent all his nights studying to be the Budget Hun. His lips were firm on hers, moving against hers, and she felt the warmth he always generated start again. She kissed him back, sliding her arms around his neck. She opened her lips and touched his with her tongue, and he slid his tongue into her mouth, tangling with hers, stroking inside her. The heat was everywhere in her now, and she clutched at him, leaning into him. He brought his hand up to the back of her head, lacing his fingers into her long dark hair to hold her close.

When he moved his hand down again, her hair became tangled in his sleeve buttons.

She felt it first as a tug and broke the kiss.

"Richard," Emily said, and he said huskily, "I know," and found her mouth again. He moved his hand down her body and she felt the hard pull against her hair.

"No, Richard! Wait! My hair..." She dropped her head back to ease the pull on her scalp.

He bent to kiss her exposed neck, moving kisses down into her cleavage. He also moved his hand to her rear end.

"Ouch! Richard, stop it!"

"What?" he asked huskily, his hand moving across her rear. Her head swayed with his hand. It really hurt.

"My hair." She held on to it, trying to take the pressure off her scalp. "You—"

"You have beautiful hair." He lifted his hand to run his fingers through it and the pull stopped.

"Thank God." She let her head drop forward as the pull eased, tears in her eyes from the pain.

"You're crying," he said softly, touched.

"My hair's caught on your sleeve."

"You're so beautiful." He bent to kiss her again.

"Dammit, Richard, my hair's caught on your sleeve!" Emily yelled.

"What?"

She pulled away from him, holding on to his arm so he wouldn't jerk her hair out. A lock of her hair was wound around his sleeve button.

"Don't move." She blinked back the tears of pain. "This really hurts."

"Why didn't you tell me?" He gently untangled her.

"I did!"

The mood wasn't broken, it was shattered. It took every ounce of self-control she had not to murder him where he stood.

"It's probably better if you go now," Emily said, backing away as Richard moved to hold her again. "I've got to be at work tomorrow. I'm meeting with advertising on the package design and you know those ad guys… Somebody's got to watch them every minute." She'd moved to the door as she spoke, and she opened it now. "I had a lovely evening."

"How's your head?" Richard looked disappointed and rueful and faintly annoyed.

She rubbed her scalp where the tug had done the most damage. "I'll take an aspirin. It'll be fine."

"Let's try again." He smiled down at her. "Come out with me again."

Emily closed her eyes. "Why don't we talk about it later?" Her head really did hurt. *Go away,* she thought. *I told you I needed an aspirin. Go away so I can take one.*

"How about Friday night?"

"Richard. You don't listen. I told you my head hurt. I told you I needed an aspirin. I told you we'd talk about it later."

"Saturday?"

"Never." Her voice rose almost to a shriek. "Never again. Not until you learn to listen. Take classes. Get a hearing aid. But get out of my life until you can hear me when I speak." She pushed him out the door and slammed it in his face.

I don't believe this, she fumed. *How can one sweet, charming, intelligent, sexy, good-looking guy be such a lousy listener? God, my head hurts.*

I am never going near him again, she thought as she turned away from the door. *Not even if someone ties him down and forces him to listen to me. Never, ever again.*

CHAPTER THREE

JANE'S REACTION WAS predictable.

"I don't see what's so funny about this." Emily frowned as she watched Jane laughing hysterically in the chair in front of her.

"Tell me the part again where he patted your rear," Jane gasped. "The part where your head bobbed up and down with his arm."

"You're disgusting." Emily sat down at her desk and tried to ignore her.

"I'd have paid money to see that."

"It hurt."

"Poor baby. So when are you seeing him again?"

"Never. I threw him out."

Jane stopped laughing. "Are you nuts? It was an accident. He didn't do it on purpose."

"He doesn't *listen* to me." Emily's teeth clenched as she thought about him.

"Well, you don't listen to me, and I'm sticking with you," Jane pointed out.

Emily looked up, outraged. "I listen to you."

"Good. Then my advice is, go out with him again."

"No."

"See, you don't listen."

"Jane…"

"All right, all right." Jane got up to go. "How is this going to affect your working relationship?"

"What working relationship? He doesn't listen there, either."

Jane shook her head. "You're making a big mistake. Aside from this one little flaw—"

"*Little* flaw?"

"—this guy is perfect for you. And you're going to let him get away." Jane shook her head again as she went back to her desk. "Big mistake."

"I'M REALLY SORRY, Emily," Richard said when she went to his office to check on some cost figures.

"Richard, it's not important." Emily sat and reached for the papers she needed. "It could have happened to anyone."

"Anyone else would have listened." He looked down at her, regret palpable in his eyes. He looked big and broad and solid and dependable and sexy. Also crazy about her, and devastated that she was unhappy with him.

Emily closed her eyes. She could feel herself weakening. *No,* she thought, and opened her eyes.

"I don't think we should date, Richard. I'm just

not comfortable with the idea of working together and dating."

"Emily—"

"Listen to me," she said, and he flushed.

"You're right." He sat down. "About the listening, not about the dating. But if that's the way you feel, I'll listen."

"Thank you. Now about the estimates..." She found the figures she needed and then left before he could do something to wreck her defenses. It was a close call.

During the next week, Richard found several pretexts to call private meetings with her, but she either sent him memos or brought Jane with her, much to Jane's disgust. Eventually he got the hint, and for the next three weeks, she didn't see him at all. She missed his sweetness and the breathless heat she fell into whenever he was close, but she didn't miss his bossiness at all. She didn't have a chance to; he bombarded her with memos that needed answers, forms that needed filling out and reports that needed filing yesterday. Ninety percent of the work, she thought, was unnecessary.

Emily took his last report request out to Jane.

"This is ridiculous. He *has* all these figures. If he sends anything else, send it back. Who does he think he is?"

Jane took the report. "I don't want to tell you this, but he wants you in his office."

"What did he say? 'Have her washed and sent to my tent'?"

"Karen just said he wanted you in his office ASAP."

"This stops now," Emily snapped and turned on her heel toward the elevators.

"Don't bother to announce me," she told Karen, and opened Richard's door without knocking.

He was sitting at his desk, comparing figures from two neat stacks of reports. His desk was obsessively tidy; a small bottle, two stacks of papers, one pen, a pitcher of water and a drinking glass. Nothing else. *He must be a Martian,* Emily thought. *How can anybody work in such obsessive neatness? He doesn't even take off his suit jacket.*

But he does look great.

"I bet your mom was really strict, wasn't she?" Emily asked.

Richard looked up from his desk, surprised and slightly annoyed.

"You summoned me." Emily put her hands on her hips. "I came running as soon as I heard."

"The new formula came up from the lab." He gestured toward the bottle on the desk. "Your idea about the, er, tingle."

"Why did it come to you?" Emily asked, exasperated. "You don't give a damn about tingle."

"I don't know." Richard pulled his eyes away

from her and turned back to his reports. "Just take it."

"What I like most about working with you is your charm." Emily picked up the bottle. "Don't you ever summon me again. You want me, you come down to see me." She turned to go.

"Emily, wait."

She took a deep breath and turned back, fire in her eye.

Richard ran his hand through his hair. "I'm sorry. I get caught up in something and I forget my manners. Let's try again. I didn't mean to summon you. I just wanted you to know the perfume was here. If they send it up here again, I'll send Karen down to you with it."

"Thank you." Emily brought her chin up. "I'd appreciate it."

Richard nodded, then really looked at her, deep into her eyes. His own eyes softened, and there was an appeal there that was hard to resist.

Emily swallowed. "I'm sorry. I'm just touchy about…being bossed."

"I know. And I keep forgetting and trying to boss you. And not listening." He smiled at her, and she smiled back automatically. Even if he was a deaf Hun, he had a sweet smile.

He put down the report. "Please try the perfume on. Let's see if it works."

"If you will," she said, and he took the bottle

from her and dabbed a couple of drops on the back of his hand.

She sat down across from him. “It probably won’t work there. I think R & D said it needs heat for the chemical reaction.” She picked up the bottle and pulled out the stopper, then stroked it into the hollow between her breasts. He watched her, mesmerized, and then said in a strangled voice, “I wish you wouldn’t do that.”

“It’s the warmest place I’ve got,” she said, and when he raised his eyebrows, she added, “For perfume, anyway,” and then blushed.

He rubbed his fingers over the perfume on his hand. “There *is* a slight tingle. A little warmth.”

The skin between her breasts grew warm and began to prickle slightly. Emily rubbed her finger over the tingle and shivered. It was somewhere between a tickle and heat, and she felt her skin respond and tighten. “Make a note never to put this stuff on any erogenous zone. This is like Spanish fly.”

He was staring at her blouse, and she looked down and saw that her nipples were pushing against the thin silk. She flushed and hunched her shoulders so her blouse wouldn’t be stretched so tight across her, but all she accomplished was to push her breasts together, deepening her cleavage and his confusion.

It also created more heat between her breasts, and the perfume started to sting.

"Is your hand burning?" she asked him, and he tore his eyes from her blouse.

"What? Uh, yes, a little."

"They've made it too strong." Emily drew a breath. "Way too strong." She shifted in her chair and ran her fingertips into her blouse while Richard watched, fascinated.

"Are you all right?"

Emily bit her lip. "Oh, yes, sure."

The stuff was really blazing now. She shifted uneasily in her chair.

"Emily?"

It was too much. She tore open the top buttons of her blouse and reached over the desk, ripping his pocket square from his suit jacket, giving him a brief glimpse of white lace stretched over full round breasts before she drenched his handkerchief in the water pitcher and plastered it on the fire on her skin.

When the burning eased, she said, "I am personally going to slaughter the folks in R & D."

"Are you all right?"

She winced as she blotted the perfume off with the dripping cloth. "Almost. How's your hand?"

"Not bad." He flexed it a little. "Hardly noticeable, really."

"It must be the heat, then." She pulled away

the cloth and examined the red patch on her skin. "Well, no scars, anyway." She looked up to see him staring.

"No, it looks great," he said.

She pulled her blouse shut. "Sorry about your pocket hankie."

He finally gave up and laughed. "Anytime. Shall I send the bottle back?"

"No." She picked up the bottle. "I want to deliver this personally."

"My sympathies to R & D, then."

She stopped, intrigued. "Why?"

He grinned at her ruefully. "Of all the people in this company, you're the one I'd least want coming after me. You take no prisoners."

"Good." She smiled back. "Remember that."

"LET'S GO TO LUNCH," Chris said when she stormed into the lab. "My place."

"Croswell, the perfume peels skin off. Fix it, or your job will be someone else's."

"What do you mean, peels skin off?"

"It burns. Didn't you test this stuff?"

"Yes, of course, we did." Chris took the bottle back. "On wrists and behind the ears. No problem."

"Well, it's a problem other places."

"What other places?"

"Just fix it," Emily snapped.

He shook his head. “You need to relax. Dump the twelfth floor and come out to dinner with me tonight.” He leered. “You can show me the other places.”

“You won’t be eating dinner, Croswell. You will be fixing the sizzle in that bottle.”

“Oh, come on, Emily,” he said, and then stopped, chilled by the look in her eye.

“I am not without power here,” she said coldly. “Do you believe I can have you fired?”

He thought about it. “Yes.”

“Do you believe I will have you fired if you do not fix that perfume and if you do not stop harassing me?”

He looked at her eyes. “Yes.”

“Then I suggest you get to work,” she said, then left, slamming the door behind her.

Jane followed her into the office when she got back.

“What did he do now?”

“Could I get somebody fired for harassment?”

“Richard?” Jane was shocked.

“No!” Emily said, outraged. “Of course not! It’s that idiot Croswell.”

“Thousands would cheer.” Jane sat down.

“Do I have that kind of power here?”

“Sure. Especially if Richard found out.”

“I don’t want him doing my dirty work.”

“What did Croswell do?”

"Nothing he hasn't been doing for the past two years. I just finally broke today. I was so mad. I'm still so mad."

"I can tell. Do you think he'll stop?"

Emily thought about it. "Yes. He knows I'm serious, and he believes I can get rid of him."

"You can. George's bluster notwithstanding, the company doesn't want to lose you."

"It's nice to know I'm valued."

"You're not." Jane crossed her legs and looked confident. "They just know that if you go, I go, and then who's going to run this place?"

"True." Emily sat down. "Has advertising got the bottle prototype yet?"

"Should have it by tomorrow." The phone rang and Jane moved to pick it up.

Emily stared out her window, and thought about how outraged she'd felt when Jane suggested that Richard was harassing her. He would never do that. He might not listen, but he would never deliberately use their personal relationship against her at the office. He had morals. He had ethics. He had—

"Laura's on one," Jane said, and Emily picked up the phone.

"What have you got?" she asked.

"Two possibilities. One's a sure thing—big stars, big promotion, everything. It's a glitzy caper movie, lots of designer labels, but very classy."

"Sounds like we could get lost in the labels. What's the other one?"

"This is a real gamble." Laura paused. "There's this kid from UCLA, shooting his first film. It's about these two business types who become sexually obsessed with each other. And there is a scene where the woman gets dressed that would be perfect for the product."

"Not if no one ever sees the movie." Emily swung around in her chair to stare out the window. "How much for the big one?"

"You're not going to like this," Laura said, and named the figure.

"The whole damn movie couldn't have cost that much," Emily protested.

"Actually for these guys, it's chicken feed. Do you want me to negotiate?"

"No." Emily swung back to her desk. "They've put a watchdog on me here. I'd never get away with spending anywhere near that much. Tell me more about this kid."

"I'll do better than that. I'll send you some scenes from the film. He really needs the money, so he's cooperating. They're shooting the scene where she gets dressed next week, so if you like the film, get a bottle of that stuff out here fast."

"What's his price?"

"He doesn't have one. He's trusting me to get him a good deal."

"Which you will. So how much is the kid going to cost me?"

"See the film clips." Laura's voice purred with reasonableness. "Then we'll talk."

"The film is that good?"

"The film is that good."

"Rush it out here, then," Emily said. "And I'll see if it does anything for me."

After she'd hung up, Emily thought about the movie. A brand-new movie with a hot new director. Another *Sex, Lies, and Videotape.* They'd get free publicity for having had the forethought to find the newest breakthrough movie. If it was as hot as Laura said, and Laura didn't make mistakes, this could be all they'd need to put Sizzle into the stratosphere.

Richard's last memo had absolutely ruled out any possibility of product placement. She'd tried to explain again, but he hadn't listened. Her lips tightened at the thought. He hadn't listened.

She buzzed Jane.

"I'm expecting a videotape from Laura tomorrow. Whatever you do, make sure Richard doesn't see it."

"Gotcha," Jane said. "What is it? A dirty movie?"

"If we're lucky," Emily said.

The film arrived the next day, but it was after five before Emily had a chance to look at it. Richard had also ruled out buying rubies, so she'd been searching for loose stones to rent, which was almost impossible. At five-thirty she gave up and ran for the elevator. When the doors opened, Richard was the only one inside.

"Did you find any rubies to rent?" He smiled at her, and she ignored him. *I've had a lousy day trying to solve the hopeless problem you created for me. There's not enough charm in the world,* she thought.

After a few moments, he tried again.

"A dirty movie?" He gestured at the videotape in her hand.

"I don't know." She tried to shove it into her pocket. "An old friend sent it to me. I'm going to rent a VCR and find out."

"I have a VCR. Come home with me. We'll get a pizza and watch your tape."

Emily shook her head. "I don't even know what's on it."

"Then we can find out together." Richard took her arm and walked her to the street, hailed a cab and put her into it. He gave the cabby his address and then climbed in beside her.

"What do you want on your pizza?" Richard asked.

"I have a choice?" Emily said.

RICHARD'S APARTMENT WAS surprising. It was as neat as she'd expected, but instead of the grim glass-and-steel decor she'd visualized for him, it was leather and brass, rich and masculine, but still warm.

"This place is great," she said, and he smiled at her, pleased.

"I'll open some wine." He pulled a bottle from a well-stocked wine rack. "Then we can order the pizza."

Emily moved to stop him. "Really, don't go to any trouble. I just need to see a little of the tape, and then I'll go."

He eased the cork out of the bottle and poured the wine into two glasses he took from an overhead rack.

"No trouble." He handed her a glass and lifted his in a toast. "To Sizzle."

Emily sighed. "To Sizzle," she echoed, and drank while he watched to see if she liked it. The wine was full-bodied and tart, and she drank again. "This is wonderful," she said, and he smiled at her, relieved, and refilled her glass as she protested.

"No, really. I won't be able to see the tape. Where's your VCR?"

"This way." He led her through double doors off the living room.

The first thing she saw was his big brass bed, a riot of curling, twisting, gleaming metal. "It's beautiful," she said, staring at it. He'd covered it with a thick white down comforter, and she had a brief vision of herself stretched across it while…

"It was my grandmother's." His eyes met hers and she had a fleeting thought he might have been thinking the same thing that she had been.

Stop fantasizing, she told herself.

Richard went to a tall cabinet in the corner of the room and opened the doors to reveal a large TV and VCR unit. He slipped in the tape and turned on the TV.

"You'll have to sit on the bed," he said, turning back to her. "I don't have any chairs in here. Unless you'd like a stool from the kitchen?"

"No, the bed's fine." Emily perched primly on the edge.

Richard punched the play button, looked at her uncertainly for a moment then left her.

A clapper appeared on the screen with the scene number, and then it was pulled away. A man and a woman stood facing each other, dark and slender, dressed conservatively, talking about a business deal they were working on. Then the woman smiled and said, "This isn't what this is all about." She kissed him slowly, and the scene exploded with eroticism as they undressed each other and made love. Emily forgot she was in Richard's bedroom and sat mesmerized by the tape, drinking slowly from her wineglass and becoming more and more flushed as the couple on the screen became more and more passionate. It was the most erotic love scene she'd ever seen.

The next scene began, a chase scene through what looked like San Francisco, and Emily tore her eyes away from the set. Richard had come back and was watching her, and she suddenly became conscious of how flushed she was and how fast she was breathing. She put down her glass and got up from the bed.

"Well," she said, then stopped. He, too, had put his glass down and was coming toward her. "Uh, Richard," she began, and he put his arms around her and pulled her close. "I don't think so," she said, and he kissed her, his lips soft but firm on hers, holding her against him while she drowned in his kiss.

When she came up for air, she was reeling. "Wait a minute," she gasped, and he kissed her again, running his hands across her back, pulling her hard against him. She shoved him away.

"You never listen," she said.

He stopped and said, "I'm sorry," and tried to get his breath back, looking at her with a dizziness compounded equally from lust and adoration. *He looks great when he's dizzy,* she thought. *I'm dizzy, too. What am I doing?*

Then he touched her and said "I'm sorry" again, and she gave up and said, "That's good enough for me." She moved against him, running her hands across his chest and up and around his neck, pulling his mouth down to hers, kissing him hard, biting him on the lip. He kissed her back and then pulled his face away from hers and picked her up, dropping her into the middle of the thick white comforter and rolling onto it beside her. He kissed her neck, then the hollow of her throat, and then the warm place between her breasts, while she ran her fingernails over his back through his shirt. His lips left a trail of heat on her skin.

"Sizzle," she said, and laughed, and he did, too, and kissed her again.

She felt the heat flow into her bone-deep, felt the sizzle everywhere he touched her, and she rolled as close as she could to him to feel his body hard next to hers.

He unbuttoned her blouse, kissing the tops of her breasts above the lacy bra and making her shiver while he slid his hands beneath her back to find her bra clasp.

"It's in front," she whispered, but he still ran his fingers along her back. "Richard, the hook is in front."

"What?" he murmured into her ear, not listening.

She closed her eyes in irritation, but then he moved his tongue into her ear, and the sizzle down her spine made her forget her irritation. She unhooked her bra herself and then unbuttoned his shirt and ran her tongue over the hard muscles of his chest, and when he finally pulled her bra off, she rolled into him, relishing the heat of their bodies against each other.

He pushed her back gently. "I've been waiting for this a long time," he said, and bent over her, touching her nipples lightly with his tongue, first one then the other, finally sinking his mouth over her breast and sucking until she cried and twisted in his arms, the heat and need so great she had to move against him, hard against his mouth and hands, because he felt so impossibly good wherever he touched her. He moved his mouth to her other breast and tormented her until she was almost unconscious with lust for him. Then he slid his hand under her skirt to stroke the smooth silk between her legs.

Any thought Emily might still have cherished of saying no disappeared. She writhed under his hand and reached for him, stroking down across his stomach with her hand until she felt him hard beneath the fabric of his clothing. She pressed against him, and he moaned and kissed her, thrusting his tongue into her mouth.

When he moved his mouth to her throat, she gasped, "Richard, I—"

"Not now," he said, and moved his hand down her body.

Not now? Emily felt herself grow even hotter

from anger. *Not now?* Who the hell did he think he was?

He pushed his hand into her panties and then slid his fingers into her, and she forgot she cared who he was and moaned at the sheer tormenting ecstasy of his hand.

His doorbell rang.

"Make love to me now," she said to him. She crawled on top of him, pushing herself down on his hand. "I can't believe how much I want you."

"Wait." He moved his hand away. "I'll get rid of whoever it is. I'll be back."

"No," she said, trying to hold on to him, but he slid out from under her, kissing her breast as he went and leaving her gasping on the bed. After a few minutes, she pulled herself up and saw herself in the mirror at the foot of the bed. Her French twist had loosened, her eyes were half-closed with lust and her mouth was bruised from his. She was naked to the waist, flushed with need for him.

And he was in the living room, talking to someone.

"I don't believe this," she muttered. She slipped off the bed, put her bra and blouse back on and tucked her hair back into some kind of order. Then she ejected the tape from the VCR and went into the living room.

He was standing at the door talking to George, whose eyes went wide when he saw her.

"Thanks for letting me use the VCR," she said, pulling on her coat. "See you tomorrow." She ducked around them both and walked rapidly toward the elevator. The doors slid open at once, and she got in.

I can't believe I did that, she thought. *I can't believe I* almost *did that. With Richard Parker. Who is beautiful, but sort of cold. Only he wasn't cold tonight. Oh, my God,* she thought. *I really want him.* She leaned back against the wall of the elevator and thought about how wonderful making love with him would have been. Except that he had to answer the damn door. She'd said no, don't, but he knew best. He didn't listen. The hell with him.

She caught a cab home and then dreamed of him all night, making love to her to the sound of doorbells.

"AND WHAT DID WE DO that was so special yesterday?" Jane asked archly.

"I had a bad night," Emily snapped. "Say what you mean."

"Three dozen roses in a crystal vase on your desk. Here's the card. It's sealed so I couldn't read it. You will, of course, show it to me because it would be too cruel of you not to."

The card read, "I'm sorry. Let me make it up to you. Richard."

"Fat chance." Emily dropped the card into

the wastebasket. She handed Jane the videotape. "Watch this tonight and see what you think. For product placement."

Jane promptly fished the card out of the wastebasket and followed her into the office as she read it.

"Richard, huh? What did he do?"

"It's what he didn't do." The roses were lovely. She handed them to Jane. "Send these back to him."

"Boy, he must have really screwed up," Jane said, taking the vase.

Jane buzzed her twenty minutes later. "The Hun is on line three. Be gentle with him."

"Ha." Emily punched three. "Yes?"

"Emily, I'm sorry about last night."

"You should be."

"Let me make it up to you."

"Not even with rubies. Any man who would leave me for George—"

"I just wanted to get rid of him so we wouldn't be interrupted."

"And when the Girl Scouts came selling cookies, you'd talk to them, too. And Jehovah's Witnesses, and some guy working his way through college by selling encyclopedias."

She heard a faint buzz, and he swore. "Hold on a second," he said. "I've got another call." And the line fell silent.

Emily clutched the receiver in a death grip and then carefully returned it to the cradle.

Jane opened the door. "I saw the light go out. What happened?"

"He put me on hold."

Jane swallowed. "Oh, boy."

"The lousy son of a bitch put me on hold."

Jane went out, closing the door behind her.

Emily stared straight ahead, rigid with anger.

Jane buzzed her again. "Richard on two."

Emily picked up the phone.

"Emily, I…"

"Don't you *ever* put me on hold again."

"Jane said that was a mistake," he said ruefully. "Let me make it up to you."

"You can't make it up to me. Not with dinners, not with roses, not with rubies. You are a controlling, cost-effective, power-mad, anal-retentive, deaf son of a bitch!" She ended on what from a lesser woman would have been a shriek and slammed the phone down. Then she buzzed Jane.

"I am not taking any calls from Richard Parker no matter what he has to say. If he wants to communicate with me, tell him to send a memo."

"Right," Jane said.

"MEETING IN THE conference room at five," Jane said as Emily got ready to leave that night.

"What?"

"Memo just in from George's office." Jane handed it to her.

Emily groaned and crumpled the memo. "I'm tired. I want to go home."

"Well, you can as soon as you've done the executive bit."

"I wish I was a secretary."

"No, you don't." Jane put her coat on. "You're a terrible typist. You'd starve. See you tomorrow."

Emily kicked off her shoes and sat in the gloom of her office. *I'm so tired,* she thought. *And my panty hose are driving me nuts. I hate panty hose. They're an invention of the devil. I'm never wearing them again.* She took them off as a gesture of independence and threw them away. There was a run in one leg, anyway.

Instantly she felt better, cooler. She leaned back in her chair and spread her legs apart to cool them, reveling in the relief from the scratchy heat of the hose. It reminded her of other ways of feeling good. It reminded her that she was still so frustrated from the night before she wanted to kill.

It reminded her she still wanted Richard.

No, she didn't. She was going to forget him and go home.

She looked at the clock. Five-fifteen. Damn.

She slipped her bare feet into her heels and went down the hall to the conference room.

"George?" It was dark in the room, and as the

door swung behind her she bumped into him, tall and broad and muscular.

Not George.

Richard.

CHAPTER FOUR

"OH, NO." EMILY turned to leave, but his arms went around her from behind, pulling her gently back against him as he buried kisses in the side of her neck.

"No doorbells this time," he whispered. "I swear."

She felt dizzy with the sudden heat he stirred in her.

No, she thought, fighting it. No way.

She kicked back at him with her heel, and he said, "Ouch!" but he didn't let go.

Emily meant to say no. She knew she could pull away easily, that he wouldn't stop her. But his mouth was so teasingly gentle on her skin, and he was so hard against her, and finally she just wanted him so much. She gave up and turned and found his mouth in the dark and licked his lips, thrusting her tongue into his mouth as she thrust her hips against his. She heard him gasp and felt his body shudder under her assault, and then he picked her up and sat her on the edge of the conference table, moving his body between her legs. She wrapped her legs around him and pulled him tight against her as his fingers fumbled at the buttons of her blouse. She tried to undo his shirt, but he was leaning down to her breasts, running his tongue across her.

Then she heard voices in the hall. The cleaners.

"Not again," Emily said.

And Richard said, "No. Nothing stops us this time." He pulled away from her and slid his hand under her skirt to pull off her bikini panties.

"You put me on hold again, and it will be the last time you ever touch me," Emily said with blood in her voice.

"If I have to, I'll make love to you while the cleaners watch," Richard said, and she lifted her hips to help him slide her panties off.

"I wish I could see you," he said. "You're so beautiful, but it's too damn dark in here." His hand slid between her legs, and he stroked her there, tormenting her, kissing her shoulders and neck, until she laced her fingers in his hair and pulled his mouth to hers.

When he stopped, she said, "No, don't stop," and tried to pull him back to her, but he kissed her and pulled her to the edge of the table. She realized that he was fumbling with a condom and she laughed until he slid hard into her with a suddenness that made her cry out. His hands, clamped on her hips, pulled her to him again and again, and he leaned into her each time, to stroke as deeply as he could, building the heat and pressure in her until she cried out and twisted in his arms, and he drove harder and faster to spur her to explode again and again until she collapsed in his arms and lay there shuddering, her legs still wrapped around his waist.

Someone knocked on the door. "Anybody in there?"

"I promise," he whispered to her, and picked her up off the table by wrapping an arm around her. He backed up until he felt a door behind him. She unwound herself from him to stand beside him, and he opened the door and pulled her inside, closing the door after them. He heard it click shut just as the cleaner turned on the light in the conference room.

"Where are we?" she whispered dazedly into his shoulder. A little light filtered around the edge of the door.

"We're in a closet," he whispered. "I hope to hell it isn't a broom closet."

"They don't use brooms," she said, and an electric sweeper began to whine outside the door.

There was no room to sit down, so he held her against him and she moved so that her breasts pressed into his chest. "I wasn't finished, you know," he whispered in her ear, and picked her up, easing himself back inside her, pinning her to the closet wall with his body. She wrapped her legs around him again, and he throbbed against her. He was being gentle and slow, and she bit him on the shoulder. "Harder," she said, and he slammed himself against her, pulsing into her until she cried out weakly. He muffled her cries with his own, thrusting his tongue into her mouth in the same rhythm that his hips thrusted against hers. Emily came again as she never had before, the muscles inside her clenching and expanding over and over while his tongue stroked her mouth. Then she heard him moan and felt him slump against her, holding her to the wall while he shuddered.

"Richard," she said, and he kissed her.

"We've got to do this in a bed," he whispered, touching her hair. "It's so much easier."

They held each other, kissing and touching wordlessly, until the cleaners left.

"Come home with me," he said.

"I can't." Emily put her head on his chest. "I don't have anything to wear tomorrow."

And I've got to think about this, she told herself. *Because this is more than I expected. This is more than I ever dreamed of.*

But when they reached the street and he hailed a cab, he got in beside her and gave the driver his address.

In the back seat of the cab, he couldn't seem to

stop touching her, not to arouse her but almost as if he had to prove she was there beside him. He looked at her as if she was a miracle, touching her cheek, her hair, holding her hand. The smile in his eyes was more than just heat and lust. She felt loved and desired and claimed.

The claimed part bothered her.

"Richard…" she began.

"I want to make love to you all night." He kissed her sweetly. She felt dizzy every time his mouth touched her.

"No, listen," she said, and he laughed and kissed her again.

He was a great kisser.

He was a terrible listener.

When Richard got out at his apartment, he turned to help her out, but Emily pulled the door shut in his face and told the driver to go on. *I want him again,* she thought, *but on my terms this time. Because if I don't establish some kind of equality in our relationship pretty soon, I'm going to spend the rest of my life being ignored, humored, dictated to and put on hold.*

Even to be with Richard, that's too big a sacrifice.

Richard.

Oh, my God, Richard.

She leaned back in the cab and thought about him again and the way he'd moved against her, inside her. She closed her eyes and savored the memory. It was going to be a lot of work to get him to take her seriously, but he was worth it. He was worth everything.

"YOU'RE LOOKING VERY chipper this morning," Jane said.

"Thank you." Emily smiled smugly.

"Your underpants are on your desk."

"What?"

"The cleaners found them in the conference room and put them on the lost-and-found bulletin board. Real clowns, those cleaners."

"Does anybody know?"

"Absolutely not. I was the first one here. And I only knew they were yours because I bought them for you."

"You get a raise."

"Thank you. I deserve one. So who was the lucky man?"

"What man?" Emily said brightly, and went into her office.

An hour later, Jane buzzed her on the intercom. "The Hun would like to see you in his office. ASAP."

I bet he does, Emily thought. *He snaps his fingers, and I scurry up the stairs, and then he makes love to me on his office desk until I lose my mind. Well, actually, that last part sounds great, but I'm not going to his office. It's time to make Richard start listening to me right now, because once we're married, it'll be too late.*

Married? Emily swallowed, sandbagged by her own subconscious. *Well, yes. Married. But on my terms, not his.*

"Tell him I'm busy," she said.

"Okay," Jane said.

Emily spread the gem photographs that advertising had sent her across her desk. *There really isn't any choice,* she thought, as she compared the paste to the gems. The fake stones were pale and dull, refusing to catch the light, while the rubies sparkled from inside and pulsed with color. She scribbled notes for a memo to Richard. *Even he's got to see the difference here,* she thought. *Even he should be able to spot the sizzle of the real thing.*

The door opened, and without looking up, she said, "Jane, I've got a memo for Richard the Hun here."

"Good," Richard said. "I'll take it."

She looked at him over the top of her glasses. "Didn't it occur to you to have my secretary announce you?"

He closed the door behind him and walked to the desk. "Your secretary is gone. And I need your memo on the stones now. I've got a report to make, you know." He smiled down at her. "My reports go in on time."

You are one arrogant SOB, she thought.

As if he'd read her mind, his smile widened, and her heart leaped to her throat. He leaned over and put his hands on the desk, and she remembered the last time he'd leaned over her, remembered where his hands and lips had gone. Her heart beat faster, and her breath came a little quicker.

Oh, no, you don't, she told herself.

She forced herself to lean back in her chair and look up at him calmly. "I'll have Jane send the memo right up," she said, trying to keep the huskiness out of her voice. "It has my recommendations and the estimates."

"What do I have to do to get it now?" he asked softly. *I haven't fooled him,* she thought. *Damn him. I've got to take control.*

Jane's voice came over the intercom. "George on line two."

"I've got it." Emily slid her chair back slightly to pick up the phone.

"Emily," Richard said, trying to be stern. "The memo."

Richard the Hun in action.

Emily suddenly found herself enjoying the situation. She covered the mouthpiece with her hand and grinned at him. "I'm busy. Get on your knees and grovel." Then she turned back to the phone. "George! How wonderful to talk to you. You know,

I was just saying to Jane, George and I don't talk enough."

"Emily?" George said.

"That's me," Emily said, batting her eyes at Richard. "What's up?"

"Well..." George sounded confused. "I was just wondering how it was going with Richard? Everything all right?"

"Just great, George." She stuck out her tongue at Richard. "Couldn't have asked for a nicer guy to work with. Always asks, never orders. Great listener. Considerate, undemanding, a real liberated kind of guy."

Richard raised his eyebrows at her. "You want to play games?" he asked. Then he walked around to her side of the desk and got down on his knees.

"What are you doing?" Emily said.

"Going over the last project totals," George said.

"Cooperating," Richard said. His hands slid over her knees and up to her waist, taking her skirt with them. Emily tried to put her knees together, but he thrust his body between them, spreading her legs farther apart and pulling her hips toward him.

"Stop it." Emily tried to shove him back with her free hand.

"Now, Emily," George said. "Relax. I'm not interfering with your project."

"Relax." Richard put his mouth against the softness of her inner thigh.

Emily moved her hand to his head and tried to push him away. *Great day I picked to stop wearing panty hose and start wearing stockings,* she thought wildly. *Oh, God, what is he doing? We're in my* office, *for heaven's sake.*

"Emily?" George said. "Emily, don't be difficult about this."

She twined her fingers in Richard's hair and jerked his head up. He winced and pulled her hand away. "The garters are a good idea," he said. "Don't ever wear anything else." And then he lowered his head again, clamping her hand at her side.

"Emily, will you please listen to me about this?" George said.

"I'm listening, George." She tried to roll her chair away from Richard, but he pulled her in closer. His lips were tickling her inner thighs, his tongue flicking in and out. The tickling made her giggle, which was bad for her phone image, she knew. Of course, if George could see her now, her phone image would be the least of her problems. She tried hard to concentrate on George's rambling, but Richard was much more interesting.

"Richard can do a lot for you, Emily," George was saying.

"No kidding," Emily said, trying to decide if she was more concerned about preserving her dignity or having great sex in the middle of the morning.

It wasn't much of a decision.

Richard let go of her hand and reached under her skirt, pulling the silk of her bikini panties to one side.

"Emily?" George said as Richard slipped his tongue inside her.

"I'll talk to you later!" she cried, and slammed down the phone. Richard darted his tongue in and out of her, and Emily fell back in her chair, lacing her fingers in his hair and pulling him closer, lost in the waves of heat he was stirring in her.

Jane knocked on the door, and before Emily could stop her, she came in, frowning at some papers in her hand. Richard fell back under her desk, pulling Emily in her desk chair after him, and Emily gasped and glanced down and then laughed out loud. The great Richard Parker, hiding under the desk. Between her legs. With a condom in his hand.

"What's so funny?" Jane asked.

"Oh, how the mighty have fallen," Emily said, and Richard slid his hand between her thighs and pinched her.

"And what's wrong with you? You're all flushed."

"I think I have a fever." Emily swallowed. "I may lie down for a while." She felt Richard's head between her legs again, the softness of his hair on her thighs, and then she felt his tongue on her skin, moving upward again.

"I really have to lie down," she told Jane. "Hold all my calls for an hour."

"Let me get you an aspirin," Jane said.

"No, I have everything I need right here. Just go away." His fingers were pulling at the silk again.

"Emily!" Jane looked concerned. "You're really ill."

He slipped his tongue inside her.

"No." Emily grasped the edge of her desk. "Go away and leave me alone." His tongue was thrusting harder and harder against her, and she could feel the waves of heat surging through her. If Jane didn't get out of the office, she was going to scream and fall off the chair right in front of her.

Jane looked hurt. "All right. Call if you need me."

Emily was beyond speech. She closed her eyes and thought only of the heat and Richard between her legs. Vaguely she heard the door close behind Jane, and then Richard was pushing the chair back, pulling her to the floor, his mouth hard on hers, his fingers pulling off her panties, and then suddenly he was hard inside her, and she moaned and bit his shoulder through his jacket. He thrust harder and harder, and she exploded under him, sobbing his name, arching closer to him as she came. When she stopped, gasping in her satisfaction, he was still there, stroking inside of her, and she opened her eyes and looked at him.

He wasn't the Richard she knew anymore; the control was gone and he was as crazed by love for her as she was for him. *He's mine,* she thought, and her whole body pulsed with his. She drew her fingernails down his back, and felt him shudder under the thick cloth of his suit. She arched and clenched under him, and he responded to her every move, and she laughed with the pure joy of knowing she could make him shiver with need. He felt so good inside her. She pulled his face down to hers and bit his lip, and he moaned and his release had a jarring suddenness.

He fell against her, his face buried in her neck, his body heavy on hers. She stroked her fingers lightly over his neck and ran them through his hair, and he moved his head against her hands.

"I love you, Richard," she said, and stopped, appalled at her stupidity. *He will now set the land-speed record for leaving an office,* she thought.

He raised himself off her, braced above her on his hands and looked down at her, his eyes half-closed, his mouth swollen from making love to her.

"I love you, too," he said. And then he laughed shakily. "I can't believe I'm saying this. I love you, Emily." He kissed her forehead. "I love you." His lips were soft on hers. "I love you." She felt his mouth move down against the base of her throat. "I love you."

He kissed her again, and she responded with all the feeling she'd been denying. He rolled to his side and pulled her over on top of him, sliding his hands down the back of her silk blouse and over the bulk of her pulled-up skirt. His hands cupped her to him, and he kissed her over and over again until she gasped for air. Then he tipped her gently back onto the floor and sighed.

"I've got to get out of here," he said finally. "If I don't, we're both going to be rolling around naked when Jane comes in to check on you." He kissed her once more, and then got to his feet, dressing himself as he stood.

He looked down at her, tousled on the floor, and smiled. "This is the way I want to remember you," he said, and reached down to help her to her feet. When she stood beside him, he pulled her to him and kissed her, pulling her skirt back down over her hips.

When he stopped, Emily sighed and stepped away, tucking in her blouse. "Do I look okay?" she asked, and he smiled and reached for her again.

Jane knocked on the door and came in. "Mr. Parker!"

"He's just leaving." Emily patted Richard on the arm. "He came for his memo, so we'll have to get it done right away. Get your steno pad."

Jane hesitated and then went back to her desk.

Richard pulled Emily close again. “Dinner?”

Emily leaned into him. “I want more than dinner.”

“You can have anything you want.” He kissed her again and patted her rear end, then headed for the door.

“See you, Jane,” he said as he passed her, and then he walked away down the hall, whistling.

Jane closed the door. “What’s going on?”

“Who are you, my mother?”

“That man patted you on the butt.”

Emily sat down. “We’re…very close.”

“How close? And how did he get in here?”

“You weren’t at your desk. Take a memo.”

“I left my desk half an hour ago. He’s been in here all that time? He couldn’t have been. There was nobody in here with you when I came in.” Jane sat down. “This is really interesting.”

“I knew I should never have hired you as my secretary.” Emily tried to look cool and disapproving but she felt too damn good. “A real secretary would have more respect.” She stretched and yawned, trying to act unconcerned under Jane’s narrowing eyes. “Take a memo.”

Jane’s eyes narrowed. “Where was he when I was in here?” she demanded.

Emily sighed. “Under the desk.”

Jane’s mouth dropped open. “Good Lord.”

"If you tell anybody…" Emily started, but Jane waved her away.

"Who would believe me? He must be incredible in the sack."

"He is," Emily said slowly, and sighed.

"So what's the problem?"

"I want a partner." Emily felt suddenly sad. "I want a fifty-fifty deal."

"Not the Hun's style," Jane agreed.

"Right. Richard is always the one in control. If I make a decision, he approves of it or says no. If he makes a decision, he just informs me of it. If I say something he disagrees with or feels isn't important, he ignores me. Today is a perfect example. I was on the phone, and he just came around the desk and put his hand up my skirt." She closed her eyes for a moment at the memory.

"And you loved it."

"That's not the point. The point is that he always decides everything, and he never listens to me. I want a little power here, too."

"Maybe you should go crawl under his desk."

"No." Emily shook her head. "Not my style. I don't know what I'm going to do. I really love him."

"Whoa. This is serious."

"Very. But he pushes me around too much. I can't live with a man who ignores what I say if he doesn't agree with it. Even if he does make my knees turn to jelly every time I look at him."

"Maybe I better meet Ben for lunch." Jane shifted in her chair. "Just what was Richard doing under the desk?"

"Just what you think he was doing." Emily sighed at the memory. "And he's very good at it."

"I'm definitely meeting Ben for lunch. I'll be back late."

"Bite him on the lip for me."

"I'll do that." Jane picked up her pad again. "In the meantime, is there really a memo?"

"Oh, yes." Emily pulled the papers toward her and read to Jane from her draft. "Memo to Richard Parker..."

JANE SENT THE MEMO TO Richard with predictable results.

"The Hun's on line two," Jane said an hour later, and Emily went a little dizzy at the thought of him.

Pull yourself together, woman, she told herself, and picked up the phone.

"Emily Tate," she said.

"Hello, Emily Tate," he said softly.

"Don't do that. Talk in your usual Hun voice, or I can't think."

"Have dinner with me tonight."

"Only if it's at your place, and we eat in bed."

"Let's start with lunch. My bed is a great place

to have lunch. I'll meet you in the lobby in ten minutes."

"No," Emily said with much more conviction than she felt. "We've got to get some work done first. Now pay attention. Did you have time to read the ruby memo?"

"Yes."

"And?"

He sighed. "We can't afford real rubies."

"We can't *not* afford real rubies." Emily tried to keep calm. "Move some money around in the budget, but I need two things, bottom line. Real rubies and a product placement."

"No," he said.

"Try," she said. "Try to cut some other corners. I need these two. I won't ask for anything else."

"Emily—"

"Try. You haven't tried yet."

There was a long silence. "If I can't, what happens to you and me?"

Emily heard the tension in his voice. "We still have dinner in bed. I don't use sexual blackmail. And besides, I want you too much to say no."

He made a sound she couldn't identify. "Richard?"

"Just trying to breathe. You have that effect on me."

"Well, I definitely want you breathing. As heavily as possible. But I want the rubies and product placement, too. You can do it, Richard. It's important."

"It's not going to work, Emily."

"You're not listening." She stopped and tried again. "It's important. The money is there. Find it. We're partners, remember? Don't say no to me. Find a way to make it work."

"Saying no to you is impossible. Can I take you home with me after work?"

"Give me time to shower and change," Emily said. "Then I'll come to your place. But no more tables, closets, desks or floors."

"Just an old-fashioned girl," Richard said. "I'll turn down the bed."

"I love you."

"Say it again."

"I love you. You're a Hun, but I love you."

"I love you, too. Make it a fast shower."

THEY MADE LOVE SLOWLY that night in Richard's huge bed, discovering each other, finding themselves so in tune with each other physically that they didn't need to speak, even though they did because they both loved the sound of the other's voice.

Any doubts Emily had were gone. She'd always scoffed at the idea of knowing without a doubt when the perfect lover showed up, the perfect life partner. Jane had told her she'd known within the first week of meeting Ben that he was all there was.

And now *she* knew.

Emily wasn't quite as confident about Richard's feelings for her. She knew he adored her—she wasn't a complete fool. But sometimes with men, adoration wasn't followed by commitment. Maybe he wasn't thinking marriage.

"We'll live here when we get married," Richard said, holding her, kissing her hair. "It's closer to work, and it's bigger than your place."

Since she'd planned to suggest the same thing, Emily really had no reason to be annoyed. But she was.

"Did I miss the proposal?" she asked coolly, pulling away from him.

He flushed. "I did it again, didn't I? Do you want me to go down on my knees?"

She relented. "Well, it was wonderful the last time you did, but I think I can make do with one from where you are."

He pulled her close and kissed her, and she felt the length of his hard naked body against hers.

"Will you marry me, Emily Tate, so we can spend the rest of our lives together like this?"

"Yes." She ran her hand down his side, feeling the rope of muscles there. "Absolutely."

He shuddered and rolled on top of her, kissing her with such heat she was lost. He slipped his fingers inside her and moaned a little at the warmth and wetness there. Then he moved against her, and she realized he was ready, and she tried frantically to push him away.

"Richard, wait, no," she said, but he was inside her, and he filled her so completely she finally fell back into his arms, back into the throbbing ecstasy of him in her.

Later, when they were trying to breathe, still clinging to each other, Emily put her head on his chest and started to cry.

"What?" he asked, sounding panic-stricken.

"You don't listen," Emily said quietly. "I keep telling you, but you don't listen."

"What?" he asked again, holding her. "I love you."

"You better." She swallowed hard. "I'm using a diaphragm for birth control."

"I know." He held her, bewildered. "I asked you if you wanted me to use a condom and you said…"

"You have to use foam with a diaphragm. Fresh foam, every…single…time."

"Oh." He held her tighter.

"I told you to stop," Emily said.

"I didn't hear you," Richard said.

"I know," Emily said, staring at the ceiling. "I know."

Later that night when he was asleep, after he'd sworn to her that he'd love a child, that she wouldn't have to stop work, that everything would be all right, that he'd take care of her forever, after he fell asleep worn out from reassuring her, Emily stared at the ceiling in the dark and thought.

This is worse than I was afraid of. This is much worse. He's got to change. I've got to do something.

But she couldn't think of anything, and she finally fell asleep, spent from love and worry and passion.

In the morning, they made love again, and Richard was scrupulous about not rushing her. He was also tender and strong and passionate, and she went into work with a lovely physical buzz spoiled only by a nasty nagging fear.

"DID YOU COUNT THE DAYS?" Jane asked when Emily told her what had happened.

"If counting the days works, I'm positive I'm safe." Emily looked down at her calendar again. "But you never know. This could be the month I decide to ovulate late or something."

"Are you worried?"

"About a baby, not yet. About Richard, very. When he almost pulled out my hair because he wasn't listening, it was vaguely amusing. Starting a baby because he wasn't listening isn't. What will it be next time? Dragging me out in front of a speeding bus?" She shook her head. "And he really loves me. I don't get it."

"I don't, either." Jane frowned. "But you were right. This is not a little flaw."

Emily shook her head in misery.

"Well, here's something to take your mind off Richard." Jane handed her a message. "Laura called before you got in. She needs to have a bottle of Sizzle by the day after tomorrow if you want it in the shoot. What do I tell her?"

Emily thought about it. Richard had said no, but this was important. She knew it just as she knew that he loved her, in her bones. Emily's instincts had taken her far, and she wasn't about to start ignoring them now.

Richard had said no.

Maybe she just hadn't heard him.

"Did we get a prototype bottle from advertising?"

"Two."

"Fill one of them with Sizzle and express it out to her."

"Do we have an okay from Richard?"

"He said he'd try to find some money." He had, sort of.

Jane tried again. "But do we have an okay from Richard?"

Emily looked at her. "I didn't hear him say no."

"Oh." Jane considered it. "Well. That's an approach I hadn't thought of. I'll get the stuff off to Laura right away."

"And call advertising and find out where they borrowed the rubies for the photo shoot. We're buying them."

"I hope he loves you a lot," Jane said on her way out. "I have a mortgage."

RICHARD WAS IN A MEETING for lunch, so Emily took Jane to the Celestial.

"You know, maybe you're going about this the wrong way," Jane said to her over the garlic chicken.

Emily thought about it. "I'm being patient."

"That's your problem." Jane stabbed her fork at her. "You've got to jar him awake so he can see what he's doing."

"He is trying," Emily began, but Jane shook her head.

"You've got to show him how frustrating it is to have no control, to have his demands ignored."

"Well, I'm doing that with the rubies and the movie."

"Not business." Jane shook her head. "He'll just assume you're going behind his back to get your way."

"Where then?"

"Where's the one place he treats you as an equal?"

"Nowhere."

"Bed."

Emily thought about it. Jane, as usual, was right. No matter how autocratic Richard was with her in other aspects, he treated her like a goddess in their private life. The times he hadn't listened to her were due to his being overwhelmed by passion, not by indifference to her feelings.

"You're right," she admitted. "So?"

"So that's the place to make your point."

"No." Emily looked at Jane, appalled. "I'm not going to withhold sex to make him agree with me. That's cheap."

"You're not listening." Jane grinned at her. "You're spending too much time with Richard. It's catching."

"All right." Emily put down her fork and listened. "Explain."

"Well, Ben and I were experimenting one night—"

"Oh, Lord, Jane." Emily picked up her fork again. "Kinky sex is not going to change his mind."

"This isn't kinky." Jane thought about it. "Well, not very. And it will change his mind. Eat your salad. We have some shopping to do."

"What kind of shopping?"

"Strawberries. Candles. And you're going to buy some of that wicked pink lace stuff I bought."

"I have a bad feeling about this," Emily said.

"Trust me," Jane said. "This will work. I guarantee you, this time, he'll listen."

CHAPTER FIVE

AT FIVE O'CLOCK EMILY sat in her office, staring at the shopping bag on the floor next to her. It held the basics of Jane's game plan.

I can't do this, she thought. *I'll feel like a fool, and Richard will laugh at me. In the nicest possible way, of course. With a great deal of affection. And then he'll never take me seriously again.*

Jane knocked on the door. "I'm leaving."

"Thanks for everything, Jane," Emily said, "but—"

"But you're not going to do it," Jane finished for her.

"It's too far out for me."

"This from the woman who talked to her boss on the phone while her lover was under her desk?"

"That was not my idea."

"Yeah. But this would be." Emily shook her head again, and Jane sighed and shrugged.

"Keep all that stuff, anyway. Eat the strawberries, but put the rest of it away. Someday you may change your mind."

"I doubt it." Emily's eyes widened as she looked beyond Jane. "Shut up. Here he comes."

Richard paused in the doorway.

"Hi, Jane." He leaned around her to talk to Emily. "Something's come up. Can I pick you up later, say, eight?"

"What's going on?"

"Meeting with George and Henry. It's money talk. I told them you wouldn't be interested. You can relax, and then we'll have a late dinner after the meeting."

"Did it occur to you," Emily asked carefully, "that I might want to go to this meeting?"

"No." Richard frowned at her. "Why would you want to come to a money meeting?"

Emily clenched her hands in front of her. "It's my project."

"I'll fill you in later. Why should you waste your time?"

"If you'd asked me first, I probably would have agreed with you." Emily drew a deep breath. "You didn't ask."

"I'm sorry," Richard said impatiently, "but since you wouldn't have gone, anyway, I don't see why we're having this conversation." He looked down at Jane. "Don't you have something to do?" he asked pointedly.

"Yes." She crossed to Emily's desk, picked up

the shopping bag and dropped it in front of Emily. "Don't forget this."

Emily looked at her and nodded. "You're right. I won't."

"What's in the bag?" Richard asked.

"Surprises." Emily smiled at him tightly. "Don't pick me up. I'll come to your place. Chill some champagne."

Richard glanced at Jane, who smiled back at him serenely.

"All right. Eight o'clock." He looked uncertainly from Jane to Emily, shook his head and left.

"I can do this," Emily said.

"Absolutely," Jane said.

Emily put her head down on the desk and moaned, and Jane patted her on the back.

AT EIGHT, EMILY RANG THE doorbell at Richard's apartment, trying to balance the shopping bag and a silver bowl of strawberries without losing her purse. Richard opened the door wearing a thick velour robe, a smile and obviously not much else. His smile faded at the sight of her. She was still in her business suit, her hair pinned up and her reading glasses on.

"Strawberries?" she said.

"Thank you." He took them and stood back to let her in. There was champagne in a bucket and two silver-rimmed glasses, chilled and waiting.

Emily took a deep breath. "Why don't we take this into the bedroom?"

"Fine," Richard said, slightly puzzled by her tension.

He followed her into his bedroom and watched her put the champagne and glasses on the bedside table.

"Have you got the strawberries?" she asked, and took the bowl from him, putting it on the table with the champagne. "Got any matches?" she asked, and began to unpack the fat white candles from her shopping bag.

"Yes." Richard took her arm. "What are you doing?"

"I thought we'd try something a little different tonight. Matches?"

He watched while she placed the candles around the room. Dozens of them.

"Good thing I have fire insurance," he said as Emily lit them all, and then turned out the lights.

The room glowed from the flames, almost as light as daylight but much softer. He moved toward her.

"We have to talk," Emily said.

"Let's talk later." Richard reached for her.

"No." Emily folded her arms across her chest. "Now."

He looked at her stern stubborn face and sighed. "All right." He sat on the edge of the bed. "What?"

She moistened her lips. "I love you, and I intend to marry you, but not until you recognize me as a partner."

He looked shocked. "I do."

"No. You decide what's important and what isn't. You don't listen." He started to protest and she held up her hand. "Did you look at the budget and try to find money for the rubies and the product placement?"

"Emily, it isn't there."

"Did you *try* to find it?"

The look on his face told her he hadn't.

"You didn't try because you decided before I even talked to you that it wasn't possible." Emily hesitated and then went determinedly on. "You don't listen to me. And as much as I love you, I can't live with a man who doesn't treat me seriously."

"I treat you seriously," Richard said, appalled. "You're the most important person in my world."

She knew it was true. She also knew he wasn't listening to her—again.

She tried one more time. "I don't think you realize how much you assume the right to make decisions for me. I can't let you do that. But if I have to fight you on this, all we'll do is waste time and money for the company."

"Emily, we've talked about this before."

"It's not just the company." She took a deep breath. "I want more control here, with you, too."

"You can have it." He held out his hand. "Now come here."

"That's exactly what I mean." She took a step backward. "You say, 'Come here,' and I'm supposed to jump."

"Okay." He stood up. "I'll come there."

"No, that's not what I want."

"Well, what do you want?" He was getting exasperated.

Emily swallowed. "I want one night where you promise to do anything I tell you to."

Richard looked uneasy. "Define 'anything.'"

"No." Emily looked at him. "If you want me tonight, you'll have to trust me. And promise me you'll do exactly what I say."

"All right," he said finally.

"Promise."

"I promise."

"Word of honor."

"What the hell are you going to do?"

"Word of honor."

"Word of honor." He shook his head. "I don't like this."

"That's the point," Emily said. "I don't like it, either, but you treat me this way every day."

"So this is to teach me a lesson?"

"No. It's to demonstrate my point. Since you won't listen, maybe you'll see instead."

"All right." He didn't look happy but he nodded. "What do you want me to do?"

She took a deep breath. "Take off your robe and lie down on the bed."

He dropped the robe and lay down naked on the bed, watching her warily. He looked great naked. *I'd be so embarrassed to do that,* she thought. *Why is it that guys never are? Must be all those locker rooms.*

"Okay. The first rule is you can't touch me until I tell you to."

"What?" He sat up.

"You swore, word of honor," she reminded him.

"I really don't like this," he said, but he lay back down again and poured himself a glass of champagne.

Emily turned and stood at the foot of the bed with her back to him, looking at herself in the large mirror over the bureau.

She looked sexless, a bug-eyed robot in a severe charcoal suit. *There's a great body under this suit,* she thought, *and Richard loves it.* She took her glasses off and put them on the bureau.

She turned around and met Richard's eyes. He looked bored and a little chilly, but he was drinking his champagne. She slowly unbuttoned her suit jacket and dropped it on the bureau.

"Take it all off," he suggested, grinning at her and toasting her with his glass.

She walked to the side of the bed and put her foot up on the edge. She was wearing black spike heels with open toes.

"New shoes?" he asked, trying not to laugh.

Very funny, she thought. *Laugh at this.* She moved her foot across to the other side of him so that her leg was arched across his stomach and buried the spiked heel in the comforter by his hip.

He winced. "Watch that heel."

She felt stupid, but it was too late now. She drew her fingertips up her leg, pulling her skirt back over her thigh to reveal her garters, never taking her eyes off Richard. The garters were pink.

Richard began to look more interested.

Okay, she thought. *I can do this.*

She reached into her skirt pocket and brought out a bottle of Sizzle. Croswell had fixed the formula, and now she was going to give it its first road test. Or in this case, bed test. She pulled the stopper out of the bottle and drew it along her inner thigh, shuddering a little at the sensation. Her whole body tightened, and she shivered in surprise. She looked down at Richard, and he met her eyes. She licked her tongue across her upper lip, more in reaction to the sensation than to seduce him, but he put down his glass and reached for her.

"No," she said, and his arms fell.

She stroked the inside of her thigh with her fingertips, feeling them glide across the smoothness of the nylon, closing her eyes, trying to concentrate on the sensation, wondering if any of this was exciting Richard in the slightest. Surprisingly enough, it was beginning to excite *her*. The Sizzle was a gentle tingle, a faint heat. She breathed a little deeper.

When she opened her eyes, Richard was still looking at her.

She unsnapped her garters with one hand.

Richard was definitely interested. She remoistened the stopper with perfume, then leaned forward to draw the perfumed glass along his throat, knowing he would be inches from the open neck of her blouse, and would see the pink lace stretched across her breasts and feel the perfumed warmth of her.

He reached up, and she pulled back.

“No,” she said. He hesitated, then put his hands behind his head.

She put the perfume on the table and slid her fingers under the nylon of her stocking, easing it slowly past her thigh and over her calf, concentrating on the feel of the nylon sliding across her skin and on her own touch. She kicked off her shoe and pulled the stocking off her toes and then dragged the wispy nylon across his chest. He clenched his hands behind his head but didn’t move.

She got up from the bed and stood beside him, kicking off her other shoe, and then she turned her back and wriggled once as she eased the zipper on her skirt down. As it slipped over her hips, she bent over to catch it, knowing that the little black slip she was wearing would ride up over her back, knowing that he would get only tantalizing glimpses of pink lace underneath.

Her skirt fell to the floor.

“This is great,” Richard said and reached for her. “Come here.”

“You promised,” she said, turning back to him. He put his hands behind his head again and smiled at her.

She moved to the bed and straddled him without touching him, dressed now in her blouse and short black slip. He watched her as she slowly moved across him, her weight on one hip, and unsnapped the garters of her remaining stocking. She reached behind and under her slip and unhooked the garter belt, dropping it on the floor.

She picked up the perfume bottle and drew the stopper across her inner thigh, feeling the heat and tingle again—sizzle. Then she dropped the bottle on the bed and stroked the soft skin of her thigh through the stocking, breathing deeper as she stroked because it felt incredibly good.

When Emily looked up, Richard was watching her, aroused and fascinated. *I can make him feel like that without touching him,* she thought. She felt powerful and exciting. She stroked again and forgot exactly what she'd planned to do, concentrating on the heat that was beginning inside her and the desire on Richard's face, moving her hand higher, until she was stroking herself through the pink lace. She closed her eyes for a moment to savor her own touch, catching her tongue between her lips, and when she opened her eyes, Richard was leaning toward her.

"You are incredible." He began to take his hands from behind his head, and she stopped instantly.

"All right," he said, relaxing again, "but hurry."

She eased the stocking down her leg, lowering her leg across him when she had pulled the stocking off. He moved against her and she felt him hard against her thigh.

"Oh, God, Emily," he said, and began to bring his hands from behind his head once more. *This is it,* she thought. *Jane did it; so can I.*

Still holding the stocking, she quickly leaned into him so that his face was hidden in her blouse, and while his mouth sought her breast, she wrapped the stocking around his wrists and pulled them back.

"What are you doing?" He tried to jerk his hands away, but she'd already tied the ends of the stocking to the brass bed frame.

"I'm helping you keep your word," she whispered, and straddled him again, bracing herself across him so that her body wasn't touching his.

"This isn't funny, Emily." He yanked at his bonds. "Let me go."

"What?" Emily asked, smiling at him gently. "I didn't hear." She slowly unbuttoned her blouse, while his eyes followed every move. She felt the silk fall open to expose the pink-and-silver lace that cupped her breasts. When she pulled her shoulders back to let the blouse fall from her shoulders, he suddenly breathed out heavily, moaning a little when the silk fell behind her onto his legs.

She reached up and pulled the pins from her hair, and it tumbled across her shoulders. She bent and trailed it across his stomach, running her fingers through her curls, and then she arched her body so she could feel her hair fall onto her back, swaying with the sheer pleasure of the touch of her curls on her skin.

"Emily, please," Richard said.

She watched him watch her as she ran her hand across the black silk slip that covered her body, sliding the sheer slip against her, and then slowly pulling it up so he could see first the strip of hot-pink lace across her hips, then the slight roundness of her stomach and finally the full swell of her breasts, straining against the pink lace roses.

When she dropped the slip to the floor, he closed his eyes.

"Untie me," he said.

"What?" Emily asked softly. "I didn't hear you."

She leaned across him and picked a strawberry from the dish. "These were the juiciest strawberries I could find," she said and leaned closer to him, her breasts almost spilling out of the lace. She stopped for a moment, savoring the feel of their weight against the brief bra. Then she held the berry before him and ran her tongue across it, licking it inches from his mouth, biting into its icy sweetness, dripping the juice across his chest as she sucked the fruit into her mouth.

"Sorry," she said, and bent down to lick the juice from his skin. Her mouth was cool against the heat of his flesh, and he writhed under her touch.

"Untie me," he said.

She ignored him.

"What are you doing?" he said.

"Anything I want to." She kissed him, plunging her tongue into his mouth. His kiss was hard and biting, hot with frustration and need. She pulled back and stared at him, her eyes half-shut, flicking her tongue across her swollen lips.

"Are you going to let me make love to you tonight?" he whispered fiercely.

"Yes," Emily said. "All night. All of me. Anything you want. When I'm ready."

"You're ready now." Richard pressed himself up against her. "I can feel how hot you are."

"I decide when I'm ready," Emily said, and pulled back, taking another strawberry from the bowl as she settled herself gently across his hips, the lace barely touching the hardness of him there. He pushed his hips up under her, and she rose, flexing her thighs so that she was just out of reach. When he relaxed again, she settled above him, watching him, still barely touching him.

With his eyes on her lips, she bit off the end of the strawberry and then drew the cut end of the fruit across her throat and over the swell of her breasts, leaving a trail of gleaming juice that seemed to sizzle on her skin. She grew dizzy at the sensation, closing her eyes and crushing the berry into the hollow between her breasts.

"I'm so hot," she said.

"I know." She opened her eyes and saw him looking at her, more calmly than before. "Go on," he said. "I want to watch."

She opened her hand and looked at the crushed berry and then put it in her mouth. Some of the juice escaped at the corner of her mouth, and her tongue flicked out and caught it. Richard watched her and breathed in deeply.

Her body throbbed. She stroked her hands up over her sides and across her breasts, reveling in their fullness. Her breasts grew hard, straining at the lace, and she brought her hands behind her and unfastened the bra, arching her back as her breasts fell free, watching Richard watch her, and glorying in his desire for her.

"You are so beautiful," he said, his voice thick with wanting her.

She rocked slightly on top of him, still barely touching him, and they both moaned at the touch. "Watch," she said, and ran her hand slowly across her round belly and into the nest of pink lace between her legs, moaning at her own touch as she slowly stroked herself. When she opened her eyes, he was smiling at her, but his eyes were black with need.

"Touch me," he said, and she leaned forward, taking another strawberry from the bowl, biting into the icy sweetness and letting the juice fall across him again, sucking it from his muscled body, running her tongue across his nipples until he shuddered. Then she arched her back, trailing the bleeding fruit across her stomach and her thighs until she was slick and shining with the juice. She held the crushed berry to her mouth and sucked it in, then moved forward again and kissed him, thrusting her tongue into his mouth and filling him with the taste of strawberries.

"Now," he said.

She smiled. Then she sat up, moving her body gently over his hips. She slid away from the bed to stand beside him. She used one finger to pull the pink lace down from her hips, letting it fall to the floor. Then she straddled him again, naked and sticky with the gleaming juice, her long hair sweeping across his chest, easing herself down over him until he was just barely inside her, barely touching her. She wanted him so much she could hardly breathe.

She looked into his eyes and saw the desire and the love there, and she said, "Now," and reached up to pull the end of the slipknot and free his hands at the same time she plunged her hips into his.

He cried out as she covered him, and he rolled her over onto her back, running his hands across her arms, her breasts, cradling her face as he kissed her savagely, all the while thrusting into her as if he couldn't stop, would never stop. She clung to him, gasping because he felt so good inside her. The feel of his body hot and strong and hard against her, inside her, pushed her out of the limbo of lust she'd been drifting through and over the edge of her orgasm, and she clawed at him and cried as it came, feeling him shudder with his own climax.

He held her tightly against him, drawing his breath in huge shuddering gasps.

"Don't ever do that again," he finally breathed. "You damn near killed me."

"I thought you liked it," she whispered.

"I did. But never again. It was too much." He kissed her, his lips soft on hers, and then began to explore her body with his tongue, licking the stickiness from her, kissing her over and over, exhausted from lovemaking but still needing her.

"I liked it," Emily said sleepily.

"I could tell." Richard pulled the edge of the comforter over them and stroked his hand slowly up and down her back until she fell asleep, but he couldn't, and when he woke her up half an hour later, still crazy with need, they made love with even more intensity than before.

When he awoke the next morning, he was alone. For a moment he thought Emily had left, but then he heard her in the kitchen.

She was dressed in his robe, making French toast from slabs of French bread and cinnamon-seasoned eggs and cream. It smelled like heaven.

He came up behind her and kissed her on the neck, and she leaned back into him.

"I never thought to ask you last night," she said. "Do you like strawberries?"

"Yes." He held her tight against him. "I especially like the way you served them. Could we do that again without the part where I get tied up?"

"Strawberries or syrup on your toast?" Emily asked.

"Strawberries," he said.

She poured syrup over the thick slabs and handed the plate to him.

"Emily?"

"Eat," she said cheerfully. "It'll get cold."

Richard sat down at the table, naked and confused.

She brought her own plate and sat across from him, pouring syrup over her toast, too.

"Big meeting today," she said.

He looked down at the syrup on his plate and sighed, and then began to eat. "Let's go in late. The meeting's not until eleven."

She chewed her toast. "I've never made this with cream before. It's really rich."

"It's great," Richard said and tried again. "Let's go in late to the meeting."

Emily handed him her coffee cup.

"Freshen this for me, would you?" she asked, smiling.

"Sure." He got up, poured in more coffee and handed the cup back to her. "Let's go in late to the meeting," he began for the third time, but she overrode him as if he hadn't spoken.

"Thanks for the coffee, love. I've got to go over a few things with Jane, so I'm going in early."

"But, Emily," Richard began, still confused.

She picked up her cup and carried it out of the kitchen with her.

"Emily!" Richard sounded outraged.

She leaned back into the doorway so he could see her. "Did you say something, dear? I didn't hear." Then she gave him a brilliant smile and went into the bedroom.

He scowled at his toast for a moment, then got up and followed her into the bedroom. She wasn't there, but he could hear water running in the bathroom.

"All right, Emily," he said to the bathroom door. "You've made your point. It's very annoying being ignored, and it's very frustrating being powerless. Now come out here." He rattled the doorknob, but it was locked.

"Emily!"

"I can't hear you, Richard," she called back. "The water's running."

The water continued to run for what seemed an eternity. When she shut it off, Richard tried the door again. "Emily, come out here! I want to talk to you."

The door opened and Emily came out, dressed for work. She kissed him on the cheek.

"See you at work, darling," she said, and slipped away from him. He followed her to the door, but stepped back when she opened it.

"Dammit, Emily."

She wiggled her fingers at him and left, closing the door behind her.

"Very funny." He stalked back to his bedroom to get dressed.

RICHARD TRIED TO CALL her when he got to work, but Jane said she wasn't in. He stormed downstairs and past Jane, but her office really was empty.

"Where is she?" he snarled at Jane.

"Who the hell do you think you are?" Jane asked calmly.

He stopped, stunned.

"She's your partner, not your property. She does not have to be here in case you want her," Jane said, folding her arms and glaring at him. "And if you have any brains at all, you'll start listening to her, because she's very good at what she does. She made four million dollars for this company in the last six months. So far you haven't brought in a dime."

Richard glared at her, his blue eyes steely with anger.

Jane glared back, unfazed. "If you won't listen to her because she deserves to be listened to, perhaps you'll listen to her to save your job. Because if Sizzle flops because you didn't give her the money to do the job, it's not going to be her neck on the line."

"She throws money around like it's water," Richard said, his glare fading. "She needs me."

"Absolutely." Jane smiled. "She's a complete loss at budgeting. But you're a complete loss at marketing. And budgeting never sold perfume yet. Emily can sell perfume, but only if you listen to her. Instead of ignoring her, listen to her and find her the money she needs. She gave up a lot of things she wanted on this campaign because of you, and that's good. She's learned a lot from you. She's been careful and focused on the two most important things, the things she felt were vital to sell Sizzle—rubies and the product placement. And you haven't even tried to help her. You just said no. You didn't even try."

Richard's glare faded to a wince. "I didn't listen, you mean."

"She'll be at the meeting in an hour," Jane said.

He started to say something, then turned and walked to the elevator. When he was gone, Jane went to the ladies' room.

Emily was sitting on the vanity waiting for her.

"He's gone," said Jane.

"And?"

"I don't know." Jane leaned against the wall. "I told him all the stuff we'd agreed on. He looked like he wasn't used to taking that kind of talk from secretaries."

"If he still thinks of you as a secretary, he's not paying attention."

"Well, that *is* his problem."

"So what now?"

"Are you going to drop your bomb at the meeting?"

"Yes." Emily scooted off the counter. "Both of them. You coming?"

"Absolutely," Jane said. "I'll run the VCR."

EMILY WAS BRILLIANT in the meeting. She introduced the perfume, had the other executives try it on so they could feel the tingle, and then began to talk about the target consumer and the marketing program. She could feel Richard looking at her, but when she looked up she didn't see the glare she expected.

She saw pride. He thought she was wonderful. *And he should,* she thought. *I* am *wonderful.*

"We're using a campaign that's analogous to Paradise, but different," she continued, putting the large mock-up advertising had done for her on the easel. "You'll note that the bottle is the same as Paradise, but it's black, instead of white, with a ruby-glass stopper, instead of a diamond-glass stopper."

They nodded.

"We're confident that the consumer will make not only the connection with Paradise, but will also subconsciously pick up the dualism here. She'll wear Paradise when she wants to feel sexy, but sophisticated and in control, Sizzle when she wants to feel sexy and wanton. She will, for example, put Sizzle places she wouldn't dream of putting Paradise." A couple of the male executives looked thoughtful and interested to mask the erotic thoughts that leapfrogged through minds. One of the female executives picked up the sample bottle.

"And since there's a little bit of angel and a little bit of devil in every woman, every woman will need both these perfumes," Emily said, and the female executive grinned at her. *Bingo,* Emily thought. *Get a note to advertising.*

"Will we be using the rubies at the openings and the showing like we did with Paradise?" Henry Evadne, the vice president, asked.

"Yes." Emily looked straight at Richard. "We bought the rubies. I'm sending the purchase order up to Mr. Parker this afternoon."

Richard raised his eyebrows.

"Did you say something, Mr. Parker?" Emily asked. "I'm afraid I didn't hear you."

Oblivious to the byplay, Henry said, "Good idea. The diamonds were a big hit. Helped add class to the product. Very good idea, Emily."

"Thank you, Henry." Emily paused. "But I haven't told you the best part."

Richard sighed. *He knows what's coming,* Emily thought.

"Sizzle is a natural for a product placement," she began. "I called L.A. to find a movie that would be big and glitzy and sexy, and I found one, but Mr. Parker felt that the fee they were asking was outrageous—" she hesitated as Richard frowned, probably trying to remember if they'd ever talked about any movie in particular "—and, of course, he was right."

He lifted his eyebrows at her again.

"So I went back, and thanks to Mr. Parker's good advice, I found the perfect vehicle."

She took a deep breath. This was the gamble.

"It's a low-budget film made by a man just out of UCLA. But he's a genius. This film could be the next *Sex, Lies, and Videotape.* It could sweep Cannes. And our product will be in it. When the press starts obsessing over every detail in the film, Sizzle will be in every magazine in the country—free."

Henry was shaking his head. "A little art movie. It could do nothing."

"Then it does nothing." Emily smiled confidently. "Life is a gamble. We gambled on Paradise. And I *know* this is going to work."

Henry frowned. "I don't like gambles. Where did the money for this come from, Richard?"

Emily tensed.

"We trimmed some of the other areas," Richard said.

Thank you, Emily said with her eyes. Even though she'd sandbagged him, he'd come through for her. In fact, he was lying through his teeth for her.

"If you'll look at this rough budget," Richard said, passing around sheets of figures, "you can see how we can afford the placement by cutting back on the print media. If the placement comes through for us, we won't need that much, anyway. The rubies are actually a capital investment and should be purchased through investment funds, not advertising."

Emily looked at the sheet he handed her. It wasn't a lie. He'd really tried. In the hour before the meeting. This time, he'd listened and tried and done it.

She loved him so much she ached with it.

Henry nodded. "Still, a movie with an unknown director and unknown actors..." He shook his head.

"But this movie is going to rewrite the cinema history books on eroticism." Emily picked up the ball from Richard. "Of course, I don't expect you to take my word for that." She nodded to Jane, who pushed the play button on the VCR at the front of the room and turned off the lights.

"They're shooting the scene with Sizzle this week," Emily said, as the two actors on the screen began to move toward each other. "Therefore, I can't show you the actual product placement, but this scene should give you an idea of the movie's potential."

She moved around the table and sat down beside Richard as the two actors embraced. The scene still had an amazing erotic effect on Emily, even the second time around. Midway through, Richard put his hand on her knee and ran it slowly up her thigh, pushing her skirt up as he stroked her.

Richard and I have got to keep this tape, she thought. *It's an instant aphrodisiac. Not that we need one. But you never know...*

When the clip was over, Jane turned the lights back on and the VCR off, and Richard moved his hand away.

Richard and I have got to have a meeting after this, Emily thought. *A very intense private meeting. Immediately.*

The executives around the table had slightly glazed looks.

Henry cleared his throat and straightened in his seat. "I'm not happy about cutting back on print, but this budget Richard has proposed is obviously still a very tight one. And the movie will certainly be, uh, stirring. Although not pornographic," he added quickly.

The rest of the executives mumbled their assent.

Henry straightened his tie and continued. "And if Emily feels strongly about the product placement, we will, of course, go with it." He smiled tightly at Richard. "We don't know how she does it, but we've learned that when it comes to marketing, the best thing we can do is listen to Emily and do exactly what she wants."

"Yes." Richard smiled. "I've learned that, too."

"Good." Henry leaned back, satisfied. "You make a good team. Sizzle, huh?" He looked at Emily and forced an offhand voice. "Have you an extra bottle? I'd like to take some to my wife. She's, uh, interested in our new products."

"Certainly." Emily picked up the prototype. "Take this one."

Jane hummed the theme from *Rocky* very faintly behind her.

THE THREE OF THEM SAT in the conference room after everyone had left.

"Very neatly done." Jane stretched. "We are incredible. The three musketeers. We had them eating out of our hands."

Richard looked at her. "You're very generous. The two of you made the brilliant decisions."

"And you made them possible with the budget." Jane beamed at him. "We're not dummies. We know when somebody's saved our bacon, don't we, Em?"

"Go away," Emily said. "Two of the musketeers have something to finish."

Jane grinned good-naturedly. "Only if I can take the videotape and go see Ben. We never did watch this. Our mistake."

"Take the afternoon off," Emily said. "I'm going to be busy."

When Jane left, ostentatiously locking the door behind her, Richard looked at Emily.

"I'm wearing Sizzle," Emily said. "It makes strong men putty in my hands. You're a strong man." She got up and sat on the table in front of him and put her hands on his shoulders. He immediately pulled her onto his lap. "See? I told you it was good stuff."

"From now on, I'm listening to everything you tell me."

"You already did. You fixed the budget."

"Not just the budget." He ran his hands up her back. "This was really a one-two punch you gave me, first last night and then this morning with Jane, but I think I've finally gotten the message." He pulled her blouse out of her skirt and slipped his hand under it, cupping her lace-covered breast. "From now on, I'm listening," he repeated.

"The hook is in the front," Emily said, and he unfastened it.

"Anything else you want to tell me?" Richard asked as he lifted her onto the table. "I'm listening."

"Yes," Emily said, pulling him down on top of her. "I love you. Make me sizzle."

* * * * *

TOO FAST TO FALL

For my uncle, who loved fast cars.

CHAPTER ONE

THE COP GREW larger in Jenny's side mirror as he approached, his sunglasses glinting ominous light as she considered whether or not to make a run for it.

She might be able to escape. The highway was a nice, straight run here, and a gorgeous 350 V-8 engine purred beneath the hood of her 1978 Camaro, just waiting for her to punch the accelerator. The deputy would have to get all the way back to his SUV before he could even consider chasing her down. By then, she'd be a speck of bright yellow a mile down the asphalt. And hell, with the snow still five feet deep on either side of the road, she could just pull off onto any old trail and he might pass right by her.

Jenny flexed her fingers against the thin circle of the steering wheel. She was tempted. She knew how to run. It had always been her first instinct, and she'd pulled it off many times. But as she watched the cop's hard-hewn jaw begin to tic in anger, she sighed and slumped in her seat. Deputy

Hendricks knew very well where she lived. He'd written her address down on three separate speeding tickets, not to mention two terse warnings.

"Good Morning, Deputy Hendricks!" she said brightly, as if she weren't easing her foot from a tempted hover above the gas pedal.

He didn't return her greeting. He didn't say anything at all. He just...*loomed,* his sharp cheekbones and hard-edged jaw a warning of danger. His lean body a threat of strength. The mountains looked small behind him.

Jenny made a valiant attempt not to squirm. "I thought I had a few more days on my tags."

His hands were loose by his sides in a pose she recognized from the other five times he'd pulled her over. One hand near his gun. One near his baton. He'd never reached for either, thank God, but this time, both his hands spasmed into brief fists before relaxing into readiness again.

"End of the month, right?" she squeaked. She'd found him pretty cute on previous stops. Now she only felt nervous.

His hands closed one more time, and then he eased them open with deliberate slowness. "Ms. Stone," he said, grinding out her name.

She aimed a big smile up at him, though her lips felt stiff. "That's me."

"Unfortunately, I'm well aware of that."

"I—"

"Just as I assume you're well aware of why I've stopped you today."

"Is it—?"

"And *no,*" he barked. "It has nothing to do with your damn tags."

She flinched at the way his voice filled her car.

In response, he cleared his throat and rolled his neck. "Excuse me," he said in a much quieter tone, though the ends of the words were clipped enough to sound razor-sharp. "While I run your information to see if you've acquired any warrants for your arrest since the last time I stopped you."

His heel scraped against the asphalt. Jenny leaned out. "Don't you need my license and—?"

He threw a hand up to stop her words and muttered something she didn't quite catch. Apparently he had no trouble recalling her name and birth date.

"Shit," she groaned as she ducked back into her seat. He'd been lenient in the past, but last time he'd clocked her going eighty in a fifty-five, he'd been clear that his tolerance had worn thin.

One more ticket, Ms. Stone, and you'll be called before a judge. You'll lose your license for thirty days, at best. At worst, you'll be charged with reckless endangerment.

"Of what?" she muttered to her steering wheel. "Chipmunks?" It had been November. Too cold for Yellowstone tourists and not snowy enough for skiers. She rolled her eyes as she heard the door of his truck open, but immediately after he slammed it, his footsteps sounded again. She watched him approach in her mirror, just as he had a few minutes before, but this time, she sank down a little in defense.

"Do you know how dangerous this is?" he growled before he even reached her window. "It's the middle of winter, damn it! You could hit a patch of ice! You could—"

"It hasn't snowed in two weeks," she argued. "The roads have been bone-dry for days!"

"Are you kidding me? There's snowmelt streaming across the road everywhere! And what if you'd suddenly come up on an elk? Or some stupid tourist stopped in the road to take a picture of a stupid elk? Are you…just…are you…?"

"Stupid?" she volunteered, hunching farther down in her seat. If she lost her license, she'd go mad. She couldn't live without her car. Or rather, she couldn't live without driving. It felt like flying to her. It felt like freedom. And it had been, three times now.

"Yes!" Deputy Hendricks yelled. "Stupid!"

"I'm sorry," she whispered. He'd never, ever lost his temper before.

He was silent for a long moment. A gas tanker drove past them, sucking the air through her open window, then hurling it back in.

Jenny shook her head. "I'm really sorry." She meant it. He'd been kind to her and she'd promised not to speed again. And now here she was.

He took a deep breath. His clenched teeth looked very white against his tan skin. "Jenny," he said, the only time he'd used her first name since she'd invited him to three tickets ago. She glanced up but couldn't puzzle out his expression behind his sunglasses. She'd never seen him with his glasses off. She worked at the saloon at night, so all her joyrides occurred during daylight hours. All she knew of him was his dark skin and sculpted jaw and wide mouth. Under his hat, his hair looked deep brown. The wide shoulders beneath his uniform jacket eased the insult of the tickets, and the cheekbones didn't hurt, either, but for all she knew he had bug eyes that wandered in different directions and brows like a twitchy mad scientist.

But probably not.

He stared steadily down at her. Jenny's heart fell. "It's okay," she said softly. "Just write the ticket. It's my own fault, and I know you've tried to help."

He watched her for a long moment, then cleared his throat and shifted. "Ms. Stone, you're not some eighteen-year-old punk with too much testosterone and too little intelligence. Why can't you just go the speed limit and save us both some pain? Why is that so hard? Even five miles per hour over and I'd be able to shrug it off. Just…why?"

She couldn't tell him, because she had no idea. Driving made her happy. The feel of the power at her fingertips. The rush of the wind past her open window when the weather cooperated. And the faster she drove, the freer she felt. Fifty-five miles per hour wasn't happiness. It was just more constriction. "I don't know," she said honestly. "But it makes me feel better that giving me tickets is painful for you. After all this time, we're practically friends now, aren't we?"

His flat mouth didn't budge in the slightest. "I meant that writing another ticket will be painful for me because I'll lose a whole morning in court testifying against you."

Her heart sank and bleated an ugly curse on its way down. She was mad at herself, and terrified about the consequences, and just a tiny bit hurt that Deputy Hendricks didn't feel some small affection for her. She'd always been polite to him. Cheerful, even as he wrote her a ticket. She wasn't a bad person.

"I warned you last time."

"I know." She felt tears prick her eyes, and blinked them furiously away. If he was going to be mean, she didn't want him to see her cry. "It's okay," she said again.

He walked away, thank God, because a tear had

managed to escape and slip down her cheek. She swiped at her jaw and sniffed hard. She wouldn't cry. It was her own fault, and even if Deputy Hendricks was being particularly hard-nosed, she wouldn't cry. She wouldn't. She deserved this, and he'd cut her enough slack. She sniffed again and scrubbed at her eyes.

The deputy cleared his throat from right beside her.

She froze in horror. He'd walked away to write her a ticket. What was he doing back so quickly?

When she snuck a glance out the window, she saw him holding out a business card instead of the thin paper of a ticket. "What's that?" she asked, thinking it was a card for the attorney she was going to need.

"Take it," he said gruffly.

She took it gingerly, barely touching the edges of the card.

"It's information about a local driving class. I want you to promise to sign up. One, you need it. And two, it'll help your case the next time I pull you over. Because I will give you a ticket next time, Ms. Stone. No questions. No leniency."

"What?" she breathed.

"I'm serious. This is getting ridiculous. You're too old for this crap, and you make a fool out of me every time I let you off."

"I don't mean to! I'm sorry! It's not like I drive

away thinking, 'Yeah! I fooled the Man!' I mean… Um…" She felt her face flame. His sunglasses stared down at her in unwavering judgment. Her attempt at a smile felt like a grimace as she held up the card. "I'll take the class. I really appreciate this. I do every time."

"Every time," he muttered. "Right."

"Each time," she tried. "Both times. Well, this is maybe the third…"

"Yes," he said. "It is the third. The third warning. The *sixth* stop."

"I just get lost in thought. I don't realize I'm going so fast. It's kind of hard to keep her under sixty."

His head turned slightly toward the hood of the car. "Maybe it's time to buy a nice sedan."

A tiny, horrified whimper escaped from her mouth.

"I bet you'd save a hell of a lot of money on gas. And it would have airbags."

"I'll slow down," she croaked.

"You'd better. Or you'll find out how easy it is to keep her under sixty when you're not allowed out of the garage."

"Yes, sir."

His face tipped toward her again at her hoarse whisper. He stared for a moment. She could see her own tiny face looking pitiful and pale in the black lenses.

"Go on," he finally said. "I'm not giving you an official warning because I don't want any record of this. It's an embarrassment. Drive safely, Ms. Stone. And *slowly.* Please? For the love of whatever it is you value?"

"Yes, sir," she whispered again.

He stepped back. She waited, but he finally shook his head. "Just go before I change my mind."

Jenny started the car, wincing at the roar of the engine. Normally, she loved that sound, but right now it seemed a little much. "Thank you," she said again. "Really. Come in for a free beer sometime, okay?"

Maybe not the right thing to say to a deputy who seemed obsessed with road safety. Shoot. Jenny released the brake and pulled away. In her nervousness, she hit the gas too hard and as she pulled off the shoulder, the tires squealed. Just a little. Just enough to make her wish she was dead.

"Oh, God," she groaned, eyes flashing to the rearview mirror as she left Deputy Hendricks behind in an unfortunate cloud of dust. Well, not a cloud. More like a tiny, harmless puff.

Heart pounding hard, Jenny drove back to town safely. And very slowly, keeping her eye on the speedometer the whole way. It didn't feel very much like flying, but it was better than being grounded.

It might be time to make a run for it, after all.

NATE PULLED INTO THE lot of the Crooked R Saloon, and his gaze was immediately drawn to the yellow Camaro parked in the far corner. He felt his left eye twitch at the sight. That woman and her damned menace of a car.

He should've given her the ticket. He'd sworn to himself that he would. After issuing that last warning, he'd ordered himself to have a steel will the next time she flew past him.

In fact, each time he stopped her, each time she drove away, he told himself that was it. He wouldn't be lenient again. If she deserved jail time, the judge would give it to her. It wasn't Nate's responsibility to decide. She was a repeat offender. She deserved whatever she got, even if she was always cheerful and sweet and apologetic.

But yesterday he'd seen her flying by again, a bright flash of yellow that shot adrenaline straight into his heart, and despite his rage and frustration and impatience, his resolve had been as weak as paper. She'd flashed that slightly crooked smile and called him "Deputy Hendricks" as if it were a private joke they shared, and…

"Fuck," he growled as he made himself turn away from her car and walk toward the front porch of the saloon.

What the hell was he doing here?

His brain had snuck up on him to issue a reminder that whatever excuse he had to be at the

Crooked R, it was flimsy as hell. But he *did* have an excuse. His cousin had needed to meet with him, so why not here? It had been thirty-two hours since Nate had pulled Jenny Stone over, so it was time for a reminder about that driving class.

Sure, she'd promised. She'd even shed grateful tears. But he didn't think for one minute that she'd called about the class yet. Why would she, when she had yet another chance to push him toward insanity? Instead of doing what he'd ordered, she'd probably attach floating neon lights to the undercarriage of her car and get her windows tinted before adding a sticker about pigs to taunt him the next time she flashed her bumper.

He was just another cop fooled by a pretty face. Hardly a rare breed. And now here he was, at her workplace like a hormone-addled fool.

Nate slid off his sunglasses and walked into the saloon, cursing himself every step of the way.

The place was packed. Five-dollar pitcher night, he realized belatedly. Not the ideal place to have a serious talk with his cousin. Then again, considering how worried Luis had sounded, maybe he'd appreciate the roar of background noise. Whatever it was, he'd made it clear that he couldn't invite Nate over to his own house.

Nate glanced around, meaning to look for his cousin, but somehow searching out a blond ponytail at the same time. And there she was, out from behind the bar, delivering a tray of pitchers. He'd never seen her outside her car. He'd never made her walk the shoulder to check for any telltale signs of inebriation. Reckless as her speeds were, her car always followed every curve of the road perfectly. Even when she spotted his lights, she eased into the stop, edging just far enough over to be safe, and never far enough to veer too deeply into the soft slope next to the highway. Jenny Stone was dangerous, but not in that way.

No, her danger lay in an entirely different set of curves.

"Damn," he cursed as his eyes roamed down her body. He'd gotten several nice glimpses of cleavage before, and had even wondered whether she'd purposefully set free a button or two as he approached. But he'd had no idea she'd been hiding a perfect ass the whole time. He almost cringed at the sight of it. Beautiful and plump and not at all good for his tenuous hold on sanity when it came to her.

And then she dealt another blow. His gaze traveled back up her body just as her eyes moved over the room. They paused on him for a moment, then moved on, no spark of recognition flashing. Not even a hint of it.

She had no idea who he was. He was just another cop when he was in his uniform, and nothing but a stranger in street clothes tonight.

"Perfect," he murmured, vowing right then that he'd talk to his cousin and then get the hell out of this place before his pride was permanently damaged by his sex drive.

Looking away from Jenny Stone, he caught sight of Luis raising a hand from a back table and headed gratefully in that direction.

"Cousin," he said as Luis flashed a tense smile and stood to give Nate a quick hug.

"Hey, Nate."

Nate had hoped to start off on a positive note, but Luis didn't look good. "You look like you haven't slept in a week."

Luis's tense smile disappeared in a flash, replaced by a pained grimace that even his goatee couldn't hide. "Shit, man. I don't know what to do."

"Is it James?" Nate asked, his thoughts immediately going to Luis's fifteen-year-old son. A ripe age for trouble, even for good kids.

"Yes… No!" Luis said. Then his head dropped. "I don't know. I'm really worried. I don't think he's gotten mixed up in it, but…he might have."

"Mixed up in what? Please tell me you haven't done anything stupid. I know the concrete business has been slow lately, but—"

"No, it's not me. It's… You know Teresa's cousin Victor came to live with us last year?"

Nate frowned. He'd met the kid once, and had his suspicions, but he'd never said a word. Teresa was a wonderful woman, quiet and strong with a will of steel. If a family member needed help, she wasn't going to ask more of him than clean language in the house and scrubbed hands when he came to dinner. "I remember," he finally said carefully.

"Everything seemed fine at first. He wasn't exactly a hard worker, but he's nineteen, you know? He took the job I offered and showed up every day. Okay, almost every day. Maybe he was a little lazy, but I kept my mouth shut about it to Teresa, because…"

Nate nodded. Teresa was as traditional a wife and mother as they came, and if she'd taken Victor in as one of her kids, that was that.

"Well, he quit a couple of months ago. Said he'd found other work. He wasn't specific, but he was paying his rent. Even bought an old car to get around in. Frankly, I was too relieved to ask any questions. I should have, though."

Nate's gut tightened in dread. He had a feeling he knew where this was headed, and it was nowhere good.

Running a hand through his hair, Luis met Nate's gaze for a moment, then let his chin drop.

"Teresa let him borrow my truck one day. When I got home, I asked what had happened to it. It was muddy as hell, like it'd gotten stuck somewhere. The kid just smiled and said he'd been helping a friend move. I let it go. Teresa said he'd probably been out joyriding on a trail somewhere, but it felt off to me. He's been cocky as hell about something lately. Two days ago, I followed him when he was supposed to be going to work. He ended up out at the cabin."

For a moment, Nate had no idea what he was talking about. "What cabin? The family cabin?"

"Yeah."

It was a run-down cabin down near South Park that had been in his dad's family for years. Forty years ago, when his father had been newly married to Nate's mom, her brother had come up from Mexico with nothing but a wife and hope for a better life. Nate's dad had rented them the cabin for a few years, and eventually they'd bought it from him. Nate had spent countless summer days there, playing with Luis and his other cousins. But these days the place was vacant and falling in on itself.

"So he's getting into trouble down there? Drinking, having sex?" But even as he said it, he knew that wasn't what had Luis glancing over his shoulder. Nate looked around himself, and caught sight of Jenny, grinning from ear to ear as she set a pitcher down a few tables away, then passed out mugs to the cowboys who smiled back at her.

Nate pulled his eyes away and leaned closer to Luis. "Listen, if he's cooking meth, I can—"

"That's not it. He's growing pot. That little bastard has a whole greenhouse set up out back."

"Are you kidding?"

"No. It's a shit job, made out of two-by-fours and plastic sheeting. I can't believe it hasn't collapsed under the snow yet, but I guess the heaters and lamps are melting it off. It's full of plants. And he's clearing out more land, like he plans to expand during the summer. That's why the truck is so muddy. He was trying to pull stumps out of half-frozen ground, because he apparently doesn't have even half a brain."

"Okay, listen. I'm glad you came to me. You're not responsible for it just because it's being grown on your land. This happens all the time these days. Somebody picks a secluded area, and—"

"It's not just on my land," Luis interrupted. "That damn greenhouse is sitting half on my land and half on federal forest. And that's not the worst of it."

Nate took a deep breath. "Do I want to know?"

"I have no idea, but I don't know who else to turn to. I need your help, Nate. It's…"

"Shit. Is James involved? Tell me the truth."

Luis slumped. "I don't know. He's a good boy,

but he loves his cousin. Looks up to him. And I found out he skipped school last week. The same day Victor borrowed the truck. Regardless of what Teresa wants, if I was sure James wasn't involved I would've just called you and had your guys go out and shut it down and arrest that little shit. But if he's pulled James into it…"

"Listen. Even if James is marginally involved, he's a good kid, like you said. He's only fifteen. He won't—"

"He's fifteen, yeah. And he's almost six feet tall, and he's got brown skin and the last name Hernandez, just like me. To a lot of people around here, he doesn't look like a good, harmless kid. He looks like an ad trying to scare people about dangerous illegals."

"Come on, Luis. People around here know you and your family."

"Yeah. And some of them probably remember when I was a kid and got up to no good."

Nate sighed. He'd forgotten about that. Luis had gone through a rebellious stage, and rebelled himself right out of school a couple of times. And into jail once after stealing beer from a local gas station. The same kind of trouble lots of kids got up to, but it was different when you were one of the few brown-skinned kids in the school.

"I'm scared, Nate. If my boy's involved and it's

on my land, it's going to look like a whole damn Mexican family operation."

"You're as American as I am," Nate snapped. "I shouldn't even have to say that. We were both born right here."

Luis raised an eyebrow, and Nate didn't bother arguing further. Sure, Nate bore the Hernandez name, as well, but it was his middle name, not his last. And he had his father's gray eyes and lighter skin than his cousins. He knew it wasn't the same for him.

He cursed and ran a hand over his jaw. "All right. Listen. Is there anywhere you can send James for a few days? Maybe a week? Doesn't Teresa's family live in Colorado?"

"Yeah. Maybe I can arrange something. But I'd have to pull him out of school. Teresa won't like that at all."

"You're going to tell her, though, right?"

Luis's eyes shifted away.

"Come on, man. You have to tell her."

"She won't like it. Better to lie. If I tell her, she'll want to let—"

A sudden shadow cut off Luis's words. "Hello, boys! You're not conspiring to lie to an innocent woman, are you?"

Luis flashed wide, panicked eyes up at Jenny, whose ponytail was still swaying from her abrupt appearance. "What?" he yelped.

She waved off his alarm. “I’m a bartender. Believe me, I see it every day. Just be kind to her, okay?” Smiling, she tipped her head toward Nate to include him in her advice, but still didn’t seem to recognize him. “You gentlemen want a pitcher?”

Luis shook his head, but Nate said, “Sure.”

Her eyes flickered down his body. “Light?”

Nate was suddenly damn glad for all the hours he put in at the gym to keep in shape over the winter. “Bring us the real thing. We’ll indulge.”

She flashed that smile again. Wide and open enough that it shouldn’t have felt intimate, but did. He’d thought that smile was something secret for him. But no. It was just her. She offered it to everyone in the crowd.

Good to know.

Nate laughed at himself as she turned away, already moving toward the bar to get their pitcher. But while he was still shaking his head at his own foolishness, Jenny jerked to a stop, frozen midstep.

Luis was leaning toward him, but Nate held up a hand and kept his eyes on Jenny as she slowly pivoted.

She frowned and cocked her head. Her eyes narrowed at him. And then her face broke into a grin wider than any she’d ever given to him.

“Deputy Hendricks?” she asked.

He tried not to feel thrilled. “Yes, ma’am.”

She laughed, her blond hair swinging as her

chin tipped up. "Oh, my God! I didn't recognize you without the shades!"

"Yeah, I noticed," he said dryly.

"It's not my fault! You look totally different. Not nearly so scary."

"Still a little scary, though, I gather?"

Instead of answering, she just stood there looking at him for a few long seconds. "My God," she finally said. "Look at you. You're a real person."

"That's just a rumor."

"Okay," she said, still smiling. Then she shook her head. "Okay. Well, the beer's on the house, Deputy."

"It's Nate," he responded.

Her eyebrows rose. "I like that."

She liked that. Thank God she finally turned away, because Nate knew he looked far too pleased with her opinion of his name.

"Hey," his cousin said, the worry in his voice making it clear he'd already dismissed any idea of the cute server. "What the hell am I going to do, man?"

Nate kept his eye on Jenny Stone's swinging hips until she was swallowed by the crowd at the bar before he gave up the vigil and met Luis's eyes. "No kidding around, are you asking me as a cousin or a cop?"

"Hell, I don't know. Both?"

"We've got two options, but whichever way we

do this, I don't want James around. If you want me to handle this as your cousin, I'll do that. We send James away to keep him out of the fight, we tear down the greenhouse, burn the plants and put the fear of God in Victor. But that means he's got to go. You have to be sure Teresa understands that. I can do this on the quiet, but he has to leave."

"Okay. Yeah. We could do that."

"But," Nate added, letting the word hang there.

Luis gave him a weary look. "But what?"

"Are you sure he's working alone? If he doesn't have a truck, how did he get all this set up in the first place? And where did he get the money? The plants, the heaters, the lamps. Do you really think he built that greenhouse and started clearing that land on his own?"

Luis had gone pale. "If James…but he doesn't have any money, and he's only missed one day of school!"

"I don't mean James. But that's the other reason I want him gone. I want to watch the place. See who's coming and going. And I don't want to see James. If Victor isn't the only one involved, if he's not the money and the brains, I'm going to have to handle this as a cop, and I can't have any reason to mention James in the reports."

Luis looked grimmer than ever.

"How do you want to handle it, Luis?"

"Christ. Victor isn't a great guy, but he's not

a criminal mastermind, either. He's working for someone. Some guy who uses kids to do the dirty work, I'm sure. Will you check it out for me?"

"Yeah. You'll send James away?"

"He's going to be out of school for a day or two next week for Presidents' Day, anyway. I'll tell Teresa that John Lopez needs help with calving over in Casper. She's always liked that guy and she keeps complaining that James needs to learn how to work harder."

"Has calving started yet?"

"Hell if I know."

Jenny arrived with the pitcher, and she paused as if she'd say something, but someone called her name from another table and she flitted away with an apologetic smile.

Nate poured two beers and slid one toward his cousin. "Teresa's going to find out about all this, you know. You can't hide it for long."

"I know." Luis closed his eyes for moment. "But I don't want to tell her until I know the extent of it. Otherwise she'll convince herself it's nothing and we should sweep it under the rug."

"It's big money these days, cousin. People get shot over it. Remember that. You could've been killed just going out to the cabin if the wrong person was waiting. There was that case up in Gallatin Forest last year. A hiker ran across a crop in a federal forest and someone shot him to keep him from talking. Luckily, the shooter had bad aim."

Luis nodded. "Yeah. I know. Damn it. That little shit Victor has put my family and my livelihood in danger. And if he's involved James…" He took a deep breath. "I can't just let it go. I'll call you when James is on his way, all right?"

"Perfect."

Luis only drank half his beer before he blew out a deep breath and stood. "I've got to get going."

Nate stood and gave him a tight hug.

"Thank you, man. I don't know what I would've done about this if you weren't around."

"Does that mean you'll stop calling me The Fuzz behind my back?"

Luis slapped his shoulder and stepped away. "Hell, Nate. You know that was because of that mustache you tried to grow to be more like me in high school. I figured you became a cop just to try to live down the nickname."

"If you want my help, you'll keep that quiet."

"Got it." Luis's smile faded. "I'll call you."

Nate sank back into his seat and topped off his beer. He wasn't going to take any unofficial law enforcement action, but he could poke around the cabin a little without stepping too far outside the rules. There might be some personal danger, but Nate was willing to risk a lot for the sake of Luis and his family. Luis was more like a brother than a cousin. Nate had a sister, but she was a few years older and had always been more of a second mother than a playmate. But Luis…if he needed help, Nate would step up any day.

"Hey!" Jenny suddenly appeared, her head tilted toward the front door of the saloon. "I hope your friend's coming back. I can't let you drive if you drink that whole pitcher on your own. I'm sure you understand. The cops around here are real uptight."

Nate raised one eyebrow and refused to meet her smile.

"Right. Ha! So, anyway…" she drawled.

"Luis isn't coming back, but I promise not to finish the pitcher by myself."

"Are you waiting for someone?"

"No. I'm on my own."

"I could…" Her eyes slid to the chair Luis had vacated, but then she just flashed a wide smile. "I'll check back on you later."

Nate looked from the chair to her. "I wanted to talk to you, actually. Care for a drink?"

"Yes! I was just about to take my break. I'll be right back."

He watched her ponytail bounce as she hurried toward the bar. If someone had asked him an hour before, and if he'd allowed himself to be completely honest, he would've said that sitting down for a drink with Jenny Stone was the goal of the evening. But at this point, he had no idea if he should be satisfied or just embarrassed that he was so damn easy for her.

CHAPTER TWO

"I'M TAKING MY BREAK," Jenny said to Benton, trying to hide the fact that she was slightly out of breath as she reached past him to grab a clean glass. "Can you survive without me for ten minutes?"

"No problem," he said, his eye on the pitchers he was filling.

Thank God. Deputy Hendricks was… Wow. He was…making her blush from across the room.

She cleared her throat and glanced at Benton, hoping he couldn't see her embarrassment. Because Nate Hendricks was so damn hot he made her thighs clench a little.

She'd spent so much time worried that he was hiding close-set bug eyes under his glasses that she hadn't braced herself against the opposite possibility: that one glance from those icy gray eyes and she'd melt into a pile of awkward mush. She'd almost invited herself to have a drink with him. She kind of had.

Jenny took a deep breath. It didn't matter. He'd

come here to see her. Or maybe not. Maybe he'd come to interrogate her. Or tell her he'd changed his mind and she needed to come down to the station with him.

Oh, Jesus, what if she was about to get arrested?

"No," she said to herself as she untied her serving apron and laid it on the counter. "Now you're just being weird."

"What's wrong?" Benton called. "You being weird again?"

"Shut up, B."

"Whatever you say, freak."

Jenny had always appreciated that Benton was like a pain-in-the-ass little brother to her. That appreciation was being strained tonight. She started away before he could say more, but not quickly enough.

"Hey!"

She turned warily back.

He tipped his head in the direction of Nate Hendricks's table. "I've got condoms under the register if you're making a move on that guy."

"Shut up!" she repeated. "It's not like that. He's my…um…deputy."

"Ah. Of course he is. That girl over in the corner there is my librarian. I still use condoms when she invites me over, though. When you sleep with one public servant, you sleep with every public servant. Or something like that."

"I hate you." Her face felt as if it were the color of the maraschino cherry Benton popped in his mouth. "I really do."

"Go get 'im, tiger."

She'd get Benton back somehow, she thought as she made herself walk toward Nate. The problem with Benton was that he was utterly shameless. Even Rayleen, the dirty old woman who owned the saloon, couldn't embarrass him, not that she ever stopped trying.

Speaking of…Jenny kept her eyes straight ahead and didn't look toward Rayleen's table. Hopefully the old lady wouldn't look up from her game of solitaire long enough to notice anything.

"Hi," she said stupidly when she reached his table and took a seat.

Nate immediately poured her a beer. "I thought you were the bartender here."

"I am, but I serve on pitcher night. I'm quick and I like the change of pace."

"You're good at it."

"At what?" she asked.

His eyes locked on hers and pushed her nerves to another level of chaos. "Being charming."

"Oh?" What did that mean? It sounded as if it could be a compliment, but his voice was faintly cool and his eyes assessing.

"Did you call about the class?"

Oh, crap. *That* was what he was here about?

"I've been really busy, but I've got it right here…." She patted the front pocket of her jeans, then stuffed her hands into her back pockets. Nothing there. By the time she patted her breast, thinking maybe her shirt had a pocket, she realized she was doing some obscene sort of macarena. His cool eyes slid down to the hand cupping her boob.

God. "It must be in my apron," she said weakly as she unclasped her breast. "I'm going to call today."

"It's seven p.m."

"Right. I meant… The afternoon slipped by."

He reached into his pocket—not cupping any sensitive body parts, she noted—and withdrew…

Not handcuffs, please. Not handcuffs.

…another card.

"I have the card!" she insisted.

"Just take it." He sighed.

She took it, noticing the warmth of it seeping into her fingertips before she set it on the table. "I'm going to call. The day just got away from me."

"Why don't I believe you, Ms. Stone?"

"It's Jenny," she said automatically. "And I'll call you Nate."

She glanced up when he didn't respond. But he couldn't take it back now. She knew his real name. She'd said it. And it felt surprisingly sweet on her tongue. It was so human. So easy. Nate. The man himself, on the other hand, was so intimidating she felt nervous saying it out loud.

"I'm honestly going to call. I appreciate what you did for me. You didn't have to. Nobody else would have."

He sighed. "You're right about that."

She started to smile, but in that moment she realized that she *was* right. No one else would've given her so many passes. No other cop would've tried to help her out the way he had. So why had he done it? And why was he here?

Warmth washed through her, trailing little sparks that settled under her skin. He liked her. As impossible as that seemed as he watched her with those cool eyes. He didn't smile. He'd barely even blinked when she'd fondled her own breast in front of him. But he must like her. It was the only explanation.

She took a needed sip of beer. "I'm sorry I drive too fast," she offered.

"You're going to have to stop, you know. One of these days someone else will pull you over and that'll be it."

"I know."

"Why can't you just slow down?"

"I don't know."

His head tilted. His eyes narrowed. Finally, he shook his head. "You really don't know, do you?"

"I don't! I mean, I obviously know how to drive

like a reasonable person. I don't speed through town. I'm careful when the highway is crowded. I've never even had an accident!"

"I know. I checked."

She looked down into her beer. "But when I'm out there alone, I just…lose myself. It's not that I think about getting out there and seeing how fast I can go. I'm not racing. At least, I'm not racing anyone else. I just want to *go.*"

"Where?" he asked, the word just a quiet drop in the river of noise that flowed around them.

"I don't have any idea," she answered honestly. "Just away. Somewhere else." She shook her head. "It feels good. To go as fast as I want to, even knowing I shouldn't."

"I get that. It can feel good. Doing something you shouldn't."

Jenny felt her cheeks go pink before she even looked at him. His soft words prompted her to peek at his ring finger. She'd checked it out before and knew he didn't have a ring, but did he have a tan line? She was pretty harmless, so what else could he mean by something you shouldn't do?

"Yes," she finally said, raising her gaze to meet his. He was still unreadable, still giving nothing away. "But it's your job to stop that, right?"

"If it's illegal, sure."

"And if it's not?"

For the very first time in any of their encounters, she saw his mouth soften and almost—almost—smile. His lips weren't so thin, she saw; he simply held them tight together most of the time. Or most of the time he spent with her.

"If it's not illegal..." His teeth flashed white against his skin as he spoke. She realized she was staring at his mouth but couldn't tear her eyes away. "Then it's every man for himself."

"And every woman?" she asked.

"Depends on who the man is," he said. And then...Nate Hendricks smiled. "Hopefully you'd get some help with that."

The jolt of it went through her like a shock wave before settling into her belly. *This* was the man named Nate. Charming. Wicked. Utterly adorable. The delicious feeling dipped a little lower in her body.

"Oh, shit," she breathed.

The smile disappeared. "What?"

"Nothing."

"What is it?"

Wow, she really knew how to play a flirtatious moment. He was frowning now, looking both suspicious and a little worried. With the thousands of people she'd watched flirt over the years, Jenny would've expected more from herself than a muttered scatological curse. Now he was leaning back, edging away from her.

"I've never seen you smile before!" she said quickly.

He frowned harder.

"I mean, usually when I see you, you're really pissed off."

"I take my job pretty seriously," he said gruffly.

"You don't have to tell me that! Whew. You're Mr. Serious." She was babbling and couldn't stop. "Ha! You kind of scare me, you know."

"Ah. Well." He glanced toward the door. "I see."

"I mean…not in a bad way!"

"I scare you in a good way?"

That sounded weird, but the words still pulsed through her. He did scare her in a good way. The good way that made her feel nervous and aware and a little too alive. Or just alive enough. It felt like driving fast, flying through the world.

"Yes," she heard herself say. "In a good way."

He stopped edging away from her.

When she was little, she'd tried ski jumping once at a tiny resort in Idaho. In retrospect, it had been the very smallest jump for the very smallest kids. No more than five feet high, but she could still remember standing at the top of that slope, trying to trust that gravity didn't always have to be a brutal lesson. Her heart had beat so hard she'd felt her whole body pulse with it. She felt that now. She'd edged forward too far and there was no way to stop.

His gaze dipped down her body so quickly she almost missed it. “Are you scared right now?”

“Yes,” she whispered.

“In a good way?” His pale gray eyes weren’t icy anymore. Now they glinted like metal. Jesus, he looked dangerous. He should ditch the shades and glare criminals into obedience. Criminals like her. She had the sudden, stupid idea that she’d like to speed past his sheriff’s truck again, as soon as possible. Right now. Tonight.

Her nipples tightened, and she was torn between hoping he could tell and praying he couldn’t. This was crazy. Her pulse was thumping so fast she actually felt light-headed.

He leaned a little closer and when he set his hand on the table, she was very aware it was only two inches from hers. Though their hands looked so different it was almost hard to believe they served the same functions. His skin was a deep bronze next to her paleness. His nails were cut so short they didn’t even approach the tips of his fingers.

Instead of his long-sleeved uniform shirt, tonight he wore a blue button-down, the sleeves rolled up to reveal forearms sculpted from tight muscle. Hair glinted along his arm, down to his thick wrist, and she noticed that he still wore a watch. She rarely saw men at the bar with watches anymore, but his looked old and sturdy, as if it had been passed on from his father.

She looked at that hand and she desperately wanted to touch it.

"I'm not really scary, you know," he said. Was that an invitation? But no. He probably didn't know that she was staring at his hand and wondering what he'd do if she stroked a thumb over his knuckles. Two scars stood out in pale contrast to his tan. She wanted to touch them. She wanted to touch *him.* Tonight.

The desire enveloped her with sudden, overwhelming completeness. It was just that simple. For the first time in her life, Jenny understood the animal urge that had strangers pairing up every night. She'd watched it a hundred times and always shaken her head at the stupidity of going home with a person you'd just met. But now she got it. The stupidity didn't matter. It wasn't a factor. It wasn't an impediment. It meant nothing, because sometimes it felt good to do something you shouldn't.

She wanted that. Her nerves tingled with the compulsion. So Jenny slid her hand across the two inches of faux wood that separated their skin, and she stroked her thumb over his knuckles.

His fingers twitched, and she almost jerked her hand away. But that would likely ruin her attempt to be seductive, jumping as if she'd just startled a snake. His hand started to curl into a fist before he flattened it to the table.

Jenny's heart was tripping over itself, trying to beat faster than was physically possible. She dared to meet his gaze, but looked quickly away as she felt a nervous smile flit over her face. His eyes were just so…intense. "Now you look really scary. Maybe you should smile again."

"Maybe I should. But I'm worried you won't take that class if you're not scared of me."

"Is that what you're worried about?" she asked, wondering if he really was. Because at this moment, she wanted him thinking about very different things. "My little driving problem?"

"No. I'm worried that you could be a much bigger problem than I imagined."

Smiling now, she let herself look up. His mouth was still an intimidatingly flat line, but the edges of his eyes were tight with amusement, as if he were just about to smile and was holding back.

"Jenny…" he said.

She had to look away. She looked too eager already. Grinning at him, letting her pinky finger rest against his as if she'd just happened to set her hand there. *Play it cool,* she ordered herself. Or coolish. Even something that could very generously be thought of as possibly cool by a kind observer.

Was he about to propose something? Ask her

when she got off work? Ask if he could see her afterward? He could. He could see as much of her as he wanted, because she'd never felt this kind of lust before.

Her gaze darted over the room, looking for something calm to latch onto, but her eyes caught on something decidedly not calm. That was no surprise on pitcher night. It was a saloon, after all. People came here to let loose and have fun and sometimes even cause trouble. But this was personal.

Her eyes widened at the man standing in the doorway. She shook her head.

"Maybe I could—" Nate started, but she didn't hear the rest.

"Oh, no," she breathed, as she watched the guy stop four feet inside the door and nod as if the place pleased him.

She slid her hand away from Nate's. "Oh, no," she groaned.

"Hey," Nate said, the tone of his voice suddenly no-nonsense. "What's wrong?"

Everything, she thought. Everything was very wrong. She should have run for the state line after all.

NATE FOLLOWED THE LINE of her gaze across the room, his muscles tensing to take action. But despite the dozens of people packed into the space, he didn't see any reason for alarm. There was laughter and flirtation, and maybe a slightly tense conversation between the couple at the next table, but nothing that set off warning bells.

One man stood alone near the door, his long blond hair pulled into a ponytail and a goofy smile pasted on his face. Nate slid his eyes back to Jenny and looked again. Yeah, she was staring right at that guy.

"Who is he?" Nate asked.

"My ex," she said, her mouth stiff in a way he'd never seen, not even when she'd been fighting back tears yesterday.

"Ex-boyfriend?" he pressed.

"Ex-husband," she said. "Ellis."

Nate blinked and looked back to the blond. "Recent?" he asked, realizing at the same moment that he'd crafted a false sense of familiarity with Jenny Stone in his mind. He knew her age and birthday and accident history. He knew she didn't have a criminal record, and she kept her insurance up to date, and he knew where she worked. Other than her willingness to be an organ donor, what else did he know except that she smiled a lot and liked to drive fast?

She might have five ex-husbands. She might be married right now.

Following the example set by her hand, which had pulled away from its interesting closeness as soon as she'd spotted her ex, Jenny pushed her chair back from the table. "I'm sorry," she said, eyes still on the man. "I've got to get back to work."

"Wait," Nate started, but the ex-husband was heading over now, his eyes on Jenny.

"Sorry," she said again before moving toward the bar. The man's trajectory changed and he followed her across the room. Nate's neck prickled at the sight of a pursuit, even if it was a slow one, but the ex's smile only showed friendliness. There was no edge to it. No warning. But Nate watched closely, keeping an eye on the man's face, his shoulders, his hands, watching for any hint of suppressed violence.

The guy said something, and Jenny grabbed his arm and dragged him toward the end of the bar.

"Come on!" he said on a laugh, his voice loud enough that Nate could hear. "I wanted to surprise you."

"What are you doing here?" she nearly shouted.

When they reached the bar, their words were no longer loud enough to hear past the crowd. Ellis seemed to be talking a lot while Jenny frowned and shook her head.

Nate cursed the ex-husband's timing, his own slow draw on making a move, and added a few general curses for his inconvenient interest in someone as complicated as Jenny Stone. Curling his fist, he looked down at the hand she'd touched, one faint brush of her fingertips over his knuckles. It had been nothing. The pressure barely even noticeable. So why could he still feel it?

He clenched his hand hard, forcing his nerves to let go of the lingering trace of herself she'd left behind. If he could force his mind to do the same, that would be even better, but her presence was still bouncing around in there, leaving bruises in her wake.

She, on the other hand, seemed to have completely recovered from their encounter. Hands on her hips, she was now facing good old Ellis, her clenched jaw barely moving as she read him the riot act. Either that or she had a very tense style of reminiscing. Ellis maintained his loose-limbed stance, smiling indulgently at her diatribe.

"Ellis!" she yelled, throwing her hands in the air.

"It's not like that!"

When the guy laughed, Jenny seemed to get even more frustrated, and a wild gesture caught a half-full pitcher on the bar. It slid away and shot into the air between two patrons before it crashed to the floor. A screech went up as people were splashed with cold beer.

Nate shot to his feet, already stepping forward to control the situation, but he wasn't needed. The male bartender grabbed Ellis by the collar of his shirt to haul him out, but Jenny shook her head and tried to calm the situation down.

Whatever she said, her ex-husband moved toward the door with a smile. “I’ll come by later, Jenny!” he called, still perfectly cheerful as he left the saloon.

Nate stood there, ready for violence, adrenaline pumping through his veins as the crowd broke into scattered applause. Jenny grabbed a mop and came around the bar to clean up the spill. Once that was done, she crouched down with a rag to clean the splatter from the bar stools.

Frozen in place between two tables, Nate watched her, waiting, wondering if he should offer to help. Wondering what to say. But in the end, he didn’t say anything at all. Jenny didn’t look in his direction. She didn’t even glance up. She just stood and headed back behind the bar.

Nate slid the business card off the table and left.

CHAPTER THREE

"YOU REALLY KNOW HOW to pick 'em," Rayleen cackled from her corner table for the tenth time that night.

Jenny sighed and rolled her shoulders, determined to continue ignoring the old lady.

"He sure did have pretty hair, though. Do you give it a hundred strokes at night? That's the recipe for a good marriage, you know." More cackling. Rayleen was drunk.

"He's my *ex,* Rayleen." Jenny sighed. "I don't stroke anything of his, and I haven't in a long time."

"Well, he's back now. And ex sex doesn't count, or that's what I've always heard."

Jenny finished wiping down the bar and glanced toward the last tables of lingerers. "Is that what your exes told you? Because I think that's called an ulterior motive."

"Ha!" The unlit cigarette clenched between her lips bounced as she spoke. "That's what *I* told *them.* And hell, yeah, I had a motive."

Accustomed to the white-haired lady's constant sex talk, Jenny just nodded as she looked at the clock. It was one, and Ellis apparently wasn't coming back. "All right, folks!" she called. "That's it! Closing time."

There were a few good-hearted groans as the two tables cleared out, but they all offered friendly waves as they left. Not for the first time, Jenny was glad that pitcher night ended at one. They were open until two Thursday through Saturday, and she was sure she was too exhausted to have made it another hour. Her ex-husband was the gift that kept on giving.

He'd reappeared two months earlier, calling to say he was in town and asking if he could buy her coffee. She'd wanted to say no. Just hearing his voice had made her anxious enough that she'd immediately reached for the car keys, just to know she could run if she needed to. She hadn't spoken to him in ten years, which was exactly how she'd preferred it. But guilt had made her say yes. Guilt that she'd run the way she had, leaving nothing but the wedding band she'd set on the table while he slept. Granted, their marriage had been brief and an idiotic idea from the start, but he hadn't been the one to walk out. She had.

He hadn't done well since then. She knew that much from brief snatches of gossip when old friends passed through Jackson. So she'd said yes to his invitation, heart beating with anxious regret before she even made it out the door.

She should have gone with her first instinct. Ellis hadn't grown up at all. And she'd ended up paying for the coffee, along with two muffins and a donut he'd ordered for the two of them and then eaten by himself.

Ellis had been looking for a place to crash, but more than that, he'd needed a job. Times were tough back in small-town Idaho. He'd been out of work for a year. But it was a slow ski season in this economy, and there wasn't enough work for the regulars who showed up every year, much less a stranger who'd just arrived.

When he'd asked about working at the saloon, with *her,* Jenny's heart had leaped with terror at the very idea. She'd said no before he could even finish asking.

God, she'd felt horrible about it. She still did. Like a cruel, heartless bitch. But the idea of her past and her present mixing up into one tangled mess… No. She didn't run in circles. She ran to escape. She couldn't do it.

But he'd really needed help. And she'd refused. And here he was again.

She'd assumed he'd gone back to Idaho, but instead, he'd apparently been hanging out with the group of losers who always surrounded Steve Tex, a guy who'd once been a promising snowboarder and was now a perpetual ne'er-do-well.

Jenny didn't like that. She didn't like it at all. Ellis wasn't dumb, but he'd always been naïve. Look how quickly he'd fallen for Jenny, when she obviously hadn't deserved that kind of trust.

Ellis was cute and easygoing. He liked everyone. And in the time she'd known him, he'd never shown an ounce of self-preservation. That was what had scared her tonight, because she knew the kinds of people who hung out with Steve Tex. Users and drifters and sneaky bastards. Steve's house, which had once been a mansion bought with sponsor money from his snowboarding days, was now a run-down, beat-up den of feral half adults.

She couldn't push Ellis away without making sure he understood what he'd gotten into. But damn, he'd chosen a truly inconvenient time to pop back into her life, ruining her first promising flirtation in months.

Nate had left at some point. She wasn't sure when, because she'd been too mortified to look at him. But he'd left, and he wouldn't be back. He'd even taken the card. But she had the first one he'd given her, and she'd call tomorrow. She'd call and she'd take that class and she'd never speed again, if only because she couldn't bear to speak to Deputy Hendricks after that.

An ex-husband goading her into a high-tempered, beer-smashing, barroom scene was probably one of the least effective flirtation strategies she could have employed. God, she was really the picture of success. A washed-up bartender driving a car that was more suited to a teenage boy pumped up on acne meds and energy drinks. A white-trash divorcee yelling at her ex in public and knocking over drinks. Nice.

She could probably still persuade Nate to sleep with her if she really pulled out all the stops, but who wanted to have to talk a man into bed?

Then again, considering how she'd melted with excitement at just touching his hand, maybe it would be worth a little humiliation. Men talked their way into bed all the time, didn't they? They never seemed self-conscious about it.

Groaning at her own pitiful thoughts, Jenny closed out the register and dropped the key into Rayleen's hand. "You should really be more careful with that," she said as Rayleen tucked the key into her bra. "Half the town probably knows you keep it between your breasts."

She shrugged. "If I get robbed, it'll be the most action I've seen in a while. Could be exciting."

"Yeah? Does that mean there's nothing going on with Easy?"

"Ha! I wouldn't give that old coot the time of day." But she blushed when she said it, her pale cheeks blooming with color. The old rancher came by at least twice a month to play gin rummy with Rayleen and engage in some verbal sparring. It was looking more and more like foreplay, and Rayleen's blush gave her away. She'd be getting some action sooner than Jenny would, that much was obvious.

"So who was that handsome piece of work you were sitting with?"

Jenny froze in the act of reaching for her jacket. Damn. She'd thought she was going to get away clean. "Nobody," she said automatically.

"Yeah? Hell, there's been nobody in my bed for years. If he's really Nobody, I'd have a damn big smile on my face every day, missy."

"He's a deputy," Jenny countered quickly. "He came by to give me some information on a defensive driving class. That's all."

"That's all? Then you should be ashamed of yourself. That boy has some special frisking in mind for you."

Rayleen's words created an unwelcome image in Jenny's mind: her body pressed against the hood of his sheriff's truck, him too close behind her, his hands running down her sides, then back up to cup her breasts.

"Good night, Rayleen," she said quickly. She'd already cleaned the bar and locked up the liquor. The last two tables needed clearing and wiping, and she felt guilty passing those by, but Rayleen liked to get the last few things every night. It gave her a reason to hang out until closing.

Jenny clicked the lock button on the door before she closed it behind her. The least she could do was be sure Rayleen wasn't robbed because Jenny had been careless. The woman only needed to walk across the parking lot to get to the little house where she lived, but Jenny still worried about her. Not in the off season when it was mostly locals, but during ski season, a lot of temporary workers came through, and Jackson felt less like a small town.

Walking through the lot, lost in worry, Jenny almost screamed when she heard a car door open just a few feet away. Her heart leaped into her throat, then slammed into a rapid beat as she backpedaled, but as the man stepped out of the truck, she realized it was Nate.

"Oh!" she gasped, her breath puffing out on a cloud in the icy air. "You scared me half to death!"

"I'm sorry." He held up both hands as if he were approaching someone unstable. "I'm unarmed."

His forearms looked more than strong enough to make his bare hands into lethal weapons, but she kept that thought to herself. At which point her brain came fully back online and reminded her of who he was and what had happened earlier.

Her receding panic was quickly replaced by mortification. She had no idea what her face looked like twisted between these two awful emotions, but it was bad enough to stop a seasoned cop in his tracks. He even took a step back, though his shadow stretched out to touch the toes of her shoes. Strangely, that imagined contact made her feel uncomfortable, so she took a step back, as well.

"Sorry," he said again. "I just wanted to be sure you were okay."

"Me?"

"Yes. Your ex seemed a little aggressive tonight. I was worried."

"Ellis?" she squeaked in shock.

"Yes," he said flatly, "Ellis."

"Oh, no, you don't have to worry about Ellis. He's just…Ellis."

"Well, I've never arrested him, so I guess that's a positive sign."

"Oh, he doesn't live here. He's from Idaho. He's just visiting. Or something."

Nate cleared his throat and took a step toward her. "Visiting you?"

"No!" she answered so loudly that she made her own nerves jump in shock. "I saw him once a couple of months ago, and then he showed up tonight. It's been over for ten years."

"Ten years," he repeated, taking one more step. Now his shadow slid over her feet and all the way up to her thighs. She watched it shift over the curve of her legs and bit back a shiver. She couldn't feel it, but she wanted to so badly that it almost felt like a touch.

"You were just a baby," he said.

"Are you trying to flatter me? You know my birth date. I was eighteen."

"Exactly. Just a kid."

"Amazing that they let teenagers walk around free like actual humans, much less get a marriage license, isn't it?"

His teeth flashed in the darkness as if he was smiling. She wished he were the one facing the light. Then she'd be able to read him and he couldn't see the mixed-up emotions flashing over her face.

"Are you—" he seemed to hesitate, his voice growing softer "—involved with anyone right now? Married or—"

"What?" she interrupted. "No, I'm not married! Or involved. Or *anything*."

"Okay. Good. Me, neither."

Me, neither. He could only mean one thing by that, and her suspicion was confirmed when he took one more step. Now his shadow slipped up her body all the way to her breasts. Better than that, she could reach out and touch him if she wanted to.

"I'm sorry about earlier," she said.

"You kind of checked out on me."

"I assumed you'd want me to."

His head cocked. "Why?"

She laughed. “Baggage. It’s so sexy.”

“Hmm. So you’d been hoping I’d think of you as sexy?”

“Oh…” She couldn’t do more than sigh that small word because his hand came up to cup her jaw. His thumb trailed over her cheek, and Jenny almost whimpered. This wasn’t the imagined touch of a shadow. And it wasn’t the brushing of hands. This was something so much more delicate and sweet and *purposeful.* And she’d never have imagined that Deputy Hendricks would be the one to touch her this way. A whisper of his skin against hers. Her heart trembled between beats.

“Did you?” he murmured.

“What?”

“Hope I’d think that you’re sexy?”

“I…maybe. You’re very…”

He drew closer, his face only inches from hers now. “Very what? Scary?”

“No,” she breathed. Then, “Yes.”

“Yes?” Nate bent his head, and his breath whispered over her mouth. “Are you scared right now?”

“Yes.” A lie. Or not a lie, because when his lips touched hers, her pulse sped with wild alarm and her legs went weak enough that she reached for his arm.

She sighed against his lips, and he deepened the kiss until she could taste him. The heat of his mouth, the faint hint of moisture as she opened for him, and then his tongue brushing her bottom lip. Just one little taste. Then another. Just as she was leaning closer, he pulled away.

"Oh," she whispered again, suddenly yanked from the slow heat she'd been sinking into.

"I've wanted to do that for a while," he murmured.

"Have you?" She blinked up at him, still dazed.

"Yes. You…drive me a little crazy. But I knew I'd be stepping over the line."

"Which line?"

"A couple of lines, actually. One, I was usually giving you a ticket at the time. That's a clear line. Another being that you didn't even know who I was tonight. That seemed like a definite 'Do not proceed' signal."

"You look a little different in jeans. And a button-down shirt." Worried he wasn't going to kiss her again, Jenny dared to stroke a finger along the collar of his shirt, down to where the first button was fastened. "And I'm used to looking up from about waist level."

Now she could definitely see his smile. In fact, he grinned so wide she was pretty sure she could count every one of his white teeth. "Whatever you're about to say," she ordered, "don't!"

"It's just that—"

"Don't."

"If you're more comfortable—"

"Stop! This isn't going to be as cute as you think. Believe me, I know. I work in a bar."

He shrugged. "It was pretty cute."

"No, it wasn't," she insisted, but she was laughing. Laughing and curling her fingers around the edge of his shirt, tugging him down. She didn't have to tug very hard. He ducked his head and kissed her again, and this time his tongue swept deeper. His arms snuck around her and she settled against his chest.

Jenny's nipples tightened against the warmth of his body. She shivered as his fingers spread over her back. Even past her jacket, she could feel his fingertips and imagined them against her naked skin. His forearms tightening as he—

She felt him growl against her lips and realized she'd moaned. Not only had she moaned—into his mouth—but she'd slid her hands up his back and tangled them in his short hair. He couldn't have gotten away if he wanted to. But did he want to?

No, he gripped her hips now and pressed her closer. She was tempted to raise her knee. To wrap a leg around him. Just to get closer, to feel him between her thighs.

This was crazy. She hardly knew him. It was the first time they'd really touched. Which only made it more delicious, of course. The shocking press of their bodies together. The scandalous thrill as she realized he was hard. Hard for *her.* Turned on by the taste and heat of her mouth. Aroused by her fingers tightening in his hair. If she invited him to her bed, he'd oblige her. There was no doubt in her mind. She could tell by the way he pulled her closer. The way the thick length of him pressed into her belly.

Oh, God. The thick length.

She wanted that. Needed it. And if this was a mistake, if it was stupid…hadn't she already been considering that it was time to go? Time to move on? She could leave Jackson. But first, she needed him inside her.

She turned her face away, meaning to ask, but before she could find her voice, he put his mouth to her neck and sucked gently at the sensitive skin.

"Oh, fuck," she moaned. Her weakness. If he bit her, she'd be— "Oh, *God.*" His teeth pressed into her nerves with exactly the pressure most likely to make her arch her back like a stray cat in heat. Which she did, rocking against his erection with a gasp of pleasure.

She felt his breath shiver over her wet skin.

"Will you…?" she tried, not quite sure what to say or how to make her voice work properly. She inhaled a deeper breath, trying to ignore the careful scrape of his teeth down her skin. "Would you…?"

"Yes." That one simple word and it tore through her, destroying any self-control. She hadn't even finished the sentence. Yes to anything. Yes to whatever she wanted.

He stood straight, his hand sliding to fold her fingers into his.

"Do you want to follow me—?" she started, meaning to ask if he wanted to follow her home or ride in her car. But her words were cut off by the loud rattle of an approaching engine. She waited for it to pass, but the racket just got louder, and suddenly the headlights were sweeping into the lot of the Crooked R.

Jenny didn't recognize the beat-up white panel van that turned in, but she watched it come to a rocking halt, anyway. A panel van was never a welcome sight in the middle of the night. It called to mind all the cautionary made-for-TV movies she'd seen about kidnappings and serial killers. Still, she had her own personal deputy standing right next to her. There was really nothing to fear. Nothing except…

The van door screeched open and out stepped Ellis.

Jenny groaned.

"Let me take care of this." Nate's voice had turned so hard and clipped that it seemed impossible he'd been kissing her neck so softly just seconds before. When he took a step forward, she put a hand on his arm to stop him.

"No, really. He's harmless."

"Jenny!" Ellis called with a goofy grin, as if she weren't standing in the dark with another man. Good Lord. Nothing affected him. Ten years ago, she'd thought he was laid-back and sweet. He was. He was also vulnerable and way too open.

His eyes focused on Nate for a brief moment, and Ellis offered the same open smile. If he'd noticed the intimacy between the two of them, Ellis still wouldn't be jealous. He never had been, which was why he hadn't understood her reaction to his occasional slipup.

Nate seemed to accept the man's harmlessness at that moment. The arm she'd been grasping lost a taut readiness she hadn't registered until it disappeared.

"See?" she said under her breath. "He's no danger to me."

Well, not in the physical sense. But he was becoming a terrible danger to her love life.

Her heart sank to her stomach when she realized she'd have to send Nate away. Her body practically screamed its objection to that idea. It wanted him. Now. And it didn't care what price needed to be paid for that privilege. But her brain was working with an unfortunate clarity. She'd asked Ellis to meet her at closing time, and he had, if a little late.

But maybe she could come up with some excuse. Maybe she could meet him another time.

Then again, if she talked to him tonight, it might be done and over.

They stood in an awkward silence until Jenny finally made herself do the right thing.

"I'm sorry. I forgot I asked him to meet me. I didn't know you'd be here. I should really... Damn. Maybe I could call you tomorrow?"

"Jenny, I don't know."

Ellis finally shrugged and approached with his familiar lope, so Nate lowered his voice. "I'm not comfortable leaving it like this."

Neither was she. She was still reeling from that kiss. She was still wet and aching. But she pasted on a smile. "You'd better go," she said, trying not to let her voice crack with grief.

Nate finally stopped watching Ellis and turned toward Jenny. She wanted to blurt out an apology right then. Wanted to explain or backtrack or *something.* But instead she met his gaze and smiled.

He watched carefully, giving Ellis—who'd miraculously had the good sense to stop ten feet away—one last glance before he shrugged. "All right. But I've already got your number, so I'll call you. Tomorrow?"

"Yes. Please?" she added, one tiny concession to the wailing grief of her body.

His shoulders relaxed a little. "I'll be in touch." He paused just as he was turning away and aimed a quick glare toward Ellis. "Keep your phone out, okay? Call 911 if you get worried."

"It's fine!"

And it was fine. She wasn't the least bit worried about Ellis as Nate walked to his truck and got in. He started the truck and backed out. Her only worry was that he wouldn't call. And why would he?

She'd felt nothing but guilt about Ellis earlier, but now she was irritated at what he'd interrupted.

"I told you to go back to Idaho, Ellis!"

"I don't have anything to go back to. I told you I lost my house to the bank."

"I know, but those guys you're hanging around are bad news. Jackson isn't like your town. There's money here. And *people* with money. You don't know what they're like. Kids who've spent their whole lives getting everything they wanted, and the so-called friends who want a piece of that."

He shook his head like she was being silly. "It's fine, Jenny. I've made some good friends, and I found a place to stay down in Hoback. I'm not crashing at Tex's place anymore."

She wanted to shake him. "You always get sucked into stuff, Ellis. Always." Like marriage.

He rolled his eyes as if he'd heard her thought. "I'm not a kid anymore, Jennybug."

Crossing her arms, she held her ground. "How did you lose your house?"

"I couldn't pay the mortgage."

"What mortgage? It was your mom's. She left it to you free and clear."

Ellis shifted and scratched his head, then rubbed his arms as if he'd just noticed the cold.

"I knew it," she sighed.

"Look, it wasn't some harebrained idea. The restaurant was a good opportunity and Chistopher knew exactly what he was doing! He just needed some start-up money. But then the recession hit, and…"

"Exactly. That's why people don't invest in restaurants. And yes—" She held up her hand to stop his next thought. "I'm sure Christopher is a great guy. Everyone's a great guy as far as you're concerned."

"People are okay, Jenny. You don't have to be so suspicious all the time."

No, people were not okay. She wasn't okay. Her parents weren't okay. But she'd never get him to believe that. Hell, she'd left him after a few months of marriage, and here he was, telling her people were nice. "You said you needed a favor," she sighed.

"I just need to store some stuff in your garage." He blinked slowly. "If you have one, I mean."

"What stuff?" she asked suspiciously.

"Landscaping stuff."

"Landscaping?" she scoffed.

"Yeah. I've got a good thing started. All these rich people. The resorts. You know."

"The resorts have their own gardeners," she countered. "And in case you haven't noticed, it's winter."

"I know! I'm on with a plowing company and working the contacts. Right now I'm acquiring a lot of supplies for spring and my van is jammed full of stuff. I need to get rid of some of it."

"You said you had a place! Keep it there."

"I'm at the Pineview Camp in Hoback. I have to walk to the bathroom. You think I have storage space? Just help me out. Please, Jenny?"

"God!" she groaned, tipping her head back to glare at the stars. Her breath hovered briefly, haloing the constellations in pale white before the wisps floated away. "Why did you even come here?"

He shrugged one shoulder. "Because I thought you'd help. I thought… You loved me once. I was pretty cool after you walked out on me, Jenny. I signed the papers you wanted me to sign. I never gave you any shit about it. But I was still your husband, even if you want to pretend I never existed."

Crap. His easy smile was gone now. He looked dead serious. And he was right. She did want to forget about it. She did go through life pretending he didn't exist. "I'm sorry, Ellis."

"I know you are."

A sound snuck to her ear on the breeze, something long and lonesome. A wolf, way off in the Tetons somewhere. She shivered and told herself it was a coyote.

She didn't owe Ellis anything. She didn't. They'd both been too young to know what they were doing. So why couldn't she leave this guilt behind? Why couldn't she leave any of her guilt behind?

But she knew the answer to that. Even if she'd been young and stupid, she'd known better than to marry him. When he'd asked her, somewhere deep in her heart she'd known the warmth hadn't been love. It had been relief. She'd been on her own for almost a year and she'd felt lost, and Ellis had loved her. And he'd owned a house. And she'd just wanted some security for once in her life.

Jenny cleared her throat. She told herself not to do it. She ordered herself to say no. But somehow her mouth opened with "Okay. But only for a little while."

Ellis grinned. His smile was still a little boy's grin, full of pride and joy and charm.

"Let's get it over with. You can follow me home."

"Whatever you say."

She thought of driving straight out of town

again. But this time, her past was right on her tail. Better to wait until she lost him before she disappeared.

CHAPTER FOUR

NATE'S MORNING QUICKLY went from bad to worse. Well, "bad" in the moral sense and "worse" in the sense that he was now in the mood to throw everyone in jail and sort out the details later.

He'd awoken to a vicious hard-on and indecent thoughts of Jenny Stone. He shouldn't have embraced the situation quite so thoroughly. He'd felt guilty even as he'd taken his cock in a tight grip and groaned with relief. He shouldn't have thought about her, but he hadn't had much choice. She'd driven him crazy last night. Just that first sweet sigh against his mouth would've been enough, but she'd added a hundred other moments to set his heart racing. The sounds she'd made. The touches she'd granted. She'd been wild for him. Just a little. Just enough that he knew it would be good in a million different ways.

He'd covered about twenty of them as he'd stroked himself that morning. So it had worked out nicely. Which was more than he could say for his current situation.

He'd driven his old pickup to the cabin, not wanting to grant any official status to this visit. It made him nervous, driving down the rutted, icy dirt road without his radio, but he wanted to do this right. Today, he was here as a cousin, not a cop.

But when he reached a part of the road where a rise in the terrain had caused fresh snow to blow across the ruts, he knew he'd be back in an official capacity soon. There were tire tracks. Fresh tracks from this morning. Which was why he now found himself crouched under a lodgepole pine that let loose waves of snow every time the wind blew. And it was blowing a lot.

Nate shuddered as another fine dusting of powder found its way past the back of his jacket collar and snuck icy fingers beneath his shirt.

God, if that asshole Ellis hadn't shown up last night, maybe Nate would still be in Jenny's bed. He definitely wouldn't be crouching in an icy ravine watching for signs of movement from the cabin. At the very least, he would've slept in and been soaking his sore muscles under a hot shower. Sore because he'd spent half the night working his ass off to make that woman come a dozen times.

He smirked at his own wild imaginings. Maybe he couldn't have managed a dozen, but he'd have done his absolute best. There was nothing he loved more, nothing that got him off more, than watching a woman come apart like that. And Jenny's little moans had promised a lovely reward for any endeavors. He wanted to know what she looked like, tasted like, felt like. He wanted to find out just how wet she got when he bit her neck like that. Fuck, he hadn't expected that response. She'd jerked against him as if he'd touched a raw nerve. A nerve that went straight to her—

Wind slapped him in the face, and snow shifted down his neck, and Nate hissed and eased into a different position, cursing his stray thoughts and stray erection.

He couldn't see enough from this position, anyway. He'd have to get closer to the cabin. See who was parked there, maybe even peek in one of the windows. He wasn't interested in surprising anyone right now, but in this snow, he might not be able to make out faces once someone was in a moving vehicle. And he might not be able to get a license plate number unless he walked right up and dusted the snow off.

"Damn." The tree provided easy cover, but he couldn't stay. Glancing back to be sure the truck was hidden on the road that cut off toward an even more isolated cabin, Nate eased out from under the tree, cursing a blue streak when more snow showered down. He missed his uniform hat and its wide brim. He wouldn't take it for granted again.

His boots crunched over the sheet of old, frozen snow that covered the rocky ground, and the sound seemed to echo off every surface, the only sound in this silent winter scene. But as he drew closer, he heard the hum of a propane heater and moved a little more quickly along the edge of the road.

He caught sight of a bumper. An ancient little Japanese car with a tan paint job and pitiful brown racing stripes down the side. The only thing that piece could race was a moped. He didn't recognize the car, but it matched Luis's description of what Victor had been driving lately, and Nate felt both disappointment and vindication at the sight.

There'd always been the possibility that Luis had been wrong, after all. But that was almost certainly Victor's car, and he was almost certainly doing something illegal.

Before he could ease farther forward, Nate heard voices from somewhere past the cabin and they were getting closer. Whatever Victor was doing, he wasn't doing it alone, and Luis had made clear this morning that James was already on his way to Casper.

Nate eased into a hiding place beneath another pine. The tan car started and pulled onto the drive. The kid inside was skinny and dark-haired, with a thin goatee that framed a narrow mouth. The rest of his face was covered by black sunglasses, but Nate was pretty sure it was Victor.

He watched the car pass, looking carefully to be sure the kid was alone. He was.

A second engine started. A tortured squeal of metal and fire. Nate winced and watched the edge of the snow carefully where it disappeared around the bend of the drive.

There. Harder to spot because the vehicle was white, but once it cleared the bend, there was no mistaking the familiar sound of that engine, not to mention the jagged black marks where a logo had been scraped off the white van.

"No," he breathed in utter disbelief. "No. Not happening." It couldn't be happening, because he was going to sleep with Jenny Stone, and he couldn't sleep with a woman who was involved in this situation.

But he couldn't deny that the guy in the driver's seat of the van looked exactly like Ellis. Nate memorized the license plate number as he tried to talk himself down.

Ellis was obviously involved with Victor, who was likely involved with growing illegal drugs. But that didn't mean that Jenny knew anything about it. The guy was her *ex*-husband. She said she'd only seen him once in ten years. A bad association, maybe, but not a damning one. Jenny didn't have a record. Nate knew that for a fact.

He blew out a deep breath and forced some of the tension to leave his body. This was probably just a terrible coincidence. He could press her a little harder, see if she gave any sign of guilt. She was damned open, as far as he could tell, all her emotions stamped on her face in clear relief. He'd be able to tell if she was lying.

Once enough time had passed, he slipped back out to the dirt road and approached the cabin. There were no other cars parked in front of it, and above the heater, the only sounds he could hear were distant raven caws and the faint thump of snow falling from nearby trees. The sun suddenly emerged, adding instant warmth to the air, but it glared from the windows of the cabin, turning them into two-way mirrors. If there was anyone inside, they'd be able to see Nate as clearly as if he were standing in the spotlight. All he could see were tree and sky and snow reflected in the glass.

Taking a chance, he headed toward the side of the cabin and pressed his cupped hand to the window to cut the light. Empty, but for a sagging old couch and a broken table. He didn't spot anything that looked new except one folding chair and a flashlight. Oh, and the plastic tarp greenhouse in the backyard. There was no mistaking that.

It listed slightly to the south, as if the northern winds were slowly easing it backward. His first impression was that Luis didn't have to worry too much about this operation, it wouldn't hold up under the coming spring storms. But when he approached, Nate saw that though the thing had been built slightly off-kilter, it was fairly solid. He walked around, looking for an entrance, but all of the plastic sheeting seemed to be heavily weighted down with cement blocks. Apparently, they wanted to discourage any curious cross-country skiers from investigating.

Nate didn't want to leave any indication that someone had been poking around. He didn't want to set off any alarms or raise any suspicions, so after another circuit around the building, which looked to be about fifteen by twenty feet, he stopped at an overlap in the plastic.

This seemed to be the door, if it could be called that. The propane heater hummed away nearby. A hint of warmth shimmered off the sheeting.

Nate slipped his gloved hand beneath the edge of plastic and eased it forward to create a gap. Warm air steamed past his face. He tugged a little harder. He could finally see something. The edge of a rough wooden table. Empty pots stacked in a corner. Shovels and buckets. He pushed the first layer of plastic forward and got a glimpse of what sat in rows on the table. Cheap plastic pots with tiny plants growing from them. He tilted his head. He couldn't see much, but they definitely looked like miniature marijuana plants.

"Shit."

Well, at least it was better than meth. Somebody could lose their life messing around with that. Still…

Now he had a better idea who was involved. He'd watch again tomorrow morning to see if any other players showed, and then he'd call it in. James was gone. There didn't seem to be any reason to worry he'd contributed. And it didn't have the feel of a major investment. Best to get it over and done with.

But first, he had to call Jenny.

CHAPTER FIVE

JENNY DID THREE things before she even ate breakfast. First, she showered and shaved. Everywhere. Then she polished her toenails. After all, no one had seen her bare toes since October. She wanted to make it a positive experience. Finally, trying not to grin down at her smooth legs and red toes and the little black panties she was wearing, she called about the driving class.

It was held on three consecutive Monday evenings from six to eight and the next class started in March. Jenny signed up. She'd have to tweak her schedule, but Rayleen wouldn't mind. It would give her extra ammunition to crack insulting jokes, and there was nothing that woman loved more.

Then Jenny stretched out on her couch with a happy sigh. She had the whole day off. Winter was the busiest season in Jackson, but it also meant a surplus of workers. Jenny normally worked a six-night week in the summer, but in the winter she could pick and choose, depending on how much she needed the money. There was always a pack of snowboarding bartenders waiting to fill in. And right now the rent on her little one-bedroom apartment was paid, her car insurance rates hadn't yet gone up, and she needed to preserve her sanity more than she needed to save for a new pair of heels.

At the moment, her sanity seemed to hinge on the prospect that Nate Hendricks would call, that she might be seeing some fantastically dirty action, and that Ellis would leave her the hell alone. She was scrubbed, exfoliated, shaved and polished, and ready for all three. She even had a reasonable amount of hope for two of those. And two-thirds' worth of sanity was better than none at all.

When her phone rang in the middle of a reality show cooking competition marathon, Jenny snatched up the phone and grinned at the unfamiliar number. It was Nate. She knew it was. And she smiled when she heard his voice.

"What time do you go in to work?" he asked.

She smiled harder. "I don't. What about you?"

"It's my day off. You've probably had lunch already—"

"I haven't!" Okay, that had been a hairbreadth too eager. Or maybe more than that, since he paused for a long moment before speaking. But screw it, if he wanted her to play coy, he could go to lunch with his disappointment. Last night, she'd been nervous. Now she was just pissed that she hadn't already gotten in his pants. She wanted to get it over with. Not the sex, but the nervousness. The doubts and worries. She wanted to get to the good part.

"I could call that new place on the square," he finally said. "I'm not sure if they're open for lunch."

Jenny glanced at her pitiful little kitchen, then down at her T-shirt and black panties "I could make something. If you'd like to come over."

Despite her internal pep talk, Jenny's heart began to pound before the words had even left her mouth. Oh, God. Oh, God. There was no mistaking her invitation. Was there? He had to know. What if he insisted on the restaurant? What would that mean? Her bravery started to sneak away. "If you want to go to a restaurant, I—"

"No! I mean, yes. No. I'd love to come over. For lunch. Do you need me to pick anything up?"

Condoms, she squeaked inside her mind. But she was pretty sure she had a few left in her dresser from…the Jurassic era? No. From a year ago. When she'd met that cute doctor. Ugh. Cute and…efficient.

"No," she said. "Unless you'd like wine? Since you don't have to work later, I mean. I won't be driving. Oh, I called about the class! I start in March. So don't worry that I'm just trying to distract you with—um. Lunch. Or even wine. If you want it. Or if you don't, that's fine, too. Do you need my address? No, I guess you—"

"I'll grab a bottle of wine. See you in thirty?"

"Yes!" She nearly sobbed in relief that her sudden chattering had been mercifully put down.

But she didn't have time to worry about her spazzy methods of seduction. He was coming over. He was bringing wine. She was stubble free and fragrant. And…she didn't have any idea what to make for lunch.

She started toward the kitchen, but before she'd even opened the fridge, she reversed course and ran for the bedroom. The top priority was looking delicious. She'd worry about her lack of food later.

More than half her wardrobe was jeans, but she rejected that idea out of hand. Jeans weren't easy access. They didn't encourage exploration. And she wanted to be explored like a new world with gold in its rivers. Or something.

She tried on a dress, then a skirt, then another dress. Then she put on the original dress and kicked the rest of the clothes back into her tiny closet. But as she shoved the door closed, she realized she looked like a woman who was going to dinner. Too much. Yanking the door open, she dug the black skirt out from the pile and slipped it on. She topped it with a pretty black bra and a blue sweater that always accidentally slipped off one shoulder when she wore it. "Oops," she said with a smile when it immediately slid down to expose her skin.

She shook out her hair and fluffed it with her fingers, so thankful she'd kept up with the color her friend Grace had done for her. A subtle change to her natural blond, but just enough warmth to give her confidence. Not that a man was likely to notice such things, but she wanted to feel like a goddess when she threw her head back and rode Nate Hendricks into the sunset.

"Oh, Jesus," she gasped, covering her face in horror at her own thoughts. She'd never do that, not with a man she barely knew. Just the idea of getting naked for him made her cheeks flame.

On one hand, she'd heard too many guys discussing women's bodies in the saloon. Little digs about big thighs. Crueler digs about breasts that didn't measure up or fat in all the wrong places.

On the other hand, she'd watched men fall head over heels for the plainest girl at the bar just because she made them laugh. Men who went starry-eyed at some obscure hobby he had in common with a girl who didn't draw anyone else's attention.

She didn't know what to think about men anymore. Sometimes they seemed the simplest creatures in the world. And sometimes she was convinced they were more complex and sensitive than any women she'd ever known. All she could do was take off her clothes and enjoy the experience. Since he was a man, she had confidence he'd do the same. Another of their many gifts.

But on her way to the fridge to check the contents, she made one last detour to close all the blinds. Getting naked was one thing. Getting naked with a gorgeous new lover in the cold sunlight of midafternoon? She'd rather sell her car and leave town on the bus.

NATE STOOD IN FRONT of Jenny's apartment door, clutching a bottle of wine in one hand and checking to see if his hair had dried with the other. He'd rushed through a shower, raced to the liquor store and arrived exactly thirty minutes after his call, but now he hesitated.

Somewhere between picking up the phone and walking up her stairs, he'd become confused about the visit. He'd meant to push her a little harder about Ellis. To find out what she knew, what the man had told her. He'd wanted someplace quiet where he could watch her face and listen closely to her voice for any tells. And then hopefully move on, set it aside and get to know this woman who'd been driving him crazy for months. But along the way, his logical plans had scattered like tumbleweeds. Actually, he knew exactly when his brain had started misfiring. It was when she'd nixed his perfect lunch date in favor of something more intimate.

Lunch. At her place. With wine.

His fingers squeezed the neck of the bottle and he knocked.

No reason he couldn't stay on track with his plans. Maybe they'd get intimate. Maybe they'd have sex. But she wasn't going to jump him as soon as she opened the door. He could still ask his questions. He could still step cautiously before deciding to move forward.

Then she opened the door, and he suddenly remembered the taste of her skin, and the sounds she'd made, and the way he'd fucked her in his fantasies that morning.

Her hair was down today. It slid past her shoulders in shiny blond waves. Her eyes glinted green in the sunlight, and her teeth pressed nervously into her plump bottom lip. When she spoke, Nate forced his gaze away from her mouth to meet her eyes.

"Come in!" she announced, stepping back and drawing his attention to her bare feet and red toes. Then her bare legs. And the short black skirt. His brain flashed to an image he'd had that morning, of parting her legs and putting his mouth to her pale, sweet thigh. And then higher.

Oh, fuck.

"I think this was a bad idea," she said, and he yanked his eyes from their unfortunate journey up her legs. "I shouldn't have invited you over."

"I'm sorry. I—"

"The only thing I have here is breakfast food. I can make eggs and home fries. God, I don't even have any bacon. An omelet, maybe? I'm sorry. I just wanted…" Her voice faded into an uncertain quiet.

Nate's mind was still spinning, but he latched onto her last word. "You wanted what?"

She bit her lip again, denting the tender pink flesh until he wanted to make her stop so he could lick the hurt away. His cock stirred at the thought of gently sucking her lip until she groaned. She'd open for him then. Give him her mouth. Her tongue. Her need.

"I wanted to…" She shifted, her gaze falling to the floor, but Nate was distracted by the neckline of her blue sweater slowly sliding down. The gentle turn of her shoulder was revealed in torturous increments. The hollow above her collarbone. The silky strap of her black bra. The soft skin just at the front of her shoulder. God, he wanted to taste her right there. This time he didn't look away from the tempting sight when he spoke. "What did you want, Jenny?"

He heard the soft shush of her inhaling. Her nervousness stoked his lust. "I wanted to be alone with you. Last night, we were interrupted. And I wished we weren't."

Nate set the bottle on the kitchen counter.

"Do you want a glass of wine?" she asked.

"No." That wasn't what he wanted at all. He reached slowly toward her, giving her time to move away. But she held her ground. "Your sweater's sliding off," he murmured, but he didn't fix it. Instead, he brushed his thumb against the sweet expanse of skin that had become exposed. Jesus, she was soft. He felt goose bumps rise under his touch. "Jenny," he said, thinking that he needed to ask her something. Say something. But he couldn't recall what it was. Because he could feel the way her breath came faster as he touched her, and he was closer now, though he couldn't remember moving, and his hand slid higher, up toward her neck, while she sighed and arched into him. Her neck… she liked that so much, when he kissed her there.

So he bent his head and kissed her neck. She gasped as if she'd been holding her breath for long minutes. Nick spread his fingers over the delicate muscles that tensed beneath him as she pressed closer to his mouth. He gave her what she wanted, scraping his teeth along her sensitive skin.

"Oh, God," she whispered, and suddenly they were right back where they'd left off. Jenny whimpering and Nate hard as a rock as he pressed his hips to hers. What questions could possibly exist that couldn't be answered by the taste of her, the feel of her body? Whatever concerns he'd meant to address were surely solved by her hands sliding around his waist. She snuck beneath his flannel shirt and tugged his T-shirt from his jeans.

For a split second, every neuron in his brain was focused on that one thing, that one promise of her hands and his skin and…

Christ, he finally felt her fingers on his bare back and every goal he'd ever had in life was supplanted by the need to feel her naked against him. Her breasts against his chest. Her legs entwined with his. And her sweet, tentative hand around his cock.

The thought made his hands shake as he finally kissed her mouth. Whatever this insane chemistry was, she must have felt it, too, because she kissed him back with wild need and he felt the sudden, delicious bite of her fingernails in his back.

This was the woman who needed to drive fast. Who needed speed and danger and freedom. Nate dragged her sweater up, only breaking the kiss for a moment to pull it over her head. Then their mouths were sucking and biting and licking again, and it was her bare skin now. And his hands. And she was so hot, her skin so soft as he traced the line of her spine.

She turned her head to gasp, "Your shirt," so Nate shrugged out of his flannel shirt as she helped to push his tee up and off his body. And then, thank every god that had ever lived, her stomach was pressed to his and she groaned in relief as he unhooked her bra and tugged that off, too.

"Yes," she said, her breasts pressing tight against him as she drew her hands along his shoulders and over his arms. "Oh, God, you're so damn gorgeous."

His male ego thrilled at the lust in her voice, but he shook his head. Nothing about his body could begin to compare to hers. Just the sight of her shoulders, completely bare, her hair falling around them, then the plump rise of her breasts against him. "God. Just…please, Jenny." He eased her back, giving up the feel of her for the sight.

She turned her head slightly, as if she didn't want to watch him seeing her, and he was relieved, because his eyes would've betrayed him. He was used to being shielded in a uniform and sunglasses. Impervious and unfeeling. But he knew he looked stunned right now. Overwhelmed that she was exposed to him. Her beautiful breasts, tipped with small nipples such a deep pink that his mouth watered at the sight of them.

He cupped a hand carefully over her breast. His fingers looked rough and dark against her perfect skin, her breast too small to fill his grasp. He teased her nipple with his thumb, watching it grow tighter. He heard her breathing quicken and looked up to see her watching now, her gaze locked on his thumb as he teased her.

He'd thought he was as hard as he could get, but then her eyes focused on her own breast as he rolled her nipple between his fingers…God. He wanted her watching him as he did…other things to her.

"Jenny?" He made himself stop teasing her and slide his hand away. She finally looked up, her lips parted, eyes dark. "Where's your bed?"

Her eyes stayed clouded with lust for a moment, but when they cleared, she smiled. That familiar smile, reminding him of who was half-naked in his arms: cute, maddening Jenny Stone. "Right this way," she said, taking his hand to lead him toward an abbreviated hallway. "I feel a little silly wearing just my skirt."

"You should." He devoured the sight of her naked back and the swell of her breast when she twisted to smile at him. "In fact, you should take that off right now to save yourself further embarrassment."

Her laugh made him smile like a besotted fool, or maybe that was the way she stopped next to her bed and unzipped her skirt. When she let it drop to the floor, Nate stopped grinning and reached for her hips. He groaned and slid his hands beneath her black panties to grip her ass.

He squeezed her, pulling her close so he could nibble her neck. "I'd like to point out…" he murmured against her skin, "that I came to the saloon before I ever saw your ass."

Her laugh ended in a small shudder when he sucked just below her ear. "What does that mean?"

Fuck, she was soft and plump and hot beneath his grip. "Because at some point, you're going to accuse me of being obsessed with your ass, and I'm going to remind you that I had no idea you had the most perfect ass I've ever seen, because you were always in your car."

"You haven't even seen it yet."

"Good point."

He spun her around and slipped her panties off while she laughed a breathless protest.

"Jesus Christ, Ms. Stone. Are you trying to kill me?"

"Yes." She arched into him when he pressed his hips to her generous backside and cupped her breasts in his hand. "It's part of my plan to keep you from pulling me over again."

"Letting me see you naked is not the way to keep me off your ass. Your instincts…" He snuck a hand down her stomach, loving the way her muscles jumped. "Are faulty." She parted her thighs just as he realized it was all smooth skin between them. Christ. Smooth skin and wetness and…

She cried out when he touched her clit. "My instincts seem pretty damn spectacular right…now."

He couldn't disagree. He also couldn't speak.

She was liquid heat beneath his fingers. Slickness. Wetness. He needed to feel that around him. He needed to bury his cock inside her right now, but he was still wearing jeans, still separated from her body by torturous millimeters of denim and cotton. And he couldn't let her go, because she was working herself against his fingers now, her hand pressing his closer as her other hand rose to grab the nape of his neck.

God, she *needed* this. She was on fire for it. But he felt insane with the need to sink himself deep. To lose himself inside her. He slid his hand lower and drove two fingers into her pussy.

"Ah!" she cried out. "Yes. Just..."

Her fingernails dug into his neck as he held her with one hand and used the other to tug at the button of his jeans. He finally freed his cock and immediately pressed it to the warm skin of her ass. The feel of her body soaked into him, bringing just enough pleasure to make him groan in pain.

"God. Jenny. Please."

"Don't stop," she urged as his fingers slipped out of her.

"Please," he begged. "I need to—"

"No!" Her hand tightened around his wrist. She needed it so badly. He couldn't say no. But his cock ached, feeling too thick for his own skin.

"Please," he rasped. "You want me inside you, don't you? You need it?"

She nodded.

"Then just give me one second. Please." Fuck, he'd get on his knees and beg if she wanted him to. "Give me a second and then I'll fuck you. Deep and—"

She moaned and let his hand go so he could dig the condom out of his pocket and tear the package open. His hands shook, but he managed to get the condom on in record time. He had a brief, frantic thought that he should turn her around. Ease her onto the bed. Kiss her. Take her gently. It was their first time.

But Jenny had other ideas. She raised one foot to the mattress and tossed an impatient look over her shoulder. Nothing gentle, then. Not this time. Nate bent his knees slightly, notching the head of his cock against her. He eased up slowly, pressing in, opening her for his body. When she gasped and swayed, he curved an arm around her chest to hold her steady as he pushed relentlessly in.

Her voice edged into breathlessness. She whimpered his name, but Nate didn't stop. He pressed deeper into her tightness, nearly dizzy with relief and pleasure and animal satisfaction as she squeezed around him. But when he was as deep as he could get, the satisfaction turned immediately to clawing hunger.

He pulled her tight against his chest and slipped his fingers along her slick flesh until he found her clit again. When he withdrew and thrust into her, Jenny cried out so loudly it was nearly a scream.

"Is that what you wanted?" he growled into her ear.

"Yes," she panted, the word pushed out by a hard thrust of his hips. "Yes."

"God, you feel so good," he groaned, and then he couldn't say more, because it was too much. Too good. Too hot and tight as she arched her back to take him deeper. He tried to concentrate on his fingers, determined to get her off and fully aware that if he focused on the exquisite slide of her body around his cock, he'd lose it. He'd come fast and hard, and he needed that, too, but what he absolutely couldn't live without was getting her off. Hearing her scream. Feeling her shudder around him.

God. Please.

She said his name then. Her body went taut. She threw her head back.

Please. Yes. Come for me. He pressed his mouth to her ear. "Come for me, Jenny."

She cried out then, her hips jerking against his hold, against his cock. Nate closed his eyes, determined not to come yet. Determined to let her ride every spasm as it shook through her. She sounded just as he'd imagined she would, desperate and wild and beautiful, her voice breaking into little bits of joy that burned straight through him.

He drove himself into her, finally, over and over, until his own climax crashed into him. He clenched his teeth against the painful wave of pleasure, biting back a ragged cry. When he was spent, he eased Jenny down to the bed before he slid free of her body and collapsed to the mattress.

Thank God they'd been at the bed, or he might have simply fallen to his knees like a dying man. He felt as if his soul had been scooped out. Jenny looked similarly weak, from what he could tell past the mess of golden hair that had fallen over her face. Nate reached to the table to grab a tissue and get rid of the condom before collapsing again.

He turned toward her and tried to ease some of the hair from her face. "Are you in there?"

"Sorry," she whispered before she shoved her hair back. "Here I am." Her cheeks were flushed already, but they turned pinker as he watched, and her eyes slid down to focus on his chest. "So."

He tipped his head to try to catch her eye. "Are you okay?"

"Sure."

Nate suddenly recalled the moment when he'd thought of being slow and careful. Then he recalled that he'd tossed that thought away and fucked her hard. "Jenny? I'm serious. Are you okay?"

"God!" She turned her face to the mattress and shook her head, spiking his alarm into the red-alert zone. He was reaching carefully toward her when she squeaked. "I don't know what to say. I'm not usually so…"

"So, what?"

"So…*dirty?* Oh, God. That was dirty, wasn't it?"

Relief slammed through him with a force that knocked the air from his lungs. When he could breathe again, he agreed. "Yeah. It was. Filthy, even."

"Stop!" Her shoulders shook, but he could see from the line of her jaw that she was laughing.

"If you were trying to throw me off, you went about it all wrong. That's no way to shake a tail."

"Nate!"

He cupped a hand over her shoulder and turned her toward him. She only resisted for a moment before rolling to her side. Still, she refused to open her eyes.

"Hey." He dragged a finger along her jaw, then over her lips. Her eyes finally fluttered open. "Did you mean that?"

"What?" she asked warily.

"That you got especially dirty for me?"

Her eyes glittered past her lashes as she watched him. "Maybe," she finally said.

Pride swelled so quickly in his chest that Nate worried it might press too tight against his heart and cause trouble. It certainly felt as if it was doing damage. "I like that."

She smiled. "Somehow that doesn't surprise me."

Actually, it surprised him. Not that he liked intense sex with her, but how *much* he liked it. His chest still felt strange, warm and woolly with the idea that she'd given him a glimpse of her that others didn't get. But he let her think it was as simple as she thought it was.

"Jenny…" He swept her hair back again, but this time he let his hand trail over her shoulder, her arm, then her hip. God. Her beautiful hip.

"You like saying my name," she said with a coy smile.

"It's because I had to say 'Ms. Stone' for so long. It felt like torture."

"Poor Deputy Hendricks."

Her sweet, teasing words caused a niggling in his brain. Then a tense tug. And then he remembered. What he'd meant to ask her about. The complications he'd meant to avoid. And now… What had he done?

Shit. This had been a mistake. The knot in his stomach couldn't make his body regret it, but his brain was a twisting mess.

He had to figure her out before he screwed everything up.

CHAPTER SIX

"Tell me something about yourself," Nate said.

Jenny smiled at the odd request. After all, they'd just bonked like crazed rabbits.

Her face flamed again. It wasn't that she was repressed. She'd had a decent sex life. Sometimes she even had a great sex life. But she'd never *needed* sex that way.

She usually let sex happen to her. Wash over her. But this had been something clawing out from her own soul. Something new inside her. The smell of him. The feel of his skin and hair. It had called forth something desperate.

What if she told him that? How would he respond? She smiled wider at the idea.

"Where are you from?" he pressed.

"Idaho. A town about an hour west of Pocatello."

"How did you end up here?"

She shrugged, not wanting to get into details. She'd ended up here by running. First from home, and all the chaos there. Then from Ellis, and the life she'd jumped into without thinking. And again, from a life she'd started to build in Montana and then grown tired of. She didn't want to tell him any of that, but her heart swelled with the knowledge that he wanted to know her. He wanted *her.*

Swallowing hard, she decided to tell him a little. "I left home the moment I turned eighteen. I married Ellis. Then I wandered for a while. That's all. Now I'm here."

"Why'd you leave home at eighteen?"

Because I couldn't handle taking care of a pill-popping mom, so I abandoned my dad and my sister and drove out of town as fast as my Camaro would take me. She closed her eyes and concentrated on the weight of his palm against her hip. "You know, same old story. My grandfather left me his car when he died. I couldn't wait to get out on my own. I thought it would be all fun and games."

"And then there was Ellis?"

She smiled. "And then there was Ellis. Believe it or not, I thought he was a knight in shining armor."

"But he wasn't?"

She sighed. "I don't want to talk about Ellis."

"I'm still worried. What's he doing here? Hanging around? Bothering you?"

"Nate." She opened her eyes to his worried frown. "I can see why you became a cop. You're protective. Overprotective. But I don't need that. I can take care of myself. I always have."

His eyebrows twitched. "Always?"

"Well. You know. For a long time."

"That's not what you said."

Jenny felt like squirming, caught under his silver gaze. "You know how it is."

"I don't, actually. I was raised right here in Jackson Hole. My parents and sister still live here. Sunday dinner once a month. And much bigger gatherings for holidays. That was my cousin Luis you saw with me at the bar. None of us went very far at all."

"Maybe…maybe I just like to run."

"Maybe you need to. What are you running from, Jenny?"

She pulled her chin slowly in, eyes narrowing at the strange focus of his gaze. She felt a sudden desire to curl tighter. To cover her nakedness.

"Why is he here? You must know."

Now she did cover herself. She folded an arm across her breasts as she pushed onto her elbow. "Wow. I can't… Wow. I thought you wanted to learn more about me. But you want to know about *him?* What is this? Some weird jealousy kink?"

His intense gaze finally flinched to alarm. "No! That's not what I meant. Look, I saw him. Today. I was looking into another issue and I saw Ellis's van. I called you about lunch so I could ask you about it. That's all."

"That's all?" Whatever energy she'd lost to

the sex, Jenny quickly regained through mortified rage. She leaped from the bed. "I thought you wanted to have sex with me!"

He reached for her, and she jerked away, trying not to notice his beautiful body. She hadn't had time to look, and now she refused to. "I obviously wanted to have sex with you," he said as he followed her slow retreat across the room. "Come on. We *had* sex."

"I'm pretty clear on that!" Boy, was she. She was absolutely aching with that knowledge. Inside and out, her body reminded her with every move that she'd had sex with Nate Hendricks. And he'd come here to *investigate.*

But…investigate what?

The thought added another layer of awfulness to the moment. A nice, thick layer of guilt. Ellis was up to no good, and now Jenny was helping him.

Oh, God. "Get out," she pushed past clenched teeth.

"Jenny, please."

She snatched up her skirt and tugged it on. Her heart beat so quickly it felt like nothing more than trembling. "I thought you came here for *me.*"

"I did!"

"You did not! Last night, you came to the saloon about my *driving.* Today, you came here about my ex-husband. Well, let me reassure you, Deputy Hendricks, you don't need to worry about me anymore. I called about the class. I start next month. And Ellis Stone is starting a landscaping operation, so there's everything I know. I hope all this important information was worth going that deep undercover!"

He reached for her again, and she shook off his hand, looking frantically around for a sweater that seemed to have disappeared. But Nate was still naked, and though she tried to avoid his eyes, she couldn't avoid the feel of his skin against hers when he finally caught her and pulled her close.

"I'm asking about those things because I'm trying to figure you out."

The feel of his hands on her naked back infuriated her. Because they felt good. So damn good, even while she was pissed and humiliated. She felt such a rush of fear and hate at the thought that she was able to shove him hard enough to get free.

"Then there's something seriously wrong with you. If you want to get to know me, try asking me about myself. You know, the old standards. 'What's your favorite movie? What do you do for fun?' Most men find that more effective than 'Can I see your license and registration?' or 'How's your ex-husband these days?' or 'Tell me all about your fucked-up childhood.'"

The silence that rang through the room after her last words made clear just how loudly she'd shouted. The shock on Nate's face was another clue. Jenny pressed her fingers to her mouth as if she could erase the echo of her own voice. "You should go," she whispered.

"I'm sorry," he said. "I've handled this really badly. I wanted to talk to you about it. Christ, Jenny. I meant to talk this out with you, and then I saw you, and I forgot what I was worried about."

"So you fucked me and then got right back on the job?"

"That's not… I just wanted…"

She felt a brief moment of triumph that she'd reduced him to stammering, but that was the most pitiful, stupid victory she'd ever embraced in her life, and it threw a little water on her fiery rage. "I don't know what this is about, Nate. I don't know what Ellis has done to draw your attention, aside from pissing you off, but I can't help. He showed up to see me after ten years, and I sent him on his way. End of story. Now please go."

"Jenny, I'm sorry. My brain wasn't working right after I came. I mean, after we made love. You were just so… God, I couldn't fucking think."

She wanted to melt into the floor. Disappear. Cease to exist. Yes. She'd been *so.* For him. She retreated into the living room and tugged her sweater roughly over her head, desperate to cover herself. "You need to go. Please."

"I'm sorry," he said again, but he dressed quickly. "I'll call you tonight." When she didn't answer, he left without another word, closing the door carefully behind him.

There was that ringing silence again. Jenny turned in a slow circle, taking in her apartment in a daze. What the hell had just happened? She'd invited a cute guy over for lunch, and less than an hour later, she'd been fucked within an inch of her life and then treated like a witness to a crime. Or an accessory.

Oh, Jesus, what was she was an accessory to?

She raced to her bedroom to snatch her phone from the table, then call the number she'd entered just last night. She should have checked inside the boxes he'd brought over.

"Hey, Jennybug," Ellis said.

"Ellis, what the hell is in those boxes?"

"I told you. Landscaping stuff."

She slammed her door open and rushed down the stairs. "Where are you? I need you to get over here right now and get these boxes out of my garage."

"What? I just unloaded them last night! What in the world is wrong with you?"

Jenny stomped over to the old building that was fronted by four dented, beat-up garage doors. It wasn't attached and it wasn't fancy, but in a mountain ski town, garage space was a treasured luxury. One she shouldn't have so easily ceded to Ellis.

"Get over here, Ellis. I'm not kidding. I want them out. You're involved with something. I know it."

"It's landscaping," he said with a firmness that betrayed him. As if he was trying to convince himself. As if he was bolstering an argument. But if it was the truth, why would he need an argument?

"Damn it, Ellis! I was trying to *help* you."

"You are!"

She grabbed the handle and pulled the heavy door up. "Not anymore. Come get these boxes or I will put them out in the parking lot."

He must have heard the enormous rattle of the door, because his voice lost its helplessness and turned serious. "Don't put my stuff outside. Please. You're the one who said I could leave it there."

She moved into the shadows of the garage and stared down at the boxes stacked next to her car. "I changed my mind. I'm hearing rumors. Whatever the hell you're up to, I can't be involved. This isn't a bluff, Ellis. And it's not a tantrum. Come get the boxes now."

"Fine. Just shut the door, all right? I'm down at Hoback. It'll take me a few to get there."

"Okay. You've got one hour. And whatever you're doing, stop it. Just stop it and leave." Jenny hung up and glared down at the first box. The flaps were folded over each other to secure the top, but it wasn't sealed. She reached toward it to free a corner and peek in, but changed her mind before she'd exposed the contents. Better if she didn't know. Better to have deniability. She jerked her hand back and wiped it on her sweater.

The cold hit her then. Her feet came alive with a twist of pain that shot up her legs. She'd forgotten to put on shoes and the cold was seeping from the cement into the soles of her feet. And the air snuck beneath her skirt to chase away every last vestige of sated relaxation. It whisked away even the memory of pleasure and left her with ice.

"Shit," she cursed, crossing an arm over her chest as she bit back a shiver. She reached up and pulled down the garage door, wincing when it landed with a crash. It sounded as if the day had broken in two, and that was exactly what it had done. One part had been searing and delicious and frighteningly good. The other part? Well. The other part was a jagged, broken stump. Jenny put her head down and raced up the stairs on numb toes.

NATE WATCHED WITH weary eyes as Jenny ran back to her apartment and slammed the door. He let his head fall back and stared at the roof of his truck, too stunned to do more. A gust of wind shook the vehicle, rocking it on its axles.

When she'd come out, he'd thought she was coming after him, and he was glad he'd hesitated. Glad he'd sat in his truck in the parking lot like a fool, trying to plan an apology. He'd screwed up, but she would forgive him. This thing between them was too damn good, and she could feel it, too. This strange urgency to be near her. To get closer. After what they'd just done, it was even more powerful. An unseen tattoo glowing beneath his skin, pressing him toward her.

She'd see him waiting, and she'd ask him to come back, and he'd try to explain what he felt, and what he'd meant to say.

But she hadn't looked up when she'd reached the parking lot. Instead, she'd been talking on the phone, and Nate had eased his door open and shamelessly listened.

The cold had wiped that hot tattoo from his skin, thank God, because it was the mark of a fool.

Jenny Stone wasn't a sweet, innocent bystander to a criminal operation. She was involved. At the very least, she was actively protecting her ex-husband. Warning him. Tipping him off. At worst, she was participating in this whole operation. Maybe even orchestrating it.

But no. He had good instincts. Good enough that he'd managed to collect his wits even after a bout of the most intense sex he'd ever had. He'd asked what he'd needed to ask, clumsy as he'd been. And now he had his answer.

He was a fool, but he wasn't an idiot. Jenny Stone was lying to him. Hell, she might even be playing him. But she was only on the edges of this. And if she wasn't, then she'd pay the price, and this time it wouldn't be only a suspended license.

But the investigation wasn't the least bit interesting to him anymore. He didn't want to pursue it further, and now that he'd slept with one of the players, he couldn't. He'd call Luis and give him the rundown, and then he'd go to his supervisor. If there was going to be a stakeout tomorrow, it'd be done by another deputy. Nate couldn't damage the investigation by putting himself in the middle of it. Plus, he had his hands full with damaging himself.

CHAPTER SEVEN

JENNY DRAGGED HER sorry ass into the saloon to pick up an extra shift out of pure pitifulness. She'd moped around her apartment for hours, feeling sorry for herself, and furious with Ellis, and hurt by Nate.

Ellis had denied doing anything wrong. He'd even opened one box to show her a jumble of plastic hosing. But his eyes had slid away whenever she'd tried to meet his gaze, so she'd refused to give in. He was in over his head again. In what, she had no idea, but she didn't want any part of it.

After he'd gone, her apartment had been too small. It had started snowing, and gotten dark, so she couldn't drive. Couldn't indulge the awful burning in her muscles telling her to run. Go. Fly.

If only it were summer. She could find a quiet stretch of highway and roll down her windows and forget for a few minutes. Hell, maybe even keep driving. Drive until the pain lost its hold and she felt peaceful enough to stop and start over.

She'd been here too long. She was making mistakes now. Wanting more than she deserved.

That was the reason she'd given in to Ellis. She'd known it was a mistake to allow him anything, but she'd wanted to be forgiven. She'd wanted to forgive herself, and so she'd latched onto the idea of making it up to him. The mistake of marrying him. Of letting them both believe she'd loved him. And then the panic when she'd awoken and realized what she'd done. The terrible way she'd left him, sneaking out in the night.

Ellis hadn't been a good husband. Hell, he hadn't even been a man. Just twenty-three years old and as aimless as he'd been sweet.

Jenny wiped down tables in a quiet corner of the saloon. She took her time, scrubbing at chair legs and cleaning the seats. She thought about calling home. It'd been years since she'd checked in. Maybe things were better now. Maybe her mom had finally decided to give up the pills.

But no. Someone would've gotten in touch. Her dad. Or maybe even Mom herself. But most likely, it would've been her sister, Jess, who took care of all the things that Jenny had walked away from. Who stayed because Jenny hadn't. Who was stronger in so many ways, and weak only in that she cared too much and too easily.

"Hey there, girl!" Rayleen's rough voice called.

"You lost in thoughts of last night? You've been cleaning that table for five minutes."

"Sorry," she said, grabbing the spray bottle and heading behind the bar. It wasn't busy tonight for some reason. The weather was bad, and no one wanted to head over from Teton, probably. She really wasn't needed behind the bar, as Benton had it under control, but she didn't want to go. "Benton, I can take this shift, if you want," she said as she passed him.

"Nah, I'm saving up for a new board. You go on."

Crap. She edged around the bar to put away the cleaning supplies, but Rayleen stopped her. "So he wore you out, huh?"

Jenny froze. How the hell had Rayleen found out about that? Jackson was a small town, but it wasn't *that* small. Had Nate *told* people? She tried shaking her head, but Rayleen just snorted.

"Don't bother denying it. I saw that boy follow you home last night."

Oh, thank God. She had it all wrong.

"Though why you sent that stud home and took up with Rapunzel, I have no idea. Are you playing them against each other in hopes of Valentine's Day gifts?"

"Valentine's Day?" God, she'd forgotten about that. But she'd be working, thankfully. Valentine's Day in a saloon was just like any other night, with maybe a few more desperate hookups. At least she wouldn't have to look at any happy couples.

"Well?" Rayleen snapped.

"Not that it's any of your business, but I did *not* sleep with Ellis last night."

"Like I said, you don't look like you got much sleep."

"I slept fine. And alone."

"Yeah? Then why's your neck all raw on one side?"

When Jenny slapped a hand to her neck with a guilty gasp, Rayleen cackled.

"Good Lord, girl, your face is as red as a baboon's ass!"

"Good old Aunt Rayleen!" a new voice said. "Always the most charming woman at the table."

Jenny spun to flash a grimace of a smile at her friend Grace. "Hey. When did you get here?"

"A few seconds before my sweet old auntie accused you of getting laid. And having a baboon ass for a face. I'm hoping the two are unrelated. Just how kinky did it get?"

Jenny's face was so hot she was tempted to stick her head in the ice maker. "She doesn't know what she's talking about."

Grace smiled. "No?"

"No!"

"She's lying," Rayleen said.

Grace's smile widened to a grin. "I know."

"And her ex-husband is in town."

Jenny groaned at the way Grace's eyes widened. When she opened her mouth, Jenny held up a hand. "Yes, I have an ex-husband. No, I did not sleep with him last night. Or do anything else!"

"You did something," Grace insisted. "You look like a girl caught with her fingers in the pot. Or the cookie jar. Or whatever kind of container you'd find penises in."

Rayleen howled and pounded her table hard enough to make her deck of cards jump. "I always find them in pockets!"

"Oh, good God," Jenny muttered. She grabbed Grace by the arm and pulled her closer. "The bathroom. Now."

"Ooo," Grace cooed mockingly. "So forceful."

"Yeah, I heard you like that."

"Ha! Look at Jenny getting her claws out. I think I like you this way, you nasty little thing."

"Go!" Jenny gave her a gentle shove toward the back of the room. She never would've shoved Grace a few months before. Grace looked tough as hell with her edgy hair and smoky eyes and black boots. She *was* tough as hell. But she'd become one of Jenny's best friends over the winter, and Jenny assumed that Grace probably wouldn't punch her over one tiny, little shove.

She didn't.

After ditching her cleaning supplies, Jenny

tossed Rayleen a scowl. "It's slow. I'm clocking out."

"Hot date?"

Instead of cursing at her, Jenny grabbed her coat and headed toward the bathroom. She found Grace waiting in the narrow hallway. Grace tipped her head. "There's already a party of four in there, comforting a girl who ran into her boyfriend on a date with his wife. Poor thing."

Jenny winced. "We can sit in my car."

"Sure. I'll do anything to hear this story. I don't think you've dated anyone since I moved to town."

"I haven't."

"Then let's go."

They raced through the snow to Jenny's car, and Grace was laughing breathlessly by the time they ducked and slammed the doors. "I don't think I'll ever get used to snow," she gasped. "I feel like I'm on vacation every time a storm hits. Because this can't be my real life. It's like living in a nature documentary."

"It's called winter, L.A. girl," Jenny teased, but she was glad for Grace's silly affection for snow. Grace's smile was different than it had been when she'd first moved to Jackson. Everything about her was different, starting with her hair, which was only brown and black now, and missing the vivid purple that had once streaked through it.

"So," Grace said, tilting her chin toward Jenny. "Who are you doing?"

Jenny took a deep breath. "You know that cute deputy I told you about? The one who keeps pulling me over?"

"Holy crap. No. No! That's like something out of a porn movie. Please tell me it was a frisk that went bad."

"Shut up. It wasn't like that. Well, not really. He pulled me over again, because I'm an idiot, and I maybe mentioned something about buying him a beer, and…he actually showed up."

"What do you mean, 'actually'?" Grace shook her head. "Of course he showed up. You're cute and sexy. He's probably been plotting a way to ask you out from day one."

"I don't know. But it went well, even after my ex showed up and nearly ruined everything."

"Okay. So why do you look tortured?"

Jenny rubbed the side of her neck that was slightly raw from such vigorous attention. "We had sex. It was… God, it was amazing. Spectacular. And then he started asking about my ex."

"What do you mean? Like he's jealous?"

"I don't know. Maybe?"

"Oh, that's bad news, no matter how good the sex was. If he's that controlling after one night, you need to think very carefully. No question."

"I don't know. It didn't seem that bad."

"Jenny. He's a cop. And he's already jealous. That could be a bad combination."

"Maybe," Jenny conceded, but as she said goodbye to Grace and started the car, she shook her head. It hadn't felt like jealousy or control. It had felt like genuine worry mixed with a little "Just doing my job, ma'am."

Had she overreacted? He'd been sweet. And so damn hot. And if she looked at it through his eyes… Heck, aside from all the cop stuff, she'd have been asking some very serious questions of Nate if an ex-wife had shown up in the middle of the night, causing trouble. Add to that the fact that Ellis definitely was acting a little strange, and Jenny lost a little of her hurt. Or a lot of it.

She stared out at the snow racing past the path of her headlights, but she didn't put the car in gear.

Had Nate done anything so terrible? He'd been awkward, yes. His timing had been unfortunate. But maybe he really had been overwhelmed by… what? Lust? Need? *Her?*

The snowflakes blurred into a solid white mass, and Jenny closed her eyes against tears. Pitiful to feel so moved to be wanted that way, but it wasn't gratitude. It was more like an answer to the need she'd felt for him. It struck her, ringing a chord deep inside her body. Unfortunately, it wasn't a comforting sound.

Jenny pulled out of the parking lot and turned

away from home. Storm or no storm, she needed to drive. And she needed to find out what the hell Ellis was up to. For Ellis's sake, but more than that, for her own.

CHAPTER EIGHT

"SERGEANT, ARE YOU sure you want me here?" Nate asked.

His sergeant shot him an impatient look. "It's your bust, isn't it?"

"Well, I suppose, but the complicating factors make it—"

"Look, we've got your eyewitness testimony and that of your cousin. This isn't going to be a complex case. These guys aren't usually careful. I'm sure there are fingerprints all over the place. They operate on the principle of nondiscovery, not *CSI: Miami*."

"I know, but I...further complicated things by—"

His sergeant seemed to be fighting back a smile. "I'm sure we can try the case without bringing your extracurricular activities into it."

Jesus, now he wasn't just a fool; he was a damned amusing one. "Fine."

"Just hang back, all right? I'll call you in when it's clear."

Nate paced deeper into the woods, following the path of an old camp road into silent trees. There was no wind this morning. The storm had settled all of that, blanketing Jackson in a foot of snow and stilling the bustle of the place.

It hadn't stilled his mind, though. That still raced and bucked. He tried to calm it. His sergeant seemed amused by any assertion that he'd compromised a drug case by sleeping with Jenny.

"It wouldn't be a case if you hadn't brought it to us," the sergeant had said, shoving aside Nate's concerns. So why was he so tortured by it? He paced the road and waited.

It was 8:00 a.m. Jenny probably wasn't even up yet. Not that it mattered. She wouldn't forgive him once he had her ex-husband thrown in prison. And he probably shouldn't forgive her for lying. He *definitely* shouldn't. But the thought of letting their connection die…

He was thirty-five years old. He'd dated a lot of women, and slept with more than a few of them. There was lust. There was chemistry. And then there was something that went so deep it nearly hurt. He hadn't known about that until yesterday, but now he couldn't go on pretending he didn't know.

Still, it was more than the physical. It was her sunny smile. The easy way she worked hard and still had a friendly word for everyone around her.

He'd already known about her positive attitude, after pulling her over six times. What had surprised him was the glimpse of something more. When she'd lost her temper and revealed too much about why she'd really left home so young. A shitty childhood, she'd said. He wouldn't have guessed it; she was so carefree.

But maybe that was what had attracted her to a man like Ellis. And maybe the drug stuff was just normal to her. No big deal. Hell, maybe it was a serious part of her life.

He hoped not. Not just for himself, but for her, too.

"Damn." He tipped his head up to stare at the dove-gray clouds above him. It might snow again, but the storm was gone. Now it was just the sad cold that followed. And all he could do was wait.

JENNY JERKED AWAKE at a distant screech of metal on metal. Her car was cocooned in snow, completely cut off from everything, and for a moment, she had no idea where she was. The world was nothing but white and cold and the mist of her own startled breath. But a few heartbeats later, she remembered. She was parked in a camp parking lot, her car covered in snow.

She'd driven last night. Through the snow and wind. She'd had to do it, to get enough air. Enough oxygen that she could think. She'd driven for miles and miles.

Nate truly liked her. She knew he did. She could feel it. He liked her so much that even though she had the baggage of an ex-husband who was possibly an active criminal, he wanted to give her a chance. Or he had wanted to, until she'd lost her shit and thrown him out.

As she'd driven deserted, icy roads, she'd told herself she was willing to answer his questions. But she couldn't. She had no idea what Ellis was up to. She didn't even know if she was involved. He'd used her property. She'd agreed. But to what?

An urgency had overtaken her then. A need to resolve this. So she'd turned her car around and driven toward Hoback, where Ellis had rented a place. It was too far away for skiers to drive every day, so likely the only place he'd been able to find a bed.

An hour later, she'd driven slowly through the scattered cabins of the ancient camp where he was staying. It had taken two passes before she'd spotted his van. She'd pulled into the one plowed parking area she could find and raced to his door to knock, but there'd been no answer. Either he was passed out or he was partying at someone else's place, but Jenny had come too far to give up. She'd retreated to her car to wait, and she'd promptly fallen asleep.

And now she was snowed in.

Jenny slowly cranked her window down, wincing at the ledge of snow that fell onto her arm. But a little discomfort was worth the sight of a slice of the world. Trees beyond a rooftop, and then the corner of a cabin. Ellis's cabin was across the lot and up the road a little, but his van was no longer there.

"Shit!" she cursed, her eyes rolling wildly. But then she saw the tracks in the snow and followed them quickly up the lane to the highway. There he was, already making the turn. He hadn't noticed her car because it had been nothing but a big lump in the snow.

She cursed again, using a few of the choicest words she'd ever learned serving beer to working cowboys. Pushing as hard as she could, she forced her door open and scrambled out. Her tall boots kept most of the snow out as she grabbed her snow brush and started frantically cleaning off the hood of her car. When she had all the windows cleared, she grabbed the shovel from the trunk and dug out the tires, too. She skipped the roof. She'd just have to create a snowstorm for the poor driver behind her. She needed to haul ass and catch up to Ellis.

At least she knew which way he'd turned, though she could guess he'd head toward Jackson, regardless. Once she got the car out of the lot, she turned toward town and floored it, praying to God that Nate wasn't working traffic today.

It took almost fifteen minutes to catch up, but she found Ellis, and fell in behind his truck to follow. She only meant to follow him long enough to park beside him and demand an explanation. But as she drove, she realized she might have the wrong idea. Ellis didn't want to tell her the truth. Whatever he was up to, he didn't think he was doing anything wrong. If she wanted the real story, she'd have to find it.

She immediately let up on the gas and fell back, as if she could suddenly fade into the background like a bright yellow fog.

Frowning, hunched over her steering wheel, she glared at his white van, taking no note of the beauty around her. Had he spotted her? He hadn't given any indication of it. The back panels of the van had no window, and his driver's-side mirror appeared to be aimed at the sky. That left the mirror on the passenger side of the van, but really, if he wasn't using one mirror, why would he use the other?

She fell back a little bit. Then a little more. She planned to catch up again when he got to town, but she didn't get the chance. Cresting the rise of a hill about ten minutes before town, she realized she'd lost him.

"Oh, crap," she gasped, looking everywhere

in a panic, even toward the sky, as if he'd pulled a Mary Poppins and floated off above the chimneys of the houses gathered at the side of the road.

The houses. She searched among the driveways and saw nothing. But just before she reached the small group of log cabins, she saw a road and slammed on her brakes to take the turn.

It was the only place he could have turned. The river ran along the other side. He couldn't have—There. His brake lights flashed ahead of her. Jenny slumped in relief and told herself to calm down. Ellis Stone wasn't sharp enough to lose a tail, even a really awful tail like her.

Now that she'd found him again, she slowed. Even Ellis might notice someone following him on this narrow, isolated road leading to…somewhere she'd never been.

Somewhere far off the highway. When they passed over a cattle grate into free range land, Jenny started to get nervous. Why the hell would Ellis need to be out here? This wasn't right. He certainly wasn't the snowshoeing type.

She'd lost sight of him for a few minutes, but she wasn't concerned. There weren't any side roads here, or if there were, they weren't plowed.

As the road snuck through a bare grove of aspen, Jenny finally found a sign of life. A side road, and two cabins, one with smoke tripping from the chimney. But Ellis's van wasn't there, and no recent tracks marred the three inches of new snow on the plowed driveway. Jenny drove on. Five minutes later, she found the tracks she'd been expecting and took a right onto a side road. When she eased around the next bend, she had to slam on her brakes so hard that she slid nearly ten feet and skidded along the edge of a ditch for a precarious few seconds.

But it wasn't Ellis's van coming toward her. It was a sheriff's truck. She was so sure that it was Nate that when the deputy got out of the truck and started toward her, she only felt confusion at his blond hair. She didn't even notice the two other deputies. Or the fact that their guns were drawn. Not until she turned her head and found herself staring into the barrel of a handgun.

For the first time, the thought of running had come too late, and now she was caught in a way she'd never expected.

AS SOON AS ELLIS WAS in custody, Nate counted himself done. Victor had shown up first, blasting music and so high already that he'd stared stupidly at the arresting officer for a good three minutes before alarm had kicked in.

Ellis had followed fifteen minutes later, and it was done. Nate had expected to feel relief, but he'd only felt tired as he'd trudged down to the cabin and finally gotten a good look inside the greenhouse. "Jesus," he said as soon as he ducked under the plastic sheeting. "This is the most pitiful pot-growing operation I've ever seen."

The techs had apparently been having the same conversation, because they burst into hysterical laughter. Any worries that this was connected to a big operation were completely assuaged by the sight of the mishmash of random heating lamps and leaking water containers. And the plants themselves looked—

"Good Christ," his sergeant barked. "That's the saddest crop of marijuana I've ever seen."

More laughter from the techs, and even Nate felt a smile tug at his mouth. He should've taken a closer look yesterday. If he'd seen these two dozen pitiful stalks, he'd have known that he and Luis could've quietly taken care of this problem themselves. Hell, they could've even made it look like a warning from a real drug operation. Oh, well. It didn't change the fact that Victor had abused his uncle's generosity, desecrated a place that meant a lot to the family and endangered his minor cousin. The kid deserved a good scare, not to mention a penalty.

"Got another one, Sergeant," one of the other deputies said from the makeshift doorway.

"Another what?"

"Suspect."

Nate's head jerked up at that. "Who?"

The guy shrugged. “I don’t know. A woman in an old-school Camaro.”

“She’s *here?*”

“Pulled up a few minutes after we cuffed Ellis Stone.”

Jenny was here. She’d known exactly what was going on the whole time. Damn. Just…*damn.*

He could feel his sergeant’s eyes on his face, and Nate hoped he didn’t look as green as he felt.

“Hendricks?”

“I won’t interfere.”

“Good. We’ll sort it out at headquarters.”

“Got it.” His voice sounded remarkably light considering the weight in his chest. “I’ll head over now.”

Nate felt the blankness on his own face as he walked through the trees to his truck and got in. As he pulled off the camping road, he called Luis and listened to the broken ring of a bad connection in his ear. Up ahead was her yellow car, bright against the snow and the dark green horde of sheriff’s vehicles.

“Nate,” his cousin said.

“Luis, it’s done. We’ve arrested Victor and some accomplices. The plants will be destroyed, though the rest of the cleanup will be up to you. We’re not very good at helping out with that kind of thing. But…”

He edged past her car, and he thought the danger was over, but as he passed a marked patrol car, Nate saw her in the backseat, her face shockingly pale against the dark interior. Her head turned toward him just as he turned away.

"But it's done," he told his cousin. "It's done."

CHAPTER NINE

NATE LEANED AGAINST the wall, his eyes locked tight on the interrogation going on behind the glass. Victor was no longer stoned. He was brutally sober and absolutely terrified. And he was spilling everything he knew, which wasn't all that much.

"I don't know, man. I met him at a party at Steve Tex's place, and we started talking about all the bullshit work we do for practically minimum wage. He told me he had a great idea to make a little money. He just needed the perfect spot to do it. Come on, man. Pot never hurt anyone. It wasn't like we—"

"So you volunteered your uncle's property?"

The kid had the good grace to squirm at that, but Nate was distracted by the sound of a woman's voice as a door opened in the interrogation suite across the hall. Jenny's voice. He couldn't make out what she was saying, but as the door closed again, he heard the tense note of pleading in her words.

He'd managed to avoid her. He didn't want to

see her. She was probably scared. She'd probably cried as she was handcuffed. He hated that. He always did. Even when the woman was a stranger.

The hair on his arms rose at the idea of Jenny being booked into jail. Whether she'd lied to him or not, he didn't want to watch that. He'd held her naked in his arms; he couldn't watch her be broken that way.

He was turning to make his way back to the desk he shared with two other officers when a deputy named Davidson appeared in the doorway with a big smile. He held a plastic baggie up. "Don't go anywhere. You're going to want to see this."

"What?" Nate asked, but the guy had already disappeared. He reappeared again in the room where Ellis was waiting to be questioned. Nate switched off the speaker of Victor's room and moved over to watch Ellis.

"You still determined not to say anything?" the deputy asked.

"I'm not a snitch," Ellis said, but he didn't sound defiant; he sounded sad.

"No? You're not much of a drug dealer, either."

"It's not like that. Pot helps people, you know?"

"So you thought this stuff was going to improve people's lives? Because you got that all wrong." Davidson smiled toward the two-way mirror and pushed the baggie forward. "You know why your pot plants look so shitty and woody?"

Ellis was apparently smart enough not to defend them and claim the plants as his own. "I don't know what you're talking about."

"No? How much did you pay for these plants? Or maybe you bought them as seeds, I don't know. But you don't strike me as a guy with a green thumb. So, where'd you get the plants?"

Ellis stared down at the table.

"I only ask because I'm concerned about you. Maybe you paid too much. Maybe you got ripped off. Because, Ellis…" Davidson leaned forward, his fists on the table and a grin on his face. "The reason your plants look so shitty is that you didn't buy marijuana. What you have going is a thriving hemp farm."

Ellis's head snapped toward Davidson. "What?"

"Not a drop of THC in them. Or not enough to show up on a field test, anyway. You could smoke every one of those plants, and all you'd get was a sore throat."

"That's not true," Ellis said, aiming a pleading look at Davidson.

"No? Bet you got a great deal on them, huh? Something special just because you're a nice guy? Did you even know the man when you handed over the cash?"

"You're lying. He wouldn't—"

Davidson shrugged. "This interview is being

recorded. I'm not allowed to give you false information about your case."

Nate rolled his eyes. That wasn't true, but apparently Ellis believed it, because his gaze slid to the baggie as the tips of his ears turned red. "He said..."

"Who?"

"A guy named Frank. We were friends. I *thought* we were friends. He wanted to help me out. He—"

"Frank who?"

Ellis hung his head, dropping his forehead into his hands. "I can't believe any of this is happening. Victor said no one ever went out there. I only had two hundred dollars left to my name. Everything else was gone. I just needed a new start. A way to make enough money to get in on a new landscaping business."

"And Frank?"

"Frank had a truck full of plants. He said he'd give me the ones that weren't doing so well. Two hundred then and another two hundred a month later. I picked up a little work. It was working out fine."

"Yeah, real fine," Davidson snapped. "You were running a drug operation in my county."

Ellis raised his head, a flash of hope relaxing his mouth into something that was almost a smile. "But it isn't pot! So I'm good, right? I can go?"

When he stood, Davidson guided him back down to his chair. “Not so fast, Stone. There are still a few good charges in there, starting with destruction of federal forest.”

“What?” he asked blankly.

“The field you were working on in back? That’s federal land. So there are still charges that can be brought. But maybe they’d go away if you decide to cooperate. I need the names of everyone involved.” Nate felt a moment of sharp fear for James and Jenny, but Ellis only looked confused.

“Everyone involved? I saw you putting Victor in a car. And I already gave you Frank’s name.”

“What about the woman?” Davidson pressed, and Nate’s shoulders tightened to rock.

“What woman?” Ellis asked.

“I believe she’s your wife,” Davidson said dryly.

“Jenny?” Ellis shook his head. “Jenny had nothing to do with this.”

“Come on. We know she’s involved.”

“No way.” Ellis swallowed and his eyes shifted away. “Look, I admit, I asked if I could store a few boxes at her place, but it was nothing illegal. Just hoses and irrigation stuff. That’s all. And I already moved those boxes, anyway. She didn’t know anything.”

“Right. That’s why she was heading out to the cabin to visit the operation.”

“Dude, I thought you said you couldn’t lie.”

Ellis laughed and shook his head. "That's bullshit. Jenny didn't know anything."

Davidson dropped it. "All right. Tell us more about this Frank."

But Nate wanted to rush in and grab Ellis by the collar and shake more information about Jenny from him. He ran a hand through his hair, aware of how hard his heart was beating, because…because Ellis had seemed sincere. And his story backed up what Nate himself had witnessed.

Was he telling the truth? Or was he holding a flame for Jenny and just trying to protect her? Nate had to find out. The need to know the truth twisted inside his gut. It felt like life or death somehow. Ridiculous, of course. He knew what it was like to face a real life-or-death situation. This wasn't life or death or even danger. It was just…his heart.

He scowled at the ridiculous, maudlin thought, not even realizing Davidson was done with his questioning until the deputy appeared in the doorway. "Can you believe this idiot?" he howled. "Hemp! Jesus Christ, he almost had enough plants to make himself a pair of those hippie sandals!"

On another day, Nate would've laughed, but this time he could only manage the strength to nod.

"Anyway, I think I know who this Frank is. We'll put out a description and hopefully track him down, see if he's carrying the real deal. But as for this genius…he's probably going to walk. I don't know how your cousin will feel about that."

Nate shrugged. "He'll just be happy it's done and taken care of. And he'll get bonus points with the wife if her nephew isn't sent to prison, I suppose."

"Yeah, I'll say."

"Hey, do you mind if I ask Stone a couple of questions just to satisfy my own curiosity?"

"Knock yourself out. We'll probably let him go before nightfall, anyway."

The cameras were still running, but at this point, Nate didn't care. Hell, even if the drugs had been real, he wasn't sure he would've cared. Ellis's arrest wasn't going to make a damn bit of difference in this community. But walking away from Jenny when she'd been in need? That was going to affect Nate's life in a hell of a lot of ways.

He opened the door. "Ellis," he said flatly.

"Hey!" Ellis said brightly, as if he were relieved to see a familiar face.

"How's it going?"

His smile vanished. "Not great, man."

"I see that."

"Shit," he muttered. "Did Jenny send you in here to kick my ass? Tell her I'm sorry, all right?"

"Sorry for what?" Nate asked, taking a seat and bracing himself for the answer. Actually, that wasn't true. No matter what the answer was, it was going to tear through Nate like a blade. Because either she'd made a fool of him or Nate had done it all on his own.

"Dragging her into this."

"Well, she's pretty pissed that you got her arrested."

"I swear to God I don't know what she was doing out there! Where did she even come from?"

"That doesn't make any sense. There's nothing out there. She didn't just run across you."

Ellis slumped. "She must have followed me. She was suspicious about what I was doing and worried I was in trouble."

"You're really saying she didn't know anything?"

"Are you kidding? She thought I was doing landscaping."

"In the middle of winter?"

"I told her I was working the plows and signing contracts for the spring. I mean, I am picking up a few shifts here and there. And hey, I was kinda doing landscaping, you know?" Ellis's laugh sounded like a broken toy.

Nate felt sick now, remembering the way he'd looked through her as he'd passed. "So she wasn't lying," he murmured.

"Jenny? No way. She'd never have anything to do with drugs. Hell, whenever I came home smelling like pot, she'd make me sleep on the couch. That shit with her mom, you know?"

No, he didn't know. He didn't know a lot of things about Jenny, because he'd been too busy asking questions about Ellis, just as she'd said.

Ellis scrubbed his hands through his hair. "Shit. I can't believe she was arrested. She only wanted to help. She thinks I can't take care of myself. She always felt like she needed to take care of me, and she couldn't deal with that. And when Jenny can't deal with something, she leaves."

"Is that what she did to you?"

"Yep. Middle of the night, she left me a letter and her ring and took off. I never saw her again until two months ago. Didn't even know where she was until last year." He sighed. "I always thought she'd come back to me, but she never even came through town again."

What had she said? She wasn't racing anything; she just wanted to go somewhere else? Nate tapped his knuckles on the table and stood.

"Hey, they're going to let her go, right?"

Nate nodded, unconcerned about giving too much away.

"So can I get out of here?"

"Not sure. Deputy Davidson will be back soon."

Ellis groaned and slumped back in his seat as Nate headed out the door.

"Hendricks!" Davidson called before he could escape. "Can you call your cousin? He needs to go out to the cabin and document which items are his and which were brought in. We also need to know if anything's missing."

"Sure," Nate said, glancing toward the other suite before he headed toward his desk. He called Luis to give him the good news and pass on the request. His cousin seemed overcome with relief, though Nate warned him that the investigation wasn't over. Still, Luis muttered something in Spanish so quickly that even Nate couldn't make out more than *Dios* and Teresa. Nate was smiling when he hung up, but his smile faded quickly. He needed to talk to Jenny. Apologize. Explain. Ask if she'd be willing to give him another chance.

It wasn't that he'd been completely irrational; it was just that he hadn't gone with his gut, a cop's number one sin. She'd felt trustworthy and sweet and bright, but he'd been so damn worried he was letting his lust overwhelm his instincts. Because there was a lot of lust. A *lot.*

Nate rolled his neck and pushed slowly to his feet. He tried to organize his thoughts as he walked. Tried to think of the perfect apology, but the only thing that came to mind was "I'm sorry. Forgive me?" Stupid, meaningless words. So generic she might just sneer and walk away.

In the end, the perfect apology would've meant

just as little, because the interview room was empty, and Jenny Stone was long gone. Nate had missed his chance.

CHAPTER TEN

SHE'D ENDED UP running. She always did, after all. So what could she do but race to her apartment, throw a few essentials in a bag and take off? She couldn't face Nate after that. It was too much.

So she drove away, deeper into nowhere, passing hardly anyone as she flew.

By the time she'd reached Idaho, she was too tired to think anymore. Too tired to decide what to do. Too tired to wind her way through any more mountains or high bluffs. She got a motel room and left her dead phone in the car and she slept.

Ten hours later, she opened her eyes expecting relief. That was the way she'd always felt before. Weeks of tension would precede her escape, but once she was gone, she felt new and happy and light.

But this time…this time she woke with shoulders knotted with stress and her teeth aching from the way she'd clenched her jaw all night. She didn't feel relieved. She felt scared. And awful. She felt as though she wanted to go home.

Home. But not the home she'd been driving toward. Not Idaho.

She missed her place. And her job. And her friends. She even missed the ridiculous shit Rayleen was going to dish about Jenny's brief trouble with the law.

Jenny didn't care about the arrest. Hell, she was a career bartender. It gave her another story to tell. Another way to schmooze tips. *Oh, you got into trouble? I got hauled in myself one time.* Plus, now she had something scandalous in common with Grace.

Yes, she could handle the notoriety of being arrested. What she couldn't handle was facing Nate.

She'd been helping Ellis, and she'd lied about it, and it turned out that he'd been growing pot. Worse than that, she'd been arrested in front of Nate's friends and coworkers. The look on his face as he'd driven past…after what they'd done together… God. After the way she'd let him into her body. The way she'd taken him with complete abandon. If she had to look him in the eyes and see disgust, she'd die inside.

Because she knew that disgust intimately. She'd felt it a hundred times. A thousand. Every time she'd looked at her own mother. Every time she'd seen her mom high and glassy-eyed and vacantly ugly.

The hair rose on her arms. It had been like looking at a dead person sometimes. As if her mom weren't even there. She'd been replaced. All her laughter. Her brightness. Her pride. Even her hot temper. It had all been replaced when Jenny was seven. First, with pain pills. Then sleeping pills. Then half a dozen different colors and shapes of tablets. Jenny had thought the lowest point had been when her mom, once a beloved first-grade teacher, had been fired from her school for drug use.

But that hadn't been the lowest. Not by far.

And now Nate thought Jenny was like *her*. Like that. And she wanted to run.

But maybe she was finally growing up. Because she didn't plan to stay gone. Maybe she was finally a stronger person.

Jenny got in her car and drove again, but this time she had a destination in mind. Her body knew the route by heart. It left her mind with nothing to do but take it in.

The little town where she'd grown up looked exactly the same. Amazing. Nothing had changed. She thought she'd forgotten it, but no. She'd forgotten nothing. There was the corner store where she'd bought jawbreakers and gumballs for ten cents every Saturday. And there was the tiny shoe store where they'd gotten new school shoes each August.

And there… God, there was the elementary

school where she'd spent so many years, and where her mom had worked for a dozen more. The school that had held happy memories until her mom had been fired, and then it had been nothing but another site of humiliation.

Jenny turned her eyes to the road and drove past it.

Their house was only two streets away. When her mom had been sober, they'd walked to school together every morning, even on the coldest days.

Jenny felt a tickle on her cheek and found hot tears when she touched her skin.

She'd needed this. She'd needed to remember. To come back.

But she stopped short of her house. She could see it from the corner. This was close enough.

It looked the same. Still neat. Still perfect from the outside.

Her father had been the gardener in the family, and the lawn had been his escape. He must still need a good reason to escape, because from this side of the block, the grass looked perfect enough to be Astroturf.

Time had gone on without her. Had anything changed at all?

But Jenny knew the answer to that. She'd changed. She wasn't running. Not anymore.

She picked up the phone and called Grace.

"Jenny, where the hell are you? We've been

worried sick! Rayleen tried calling the sheriff, but you're an adult, and they wouldn't… Sweetie, where *are* you?"

Jenny smiled at the sound of Grace calling her sweetie. Grace, who'd likely never used that word once when she'd lived in L.A. "I just…needed to get away."

"Thank God. But when you didn't show up last night—"

"Oh, shit. The saloon! I didn't even think about it. Am I fired?"

"Of course you're not fired."

"It doesn't matter. I'm awful. I've never done that before. I have to call Rayleen!"

"Oh, screw Rayleen. She's fine. You can apologize when you get here. If… You are coming back, right?"

Jenny stared down the street and swallowed hard, overwhelmed with a thousand memories of this view as she'd walked home from school.

"Jenny?" Grace whispered. "Don't be like me, okay? I didn't know I belonged here, but you know you do. You *know* that. Don't you?"

Jenny let her gaze fall to the sad little bag she'd packed. She'd spent five years in Jackson and this was all she'd grabbed on her way out the door. No pictures. No memories of the life she'd built. Just this small bag and the clothes on her back. Not because she was leaving everything behind, but because she knew she'd be back.

If there were bad things waiting—if Nate hated her, and Ellis kept hanging around, and things didn't go smooth and easy—she could handle it. "I know where I belong," she said. "I do. I'm coming back."

"Thank God! When?"

"Now," Jenny said, feeling the awful tension leave her shoulders. "I'm coming home right now."

She hung up the phone and watched a flock of birds rise from the tree in front of the house she'd spent so many years in. Her family was still there. And her past. And that was okay. She could face it. Maybe she'd call her sister soon. Maybe she'd even come back and visit, knowing she had a better place to return to. But not today. Today was part of the future she'd built in Jackson, not this past she'd left behind.

Jenny put the car in gear and drove.

CHAPTER ELEVEN

NATE SAT BEHIND the wheel of his truck like a hunter watching for game. Eyes narrowed, he stared at the road, noting each vehicle that came over the distant rise.

She had to come this way. Rayleen had called to say they'd tracked her down in Idaho and she was coming back. She'd be at the saloon that night, working the bar like normal.

Jesus, when he'd walked in the night before, he hadn't been terrified yet, only worried. But then Old Rayleen had looked up with a vicious scowl and barked, "It's about time. That little shit said you weren't coming."

"What? Who?"

"The piece of crap I talked to at the sheriff's department. He said Jenny was an adult and I couldn't report her missing."

That was when his heart had dropped into his gut with the weight of a locomotive. She hadn't answered her phone. She hadn't called anyone. Jenny was gone and she'd never even pass through Jackson again.

But no. She was coming back. His heart was racing for no reason. She was fine.

He glanced down at the box on the seat next to him, then back up to the road, and his eye caught on a flash of yellow coming on fast. Of course it was coming on fast. It was Jenny Stone.

For the first time in twenty-four hours, he felt his mouth stretch into a smile. "Jesus, you idiot," he muttered, thinking he meant Jenny and her speeding, but realizing that he meant himself.

She flew past with a whoosh and Nate shook his head and pulled around to follow her. "Unbelievable." He didn't catch up at sixty, so he hit the siren and pushed the pedal to the floor. This woman was…she was…fucking beautiful and maddening and *alive* and he couldn't let her get away.

He couldn't.

JENNY GLARED AT THE ROAD in front of her, watching for slippery patches and roaming elk and trying not to consider that she was taking a big step in her life. She was just driving home. She was just rushing to get into work. She needed to take a shower and dig out some clean clothes so she could get to the saloon on time, because she was determined to never be late again. It would take months to work off the embarrassment of having not shown up for a shift. Her stomach twisted with shame.

She'd been working since she was fifteen, and she'd never ditched a shift, or shown up drunk, and she'd definitely never behaved so badly that she'd been fired from her position of twenty years.

"Focus," she ordered herself, pissed off that she'd been thinking of her mom so often lately. "Focus," she said again, but the word ended in a wail of shock when she glanced over and saw a flash of blue-and-red lights in her side mirror. Then the cry of the siren caught up with her own wail until she shut her mouth with a snap.

Her eyes jumped down to the speedometer, but she'd already lifted her foot from the pedal, so she had no idea how fast she'd been driving.

Even she couldn't understand half of the expletives that began flowing from her mouth, though she managed to repeat a few favorites several times.

Slowing, she pulled to the shoulder, then edged onto gravel out of fear of the semis that frequented this highway. By the time she stopped, her hands were slippery with sweat and she wiped them over and over on her jeans.

Please don't let it be Nate. Please don't let it be Nate.

She'd rather it be an unsympathetic stranger who'd throw her straight into jail than to have to face Nate like this. Cowardly and shamed and throwing all her promises about speeding back in his face one more time.

Jenny scrambled to open the glove compartment to grab her insurance information, but she crumpled it in her hand when she heard the thud of a closing car door. Tears clouded her eyes. She didn't want to look. She couldn't.

But she did. And when she saw Nate walking toward her, his sunglasses off, her tears dried as if they'd never formed. This was too horrifying for crying. All she could do was stare straight ahead as she rolled down her window. All she could do was wait for it to be over.

His body blocked the window. "Jenny," he said. She didn't look. "Hey."

She shook her head and held up the insurance information. "I'm sorry," she rasped.

He didn't answer. She didn't breathe.

"Damn it, Jenny, I don't need that."

Right. She dropped her hand and stared down at it. "I'm sorry."

"Stop saying that."

When she finally tried to draw a breath, she couldn't force it past the lump in her throat.

"Please look at me."

No. She didn't want to see his face. She didn't want to see his eyes. Why did this have to be the one time he wasn't wearing glasses?

"Please," he said again, and she looked up. Just so he'd get this over with and let her go. She couldn't bear it another—

"What's that?" she asked, blinking in shock at the big red velvet box in his hands. Special handcuffs just for her? But it wasn't just a box. He held it toward her and she saw that it was heart-shaped. "What are you doing?"

"It's for you."

"But why?"

"It's Valentine's Day."

"It is?" But of course it was. The fourteenth. She'd lost track. Valentine's Day.

"You don't have to take it. I understand if you can't. But I want you to know how sorry I am. And—"

"You?"

He flinched. "I was out of line. And when I came over, I wasn't as up-front as I should have been. Then yesterday at the cabin… Shit, Jenny. Can you forgive me?"

She couldn't process what he was saying and found herself simply staring up at him until his shoulders slumped.

"I get it. Maybe we could talk in a week or two."

"No, I—"

He pushed the box past the window and she grabbed it automatically. "I understand. But the chocolate is yours. And this." He presented a smaller box he'd tucked under his arm. "It's for you, too. I'm really sorry."

She took the smaller box, then watched in utter confusion as he walked back toward his vehicle. "Wait!" She let the box of chocolates slip to the floor of her car as she shoved open her door and scrambled out. "Nate!"

He paused near the flashing lights in the grill of his truck and watched her approach.

"I swear I didn't know what Ellis was doing!" she said on a rush. "And I'm so, so sorry I got caught up in it, and your coworkers saw that. I was just following him. That's all. I wanted to find out if—"

"Jenny!"

His exasperated voice snapped her thoughts in half. What did he want from her? His mouth was so tight and serious, his jaw working like a beating pulse. "I'm sorry," she whispered.

"You don't have to apologize," he groaned as his hands closed over her shoulders. "I'm the one who's sorry. I pulled you over because I needed to tell you that, and..."

"And what?" she asked softly, afraid if she spoke too loudly it wouldn't be true. She'd realize she'd misheard him. He'd shake his head and change his mind.

His hands slipped slowly up her shoulders, to her neck, to cradle her jaw. "It's Valentine's Day,

Jenny. And I wanted to tell you that this means something to me. *You* mean something. Even if you never want to see me again. You make me feel a little…lost. When you're not around, I feel lost. But then when you touch me… God, when you touch me, I feel found again."

"Oh," she breathed, staring into his beautiful eyes until her vision blurred and she had to drop her head.

"Don't cry. Please. Yell at me. Or tell me to go to hell. But don't cry."

"I'm sorry." She sniffed, but the tears flowed harder when he kissed her forehead and wrapped his arms around her. Jenny buried her face against his neck, and the scent of his skin finally stopped her tears. The warm smell of him invaded her like a soul sneaking inside her own.

She wanted him. She didn't want to give him up. He was part of her home now. "This means something to me, too," she said into his skin. "It means something…good."

He squeezed her harder, and whatever words he whispered beneath his breath, she couldn't understand. Spanish, maybe, or—

"Ow." Something poked her in the ribs and she pulled back to look at the box she still cradled. "What is this?"

He let her go and gestured to the box, then shifted back and put his hands on his hips.

For the first time since she'd met him, he looked genuinely nervous. He watched the box instead of watching her. Jenny, never one for savoring the process, tore open the beautiful silver wrapping paper and pried open the box. Inside was a card.

She flipped it open.

"It's good for two sessions. At a racetrack. It's over near Pinedale, I don't know if you've ever heard of it. But you can take your Camaro there and go as fast as you want. But you have to promise to wear a helmet, okay?"

"Oh, Nate," she said. "Oh, God."

"Or if you don't like that, I'll get you something else. I was going to buy you flowers, but I didn't know… You're into cars. I didn't know if—"

"Oh, God." She was suddenly dizzy. A semi flew past, sucking the last of her equilibrium from her head. She had to touch him. To lean into him. This man who…understood her. Despite everything. After the shortest of time together, he got her. "It's perfect, Nate. It's so damn perfect, and I didn't get you anything."

"You got me *you,* Jenny. You came back. You were running, weren't you? You were gone."

"I don't know. But I'm back."

"That's all I can ask for. That and maybe…a night this time? Instead of an hour?"

"Yes."

How many Valentine's Days had she spent behind the bar? How many lonely people had she watched hook up, not wanting to be alone on this stupid holiday everyone claimed for love? She'd seen it for so many years that the day had ceased to mean anything. But this year, for the first time, there'd be someone waiting just for her. In a home she'd finally chosen as her own.

CHAPTER TWELVE

IT WAS PITCH-BLACK in her room, and cold from the window she'd cracked open to the early spring day, but beneath the blankets, Jenny was warm and toasty and half-asleep as Nate's hand curled over her hip.

"Mmm," she sighed, snuggling into his chest as he slipped into bed beside her. "I missed you."

"I'm sorry," he whispered against her shoulder. "I really, really wanted to be there."

"I'll go again. You can come with."

"I know, but it was your first time. How was it?"

She smiled into the dark, remembering that crazy rush of adrenaline as she'd lapped around the racetrack that first time. The instructor's voice in her ear as the stands flew by in a blur. And then the silence when she'd gotten the hang of it, and all she could hear was her own heart beating hard. She'd driven faster than she ever had. She'd flown free and it had been… "It was beautiful," she whispered.

"I wish I could've seen it."

"Saving lives is more important than watching me drive."

"It was more like two hours of directing the public around the people who were actually saving lives. And the accident looked far uglier than it was, thank God."

"Good." She snuggled tighter against him with a sigh.

"And tonight's defensive driving class?"

She laughed at the official way he said that. "Oh, that was a whole other level of exciting. I learned how to go slow and steady. Did you know that saves a ton on gas mileage?"

His teeth pressed her neck, and she was suddenly very aware of his body behind hers. The length of his cock branded her ass. "I'd like to know more about this. Slow and steady, huh?"

His hand slid down her hip and cupped her sex.

"What do you know about slow and steady?" he breathed into her ear.

"Oh," she sighed as his fingers slid along her seam. "Oh, I…learned that I have to be…aware."

"Mmm."

She tried to ease her knee open, but his leg was holding hers down as he teased her. Keeping her closed up tight as he dragged his fingers over her sensitive flesh.

"Yeah?" he said. "What else?"

"I have to concentrate on what I'm doing and

not get distracted by…" She tried to tip her hips up. His fingertips dragged over her clit. "Oh, God."

"Distracted by what?"

"By…" She didn't even know what he was talking about by that point. All her concentration was on his hand and the way it slipped over her, sliding easier and easier the wetter she got. God, if she could just get her legs apart, his fingers would just naturally slide right inside her.

"Oh, Jenny. I don't think you learned anything at all. Shhh. Slow down."

She rocked against him as he circled her clit. His other arm was tight across her chest, holding her in place.

"Please," she whimpered.

"It's okay. You can go slow, can't you? For me?"

"No," she panted. "No, no." She was so close now. So close. He could say anything he wanted, as long as he kept touching her that way.

His hand slipped up, gliding over her belly.

"No!"

But he held her tight with his arms and his leg and he teased her nipples as if they had all the time in the world. She was sobbing. Begging. Almost angry by the time he touched her clit again. And she arched into him with a desperate cry.

"See how nice it can be to go slow?" He stroked her. Stroked her again. She was so close. So close. "See, Jenny?"

"Please," she cried.

He finally let her loose. She twisted away, and he caught her and pulled her toward him as he turned to his back. "Now," he growled, breathing almost as hard as she was. He gripped her hips and moved her to straddle him. "Show me how you felt at the racetrack."

He gripped his shaft and pulled her down, and his cock surged into her.

She screamed.

"Show me," he urged, his palm flattening to her belly as he thumbed her clit.

"Oh, God," she cried.

"Show me how you learned to go hard, Jenny."

She dropped her hips and showed him. And Jenny knew she'd found a better way to fly.

* * * * *

ALONE WITH YOU

Acknowledgments

Thank you to Harlequin HQN,
Angela James and Kim Whalen for the chance
to join Jennifer Crusie and Victoria Dahl in
bringing Valentine's Day romance to our readers!

For Stuart. Chocolates and flowers are nice,
but nothing's better than plain old everyday love.
Thank you for twenty years of it and counting.

CHAPTER ONE

"ASHGABAT." THE SEXY stranger's breath blew warm over her neck as he whispered the word near her ear, and Darcy Vaughn chased a full-body shiver with a big gulp of martini.

"Ashgabat," she repeated for the trivia host, since he hadn't been wrong yet.

"That's correct!" The other teams around the bar all groaned, and Darcy smiled sweetly at Kent and Vanessa, formerly the reigning know-it-alls of Tuesday-night trivia.

She and her sexy fountain of random facts were kicking butt tonight.

Her regular partner hadn't called to cancel until after Darcy had ordered her margarita and nachos, so she'd left it to the waitress serving as trivia host to pair her with another customer flying solo. She hadn't expected the guy rocking the scruffy, blue-collar look to raise his hand and join the academic fun, but figured he'd contribute on the sports questions. Despite working at a sports bar, Darcy wasn't much of a fan.

But now she knew a few things about her trivia partner. His name was Jake. He had brown eyes the same shade as his close-cut hair, smelled delicious and had a body made for selling charity calendars. He also knew a little something about which capital city sat between the Kara-Kum Desert and the Kopet Dag Mountains. Being able to cough up Turkmenistan trivia was almost as sexy as the way he rested his arm across the back of her bar stool every time he leaned in to whisper an answer in her ear.

"Ten-minute break," the host announced.

After hitting the restrooms, the teams eventually settled back on their bar stools to wait for the host, who'd disappeared into the kitchen. When the silence stretched toward awkward, Darcy turned to Jake. "So, let me guess. You're taking a break from exploring the world after an expedition to Turkmenistan to find an ancient, possibly cursed relic went bad."

His smile should've been illegal. "And that must make you the Russian spy sent to charm the relic's location out of me with your knowledge of U.S. presidents and the Periodic Table of Elements."

"I have ways of making you talk," she joked, though it came out a little more suggestively than she'd intended.

"I bet you do."

Darcy realized, with the way they were gradually leaning in closer to each other and the innuendo, they were in heavy flirting territory and she panicked a little. Guys didn't usually come on to her in bars. At Jasper's Bar & Grille, where she waited tables and occasionally worked the bar, most of the guys were looking at Paulie, who managed the place. She was tall, had a killer body—including great breasts—and knew everything and anything about sports.

Darcy was on the short side of average. Her breasts were on the small side of average. She pretty much ran just left of average overall. Her hair was nice, though. Dark and thick, with just enough wave to keep it cute in a ponytail.

"So, Darcy, what do you really do when you're not answering trivia questions or charming Indiana Jones types out of their relics?"

"I wait tables." She shrugged. "It's a good cover. Lots of eavesdropping opportunities. What do you do when you're not sifting through ancient ruins?"

"Some business consulting. Boring stuff."

"Do you get to travel a lot?"

He shook his head. "Honestly, I don't fly, so a few sledding trips to Canada and a really misguided summer in Florida during my youth are the extent of my travel. Not trusting airplanes to stay in the sky killed my dreams of being Indiana Jones when I grew up."

"Yeah, well, my Russian accent sucks." They were laughing as the trivia host stepped back into the horseshoe center of the bar and poured them all another round before continuing the game.

After Kent and Vanessa got an economics history question right and the next couple blew it on geography, the host turned to them. "What famous player, inducted into the Baseball Hall of Fame in 1972, was known for the phrase 'It ain't over till it's over'?"

As Jake leaned in to whisper in her ear, Darcy blocked him with her hand. "Wait. I know this one, dammit. Finally a sports question I know the answer to."

"We should talk about it."

"Why? Don't you think women can answer sports questions?"

His mouth brushed her ear as his arm pressed against her back. "I just like having an excuse to whisper in your ear."

"Yogi Berra," she told the trivia host in a surprisingly normal voice, considering how on the inside she was a shivery, breathless mess.

A couple of drinks and a few rounds later, Jake and Darcy were declared the winners. The grand prize was nothing more than bragging rights and the his-and-hers puckered looks Kent and Vanessa sported as they went out the door.

"How are you getting home?" Jake asked as he held Darcy's sweater so she could slip her arms in. Such a gentleman.

It was an innocent enough question, but Darcy's overheated, alcohol-fueled imagination added a pronounced ungentlemanly slant to his words. "I'm walking."

"Alone?"

"It's not far."

"You've had a bit to drink." A bit more than she usually did, actually. "I'd feel a lot better if you let me walk you home."

He didn't know it yet but, unless she'd totally misread his signals, he'd feel a *lot* better because if he got as far as her front door, she was going to drag him inside and have her way with him. She wasn't in the habit of bringing men home after the first date—and random trivia partnership was stretching the definition of date—but she was going to roll the dice on this sexy, smart guy with a sense of humor. They were rare. Plus, she just really, really wanted him.

JAKE HELD THE DOOR FOR Darcy, cursing himself the entire time. Now wasn't the time to be romancing a woman, even if she was smoking hot and correctly guessed that painite was considered the rarest mineral gem.

But he couldn't let her walk home alone in the dark. And after watching that mouth smile at him all night and her teeth catching on her bottom lip when she wasn't sure of an answer and her tongue flicking out to grab a stray dab of nacho cheese, he wanted a good-night kiss. Maybe it wasn't the most traditional first date, but it counted. Sort of.

Translating a woman's body language didn't come as naturally to him as it did to other guys, but he was pretty sure he was reading Darcy right. She walked really slow, as if she was lingering to make the walk last longer, and she stayed close enough to him so their arms occasionally brushed. After the third time, he threw caution to the wind and captured her hand in his. She didn't pull away.

"Do you do that every Tuesday night?" he asked after a few minutes of comfortable silence.

"As often as I can. My usual partner couldn't make it, so I was lucky you showed up tonight."

Her usual partner? He didn't like the idea of her sharing random facts and sexy smiles with anybody else. "Her youngest was sick and her husband does diapers and homework help, but no puke buckets."

So not a boyfriend, then. "I'm sorry your friend's kid is sick, but I'm glad I got to be your partner tonight."

On the well-lit street, he had no trouble seeing the blush on her cheeks. "And I talk to you about puke buckets. That's so sexy."

"Puke buckets might not be sexy, but a woman as pretty as you who knows the Treaty of Paris ended the Seven Years' War is hot as hell."

The blush got brighter and he squeezed her hand. It wasn't a line, either. Brains and beauty were like peanut butter and chocolate—each good on its own, but downright delicious together.

Leave it to him to find a potentially right woman at the totally wrong time. And in the wrong place. The city was a quick stopover between the life in Connecticut he'd grown bored with and the exciting, new restaurant venture with an old friend. When he'd seen a flyer at the auto shop for trivia night, he'd decided to scope out how it was run and the turnout in case it was something he might want to try in the future. He hadn't expected to meet a woman he'd be reluctant to walk away from.

"This might sound pushy, but I'm only passing through here and I'm leaving tomorrow for business and I really want to ask for your number, so… what's your romantic situation?"

"No boyfriend. No husband, though there was one once. No kids and we went our separate ways years ago. How long will you be gone?"

"It'll be an extended trip, but I'll be traveling

back and forth a lot and I'd like to maybe see you when I'm in the city. You know, if you want." Which was probably a dumb thing to say considering she was holding his hand.

"I'd like that." Her voice was soft and warm and his mind jumped ahead to the possibility of a good-night kiss. "This is my building."

He was so busy imagining how her mouth would feel, he barely registered that they'd stopped walking. Would her lips taste like margaritas? He started to reach for his phone, intending to program her number into it.

"If you come up, I'll write my number down for you."

Some of the blood left his brain and headed south, but he was no fool. He left the phone in its holster. "Sounds great."

Darcy unlocked the glass door tucked between two business entrances and led him up the stairs to a very small hallway somebody had tried to make nice with a few potted plants and a bright throw rug. There was a door on either side of the hall and she unlocked the one on the left, reaching in to turn on the light.

Her apartment was small and pretty, just like her. The walls were a plain beige, but she'd hung colorful pictures on them and she had a bunch of those little pillows on the couch that matched the curtains and throw rugs that matched the one in the hall. He wasn't surprised to see several bookshelves taking up space.

He watched her tear a sheet of paper off a memo pad stuck to the fridge and then rummage in a drawer for a pen. After jotting something down, she held it out to him. *Darcy, from trivia night.* And her number.

It made him chuckle. "How many Darcys do you think I know?"

"I thought it might help you remember me when you fish that out of your pocket later."

In the light of the bar, he'd thought her eyes were a hazel color, but now—standing close enough to her to touch—he realized they were more green, with flecks of brown and gold. "I'm not going to forget you that easily."

When she blushed again and shifted her weight from one foot to the other, and then back again, he realized she either wanted him to make a graceful exit with a promise to call her later or make his move. The problem was deciphering which she was looking for.

Then she stood on her tiptoes and leaned forward, so he took the hint and moved in for the kiss.

DARCY HAD NEVER BEEN SO thoroughly kissed in her life. When Jake first touched his mouth to hers, he'd been tentative, maybe even a little shy. Now she was backed up to her fridge, her nails digging into his shirt as his tongue danced over hers.

His hands slid from her waist up to her breasts and she moaned when his thumbs brushed over the taut nipples. Just the lightest touch, but it ignited a need in her stronger than any she'd felt in a long time. And then his lips left her mouth and blazed a trail down her neck.

"All I thought about tonight was kissing you," he said, his breath warm against her skin.

"And yet you still almost always knew the right answer."

"Well, I tried to pay attention when it was our turn, but when it wasn't, all I could do was think about touching you."

Darcy took a deep breath and said the words. "I'd like for you to stay. You know, if you want to."

He straightened and looked down into her face. "You're sure?"

"Very sure."

"Then I want to." He kissed her and, when she curled her arms around his neck, he lifted her off the floor.

It startled her and she wrapped her legs around his waist, really hoping he wouldn't drop her. But she wouldn't have fallen, anyway, with her back against the fridge and Jake between her thighs, his denim-clad erection putting a little pressure in just the right spot.

Once he'd kissed her until she could barely breathe, she felt him shift his arms to hold her more securely and then they were crossing the living room. She'd never been carried before and she buried her face in his neck, hoping nothing mood-killing happened, like running into a wall or hitting her head on the doorjamb.

When he leaned forward, she clutched at his shoulders for a second, until she felt the mattress under her. He went down with her, kissing her and nibbling at her ear, with short interruptions to pull her shirt off, then his shirt and then her bra.

The feel of his warm, naked skin against hers sent shivers through Darcy and she wanted more. She reached for the fly of his jeans, but was momentarily distracted when his mouth closed over her nipple. Gentle suction, then a little bit harder, and when he slid his hand between her legs, she lifted her hips, desperate for the touch, even through the jeans she still wore.

"Remember how I told you I spent the whole night thinking about touching you?" She made an *mm-hmm* noise. "It's even better than I imagined."

They lost the jeans and socks and underwear then, and he lifted her so he could lay her down higher on the bed. She heard the rustling of a condom packet and then he covered her body with his.

Closing her eyes, she moaned as he filled her,

moving with slow, even strokes that felt so good, but weren't enough at the same time. "Faster."

"In a hurry?"

She opened her eyes to find him smiling down at her. "It's been a while."

"Good." But he didn't seem inclined to obey her demand. If anything, he slowed his pace, drawing almost completely out of her and then pushing deep. She moved her hips, trying to urge him on, but his fingers pressed into her thighs, holding her still. "Not yet."

"Who made you the boss?"

He drove into her, and her back arched off the bed as she bit down on the side of her hand, trying not to scream and wake her neighbor. Again and again he did it until she was almost at the brink… and then he stopped moving.

"More," she whispered. One small, lazy circle of his hips was all she got. "You're making me crazy."

"Good." He bent to her breast, sucking one nipple just hard enough to make her squirm. "I want you to be crazy about me."

Then he kissed her mouth while his hips moved faster and harder and she gasped against his lips. This time when she lifted her hips, he didn't stop her. Each thrust came faster and deeper until the orgasm rocked her.

With her ankles crossed behind him, she used

her legs to hold him to her as the tremors faded. He groaned her name against her neck as he pushed into her in the deep, jerky rhythm of his own orgasm.

Darcy ran her hands over his back, trying to catch her breath. After a minute, Jake disappeared to the bathroom for a minute, but then he slid back into bed and pulled the covers up over them.

She'd rolled onto her left side when he got up because that was how she lay in bed and she was going to turn to face him, but Jake curled his body around hers before she got the chance. With his right arm thrown over her, he pulled her tight against him and kissed the top of her head.

"That was incredible," he whispered, and she could already feel the relaxing of his muscles as he started nodding off.

The next thing Darcy knew, sunlight was streaming through her bedroom window and her trivia partner was leaning against the doorjamb, cursing and rubbing his toe. She winced, having kicked the cedar hope chest at the foot of her bed more than once herself.

"Sorry," he said when he realized she was awake. "I was trying to be quiet."

"Were you going to sneak out without saying goodbye?"

"No, I was going to let you sleep until the last

possible second and then kiss you goodbye on my way out so you could maybe nod back off."

Sweet, if it was true. He already had his jeans on, sadly, but she watched him pull on the rest of his clothes. He had an amazing body and it was such a shame to cover it up.

When he was done, he disappeared into the other room and then came back holding the paper with her name and number on it. He folded it before shoving it into his pocket, and then he leaned over the bed.

"I have a full day today, with a lot of travel and a meeting with a contractor, but I'll call you tomorrow."

Lounging in bed—her body happy and lazy from a night of lovemaking—and looking up into his dark eyes, she almost believed him. "I have tomorrow off, so whenever you get the chance is good."

He kissed her goodbye and then got halfway across the bedroom before he came back and kissed her again. She laughed and wrapped her arms around his neck, but didn't miss the fact that he was sneaking a peek at his watch.

"If I didn't have a meeting with a contractor, I'd crawl back into bed with you," he muttered against her lips. "And I already called a cab."

"When will you be back in the city?"

"As soon as I can." He kissed her one more

time and then made it to the bedroom door. "I'll call you tomorrow."

She heard the front door close and then snuggled under her covers, grinning like an idiot. Jake just might be the keeper she'd been looking for.

CHAPTER TWO

JAKE HAD THE cab drop him at Kevin's house since that was where he'd left the business card with the phone number for the garage he'd handed his truck over to the day before. He wanted the oil changed and a maintenance check done before he headed up to the northern part of the state.

He paused for a few seconds outside the gate of the white picket fence surrounding the pretty, maroon-shuttered Cape that had a blue minivan in the driveway, looking at his friend's world. Kevin Kowalski was a pretty lucky guy.

A pretty lucky guy whose wife, Beth, pinned Jake with a hard look the second he let himself in through the side door into the kitchen. She was sitting at the table, drinking coffee, and judging from the silence, Lily wasn't up yet. Their daughter was a great kid but, man, was she loud.

"I'm sorry," he said immediately. "I should have called."

"Did you at least leave her a note, whoever she is?"

"I kissed her goodbye this morning and promised to call her tomorrow. And I will."

Beth looked surprised, as did Kevin, who appeared in the doorway from the living room wearing flannel pajama pants and a Bruins T-shirt. "Did you tell her you're not sticking around?"

"I told her I was leaving town, but that I want to see her whenever I'm down here."

"Which won't be often," Kevin said.

"Don't kill my buzz, man. She's pretty and fun and wicked smart and I like her."

That raised both their eyebrows, but he ignored them and helped himself to the coffeepot before calling to check on his truck. It was ready, so once his cup was empty, he went to gather his things out of the guest room he'd spent the night before last in while Kevin got dressed. He would have liked to stay until Lily woke up so he could say goodbye, but he settled for kissing Beth on the cheek and climbing into the Jeep parked in the shadow of Beth's mom-mobile.

"So, where did you meet this pretty, fun, wicked-smart woman?" Kevin asked when they were on the road.

"At a bar."

"Which bar?"

"Not your bar." He'd been to Jasper's Bar & Grille a few times to talk about the new offshoot pub they were opening together, but always while they were closed. It was hard keeping Kevin's attention when the place was busy. "They were hosting an event and I went to check it out. See if it's an idea worth running with."

"I want to start advertising the launch soon. You're sure we'll hit the February mark?"

"We'll soft-launch the first and have all the kinks worked out by the big Valentine's Day shebang." He wasn't sure what that shebang was going to be yet, other than an opportunity for the guys to convince their wives snowmobiling was a great way to spend the holiday because they could have a romantic evening together at Jasper's Pub.

"I emailed you the logo design. Did you see it?"

"Not yet." He'd been busy.

"I think it's good. Close enough to the bar's for branding purposes."

Even though Jasper's Bar & Grille was a sports bar, they'd decided to keep the name and branding because a lot of the guys who loved nothing more than kicking back with a beer and watching a game at Kevin's place were the same guys who were going up north to sled. They were banking on familiarity and maybe even some customer loyalty before they even opened.

Kevin pulled into the garage's parking lot and left the motor running. He'd be going to the bar while Jake would be hitting the highway. "I'll give you a head start before I send somebody up to work on the menu development and hiring servers and that shit."

"Not a problem."

"Do me a favor, though. If it's a woman, swear to me you'll keep it professional."

Jake recoiled as if Kevin had popped him one. "What the hell is that supposed to mean?"

"It means hands off the help."

"You think I don't know that? I've managed to be professional a long time without you slapping my hand."

"Sorry." Kevin sighed and shoved his hand through his hair. "I'm just overworrying. I believe the pub's going to be a hit, but sometimes I realize just how much I've got on the line and I start thinking about every little thing that could go wrong."

"Scratch me screwing the help off the list." He had a feeling he might be off the market soon. He hoped, anyway.

Almost three hours later, Jake was lost, his GPS was confused and he was bouncing down a dirt road he wasn't sure was even on the map. And it was raining. Hard.

He was looking for a place to turn around when he saw the car. The rain must have softened the shoulder because the car had slid down into the ditch. And, as he got closer, he saw a flash of what looked like a pink sweater in the driver's-side window. Of course, it had to be a woman.

Saying every curse word he knew, just to get it out of his system, Jake hit the button for his four-way flashers and put his truck in Park. He unclipped the useless phone with no service from his pocket and tossed it in the center console, then climbed out. By the time he reached the car, he was soaked through.

He had to knock on the window to get the woman's attention away from the squabbling kids strapped in the backseat, but when she saw him, he could almost feel her relief. "I'm stuck."

"I can see that. I don't think you're very stuck, though."

"Can you pull me out?"

"I don't have a tow strap with me. I'm guessing you don't, either." She shook her head. "I should be able to push you out. You're not far off. Put it in Drive and when I say, 'Let off the brake and give it some gas,' don't gun it. Just nice and steady."

It wasn't much of a ditch, but the rain runoff had built up steam and it washed over the tops of his boots as he took his place behind the little car. After a quick check of the wheel positions, he placed his hands a little right of center on the trunk and braced himself.

"Give it gas," he yelled.

The first attempt, she was nervous and didn't

give it enough gas. The second, she overcompensated for the first and spun the tires. On the third, she got it right and he was able to push her back onto the road. Of course, once the car drove out from under his hands, he slid in the loose gravel and ended up laid out in the ditch, but he was already so wet and filthy he didn't bother wasting a good expletive on the fall.

Once he'd accepted her thanks and refused her offer of a grocery bag to put over his truck seat, he asked her for directions to the building the old hardware and feed store had been in and got his truck turned around.

He pulled up to the future Jasper's Pub, feeling like a muddy, wet rat, just in time to see a guy climbing into a truck that read Peterson Construction. Jake laid on the horn, getting his attention.

After getting out, he jogged over to the other truck and the guy, who had to be Derek Peterson, lowered the window. "I'm sorry I'm late. Got lost. Dirt road. Woman and kids in a car slid off into the ditch. If you can wait five minutes, we can go over the plans."

"Not a problem," Peterson said, which didn't surprise Jake. The kind of work he and Kevin were having done was scarce in the northern part of the state, and Peterson wasn't going to walk away from it because he was half an hour late.

Jake had to go back to his truck to get the ring

of keys Kevin had given him and one of his duffels. Then he went up the stairs on the back of the building to his new home.

Kevin had said the apartment over the restaurant space was a little outdated. What he hadn't mentioned was how damn *brown* it was. Really fake wood paneling on the walls. Brown rug. The furniture was big and bulky, with a lot of exposed wood and brown plaid cushions.

The lack of color made Jake think of Darcy. Her apartment was the kind of place that made a person feel better and…Darcy.

"Shit…shit…shit…" he muttered, shoving his hand into the front pocket of his muddy, wet jeans.

He pulled out a soggy ball of paper with a black blur where her name and phone number used to be. And he hadn't given her his.

Well...shit.

Six weeks later

"DARCY, CAN I TALK TO YOU a minute in my office?"

"Uh, sure." Her boss sounded serious, which made her stomach clench. Not that Kevin Kowalski wasn't always serious about his business, but he was a friendly, laid-back kind of guy and she loved working at his busy sports bar.

She tried to brace herself for the worst, but she knew the tears would come if he let her go. The jerk she'd thought might actually be her Prince Charming had never called, and her best friend and trivia partner was in the process of moving to Rhode Island because her husband got a new job. Bad news came in threes, and she prayed getting fired wasn't the icing on the bad luck cupcake.

"So you know I'm opening another restaurant up north," he said when they were seated in his office, referring to the northern part of the state. She nodded, since she'd been around during many conversations Kevin had had with Paulie about his plans to open another bar in prime snowmobiling real estate. "J.P., my business partner, has been up there handling the renovations and refitting the kitchen and business crap. Generic restaurant business."

She nodded again, since she knew that, too. Kevin went up occasionally to check on the progress, but because of Beth and Lily, he didn't like to be away too much.

"We've reached a point where we need to start going beyond the generic and putting the Jasper's stamp on it. Menus and policies and how to set things up for the best work flow and stuff. That's not really J.P.'s thing. I don't want to be away that long and I can't really spare Paulie."

Darcy wasn't really sure what he was asking of her, but he didn't seem to be giving her the boot. That was the important thing.

"I had planned to hire a consultant specializing in restaurants to work alongside him, but I want it to be more personal than that. I want the two places to really share a common feel, you know?"

She nodded again, starting to feel like a bobble-head.

"So." He leaned back in his chair and laced his hands behind his head. "I guess the question is whether or not you'd be willing to go stay up north for a few weeks or maybe more and help launch Jasper's Pub."

It was on the tip of her tongue to tell him he was crazy. She couldn't just go away for a month. Sure, she didn't have any pets and her neighbor could water the plants, but to just pack up and head almost to the Canadian border?

Then he told her how much he was willing to pay her, and the decision got a lot easier.

IT WAS ALMOST TWO WEEKS before they'd trained a temp to take over her hours at Jasper's Bar & Grille, and Darcy had taken care of everything that needed to be done in preparation for a month or more away from home. She even put new tires on her car in anticipation of more snow than she was used to driving in. Once she'd done Christmas and New Year's Eve with her family, it was time to hit the road.

The building wasn't hard to find, since the only

other things around were a convenience store with gas pumps, an auto parts store, a hardware store, a very expensive-looking bed-and-breakfast and—just barely in view—a couple of long, one-story motels. It didn't look like a mecca of any sort, but Kevin had assured her it was a major crossroads on the snowmobile system.

Darcy had her choice of spots in the massive parking lot, which was designed to accommodate vehicles and snowmobiles, including trucks pulling big sled trailers. Right now it was empty. She decided to return for her bags after she got the lay of the land, got out of the car and took a deep breath. This was going to be weird.

Apparently there was a two-bedroom apartment over the restaurant and she was going to be roommates with J. P. Holland. As if this job Kevin was trusting her with wasn't enough stress, she was going to live with a man she didn't know. Her boss had sworn J.P. would be nothing but professional, and if it really didn't work out, he'd put her up in one of the motels for the duration, but her practical nature shied away from wasting the money. They were adults who'd be working together.

Besides, she wasn't a big fan of men at the moment. Even though she'd tried to prepare herself for the probability, it had hurt when Jake didn't call.

The back door to the restaurant was locked. So

was the side entrance and the front door. And a quick glance at the "no service" on her cell phone killed any hope of calling the cell number Kevin had given her for J. P. Holland. Even if she drove over to the gas station and begged the use of their landline, he probably didn't have a signal, either.

Even though it was probably an exercise in futility, Darcy returned to the back of the building and went up the exterior stairs to what she assumed was the apartment entrance. To her surprise, the doorknob turned in her hand and she stepped inside, realizing belatedly she probably should have knocked.

She found herself in a very drab brown apartment improved drastically by the tan expanse of naked male back in the middle of the living room. The steam curling from the bathroom and the fact that he was scrubbing his head with a towel cued her in to the fact he was fresh out of the shower. That and the droplet of water she watched make its way from the back of his neck, down over the muscles of his back to the waistband of his jeans. And thank goodness for the jeans because that body wrapped in nothing but a towel might have made her drool.

"Excuse me," she forced herself to say.

The man spun around, lowering the towel, and Darcy's stomach dropped. Her brain couldn't quite grasp what was going on, but her body certainly recognized him, and only shock kept her from running back the way she'd came.

Jake stared at her for a few seconds, probably as confused as she was. "Darcy?"

"What are you doing here?"

He stared at her, then frowned. "What are *you* doing here?"

"I asked you first."

"I'm supposed to be here."

"So am I." Darcy's stomach knotted as she started putting the pieces together. "Oh, God. Please tell me you're not J.P."

"Only to Kevin. Back in the day, he knew three Jakes, so he called us by our first and middle initials—J.P., J.D. and J.R.—and I guess it stuck. Not a fan, but he never cared." After a short pause, he muttered a curse. "You work for Kevin."

"I've worked at Jasper's for years. Paulie and I were there before he bought it." Her voice sounded surprisingly normal considering what she really wanted to do was plant her knee in his balls before making a grand exit.

"So you're here to help me launch Jasper's Pub."

Really? That's what he wanted to talk about? He'd held her hand and made love to her and kissed her goodbye with promises of a phone call and he wanted to talk about work. "I don't think that's going to happen."

She was going to get back in her car and drive back to Concord. The three-hour trip would give her plenty of time to come up with an excuse to give Kevin about why she couldn't do him this favor, after all. Maybe she could tell him she startled a Dumpster-diving bear and she was too traumatized by the encounter to stay in bear country.

Jake blew out a hard breath and tossed the towel onto the counter. "We can make this work."

Darcy sighed. She was a nice person, really. People described her as cheerful and happy and a few of the regulars called her Sunshine. But under the sunny personality, she had a really low tolerance for bullshit. And she'd already had a shovelful from Jake Holland.

"I don't think so." She turned around and went back down the stairs.

JAKE SHOVED HIS BARE FEET into his boots before he went after Darcy, but he didn't take the time to grab a shirt or coat. She was halfway across the parking lot before he caught up to her. "Darcy, wait. Please?"

He couldn't let her go. After weeks of thinking about her and beating himself up for not putting her number in his phone right away, he couldn't let her leave without trying to explain. Upstairs, his mind had been trying to work out the business implications of her arrival, but right now he was just a man trying to catch the woman who had slipped through his fingers once already.

"I'll tell Kevin I'm afraid of bears," she said in a flat voice, reaching for the door handle of her car. "He doesn't need to know we'd met before."

"I'm sorry I didn't call you."

That stopped her. "Whatever. We both knew you weren't going to call."

That pissed him off. He wasn't that kind of guy, and maybe she didn't have any way of knowing that, but a little benefit of the doubt wouldn't hurt. "My jeans got wet and the ink ran."

"Funny how often that happens to guys."

"I swear, Darcy. I wanted to leave a message at the bar where we met, but I couldn't remember the name of the place. I even called the car garage where I saw the trivia night flyer to get the name or number off it, but they'd thrown it away. I didn't know how else to find you."

"You haven't been back in the city since then?"

"I've only managed to get down there once, since the contractors screwed up the HVAC plans and we had to scramble. I drove around a little, but a lot of those streets look the same and all the buildings look the same and I couldn't find the bar."

She wasn't allowing herself to believe him. He could see it on her face. "Look, Jake, it doesn't matter if you were going to call or not. We can't work together."

"Why not? If Kevin sent you, it means you're damn good at what you do. I'm damn good at what I do. There's no reason we can't open Jasper's Pub together by February."

"I thought being roommates with a man I'd never met would be weird." She shoved her hands in her coat pocket. "This is worse, I think."

Jake wished he had a coat to shove his hands into. When it was cold enough to see your breath when you talked, shirtless wasn't a great fashion choice. "I'm not going to lie to you. You being here feels like a second chance to me, but—"

She shook her head, but he pushed on, anyway. "*But* this restaurant and my partnership with Kevin are important to me. Important enough so I can set aside any personal stuff and keep it professional."

"You look cold."

"I was, but the numbness is setting in now, so it's not so bad."

"You should go inside."

"Kevin wants you in his corner on this project, Darcy."

"I know he does, and trust me, that matters." She was wavering.

"Let's try it for a couple of days and see how it

goes. If you still want to leave, you can tell Kevin I'm an asshole and I'll take the heat for it."

"I'm not here just because Kevin's a good boss and he asked me. It's an interesting opportunity and I was excited about it."

"It's still an interesting, exciting opportunity."

When she sighed, blowing out a frosty cloud, relief seeped through his frozen veins. She was going to stay long enough for him to make things work professionally. Personally? That could come later. Especially since it would probably be at least a week before his body thawed enough to even think about misbehaving.

"I'll stay. But if it's too awkward, I'm going to move to the motel and waste your money. If it's still awkward after that, I'm leaving."

"We'll be working too hard for awkwardness."

"I'll bring up my bags."

Because he was raised right, Jake willed the impending hypothermia away and helped her carry up her luggage, but he threw on a thermal shirt and a flannel shirt *and* his coat before he went back down for the boxes and bags she had crammed in her trunk.

On his third trip up, he realized both bedroom doors were closed and she was hovering over the growing pile of her belongings as if she wasn't sure what to do with them. "I was greedy and took the room with the queen bed, but we can switch if you want."

"Are they both as brown as the living room?"

"Yeah."

"Then it doesn't matter."

"Then that room's yours," he said, pointing to the door on the left. "At some point down the road we'll redo this apartment, but right now all the time and money are going into the pub's launch."

She shrugged, picking up a suitcase to bring into her room. "Doesn't matter to me. I won't be here after the launch."

"I'm not sure what I'll be doing. It's open-ended right now. After it opens, we might turn it over to a manager. But if I like it here, I might stay."

"Where did you come from?"

"Connecticut. But I'm a Red Sox fan, not Yankees. Connecticut goes both ways, but I was born in Mass."

It wasn't until she turned and glared at him that he realized that while they'd been talking, he'd followed her into her bedroom. He took a couple of big steps backward, until he was on the living room side of the doorway.

"This space is mine and you absolutely are not allowed in here," she said firmly. "I'm here to work, Jake. Nothing more."

"Yes, ma'am."

"Don't call me ma'am."

"Mistress?" Now, there was a word he liked. He let his gaze wander down the body his hands itched to touch again, dressing her up in his mind.

"Darcy's fine, thank you very much." She frowned at him. "Are you picturing me naked right now?"

"No."

"Okay, good."

"I'm picturing you in thigh-high, black leather boots, wearing one of those corset things that pushes your boobs up."

She snorted. "That sort of thing turn you on?"

"Never did before, but being punished by Mistress Darcy wouldn't hurt. Much."

"I think you're too bossy in bed to let a woman take charge."

"I think we should stop talking about this while I can still walk."

She slammed her bedroom door in his face, which was probably a good thing. One of them had to set boundaries because the last thing he wanted to do was tell Kevin their plan for Jasper's Pub was screwed because he couldn't keep his hands off the one woman he'd sworn he wouldn't touch.

CHAPTER THREE

DARCY DIDN'T WANT to get out of bed, even though she'd been awake long enough so she really needed to pee. But she waited out the sounds of Jake making coffee and taking a shower and the smell of slightly burnt English muffin. There was a horrible grinding sound, as if he'd thrown a bunch of rocks in the blender, and then, finally, the door closing and his heavy footsteps on the outside stairs.

She should have gotten in her car, driven back to Concord and fed Kevin the scary bear story. Even while she was telling herself the chance to be in on the opening of a new and hopefully successful restaurant was a golden opportunity, she knew deep down in some sappy part of her that she hadn't wanted to walk away from Jake so quickly.

Which was stupid and she knew it. He was a player and he'd played her. And now he was probably playing her some more to get done what needed to be done and save face with his business partner.

But when he was standing out there shivering, covered in goose bumps, but looking at her with those eyes, she'd felt just like she did before he kissed her as if he'd been waiting his entire life to kiss her and she hadn't wanted to leave.

So here she was, hiding in her bedroom to avoid the awkward sleepy morning moments like who got the bathroom and dancing around each other in the kitchen. Sure, this was going to go well.

After she showered, Darcy turned the toaster setting down slightly and made herself an English muffin and a coffee. He'd washed his mug and the knife, along with the blender, so there were no clues as to what he'd been mixing. Maybe some kind of weird protein drink or something, which would explain the abs.

No thinking about his abs, she reminded herself as she washed her few dishes and set them next to his to dry. Then, dressed in jeans and a Jasper's Bar & Grille polo shirt with her hair in a ponytail, and feeling a little more like her work self, she went down to face the day.

Because she was only going outside long enough to get down the stairs and in the back door, the key to which she'd found labeled and sitting on the counter, she skipped putting on her coat. She arrived for her first official day on the job half-frozen and cursing the unexpected windchill.

What seemed like acres of stainless steel

greeted her. She wasn't a cook and didn't know a lot about the different equipment, but it seemed as if Kevin and Jake had spared no expense when it came to outfitting the kitchen. What really mattered to her was on the other side of the double swinging doors.

Of course, the first thing she saw when she pushed through them was Jake. He was standing in the middle of the dining room, scowling down at something on the floor. When he heard the swish of the doors, he looked up and gestured her over.

"Take my hand," he said when she reached him.

"I'm guessing you haven't read the Jasper's sexual harassment policy."

"What?" Clearly distracted and annoyed, he held out his hand. "No. Just let me hold on to you and I want you to walk in front of me."

"Fine." She grasped his hand and crossed in front of him.

On the second step, her foot shot out from under her and only Jake's grip kept her from landing on her ass on the floor, or maybe even smacking the back of her head.

"I knew it," he muttered, but he didn't sound happy to be proven right about whatever he was talking about. "I crushed some ice this morning and put a few piles around the floor to melt. They told me this flooring wouldn't be slippery when it's wet."

"They lied."

"In my boots, it's fine. And in snowmobile boots, it'll be fine. But when the snow starts melting off those boots, the servers wearing sneakers like yours will be going down like bowling pins."

Darcy knew nothing about flooring and not much more about snowmobiling. "Do they make some kind of absorbent mats we could put under the tables? Maybe attractive ones that look like throw rugs?"

"Maybe we could lay down braided rugs. Homey feel and they're absorbent."

"And who's going to deal with a pile of sopping-wet, heavy rugs every night at closing? It won't be the wait staff. And they'd never dry completely."

"Good point. I'm going to have to research options. The amount of snow that might get tracked in isn't something I've ever had to factor into a restaurant plan before. Having a good mat inside the front door's always important, but snow melting off sledding boots while people eat is a new challenge."

Darcy was trying to pay attention to what he was saying, but somewhere around researching blah, blah, blah, she realized their fingers were still laced together. His hand was strong and warm and there was something incredibly comforting about the feel of it cradling hers. In fact, when she'd dreamt of him a few weeks back, it hadn't been the sex her subconscious had returned to. She'd dreamed of walking down the sidewalk with him, hand in hand.

"I need to call Peterson," Jake said. She knew Derek Peterson, of Peterson Construction, was handling the bulk of the remodeling and handling the various subcontractors.

His hand slid free of hers so easily as he walked away, she wondered if he was even aware they'd been linked. As he disappeared through the swinging doors, Darcy sighed and tried to shake it off. She had work to do, starting with exploring the waitress station setup and seeing how many different ways she was going to make him change it.

"FOR THE THIRD TIME, Jake, *big-ass* is not a cut of steak."

He grinned at her over the slightly burned, formerly frozen pizza sitting on the table between them. It was a very late dinner, so he'd gone for easy. "Sure it is. What kind of steak does a man want? A big-ass steak, that's what kind."

"We're not putting big-ass steak on the menu."

"Bet you a hundred it would be our top seller."

When she rolled her eyes and went back to sawing through the pizza crust, he laughed at her, but only on the inside. She was in a touchy mood and it was probably best she didn't know how much he enjoyed pushing her buttons. It was payback for the list of things wrong with the front end of the restaurant she'd given him. Three full sheets from the legal pad she'd filched from his office. She even wanted the commercial coffee brewing station moved—claimed it was too close to the pass-through window and would cause traffic jams—which meant contacting the electrician about circuits.

"We've been at this an hour and all we have is the Jasper Burger," she said. It was a crowd favorite at the Bar & Grille, so they'd put it on the menu and hope word of mouth spread that far north.

"And a big-ass steak."

"What about a pasta dish?"

He chewed and swallowed another bite of cheese-and-sauce-covered cardboard, chasing it with a swallow of beer. Screw the pub's menu. They needed to come up with a better meal plan for themselves. "I'm iffy on pasta."

"Right, because men like big-ass steaks cooked so rare a good vet could save them." She sounded on the verge of stabbing him with her fork, so he bit back the grin. "You're too focused on the sledders. This area's hurting for dining options, as we know since we're eating frozen pizza, so some good, reasonably priced family choices will draw in the locals and help keep the place going year-round. The big-ass steak crowd may bring in the gravy, but it's the spaghetti and meatballs and all-you-can-eat fish fry crowd that's the bread and butter."

"If the menu's too scattered, we'll go broke keeping all the ingredients on hand."

"True." She pushed her paper plate away and pulled her legal pad—which matched his—in front of her.

"How about you make a list of things you'd like to see and I'll do the same and we'll see where they cross over and go from there? We've both got the Jasper Burger and Jasper's Big-Ass Steak."

"Steak cut yet to be determined," she said firmly.

He made a few notes on his paper. She was right about the fact that he'd been overly focused on attracting the sledders and maybe not enough on building a community restaurant. The residential area was so scattered he wasn't sure they could sustain a steady business all year long, so his idea was to make as much money as possible during the snowy months and cut down to a skeleton menu and crew during the off-season. But maybe people would be willing to make the drive for a good, affordable night out.

Mostly, though, he watched Darcy making her list. She was cute when she was lost in thought. He could do without the constant tapping of her pen against the paper, but the way she bit at her bottom lip made *him* want to nibble at that spot, and with her free hand she twirled curls into bits of her ponytail.

She hadn't said anything earlier, when he'd forgotten to let go of her hand after the slippery floor experiment. She hadn't pulled away or commented on the fact, and he wasn't sure what that meant. To him, it just felt natural to hold her hand. But he couldn't take for granted she felt the same because the last thing he wanted her to do was pack up and leave.

"What?"

Damn, she'd caught him staring. "Nothing. Just staring off into space, I guess."

She went back to her list and he forced himself to focus on the paper in front of him. It wasn't working. "Did you know the potato famine lost Ireland about two million people, between death and emigration?"

Looking up from her paper, one eyebrow raised, Darcy shook her head. "No, I didn't. Where did that come from?"

"Oh. I wrote down French fries."

"Ah, potatoes. I get the connection." She started tapping the pen on the paper again. "How did you get to be such a trivia guy, anyway?"

He shrugged. "It was just my mom and me growing up and she had to work, so after school

I'd walk to the library and hang out there until she picked me up. After my homework was done I'd pull a random book off the nonfiction shelves and start reading. The almanacs were my favorites because there was a ton of information in little bite-size pieces."

"You should go on *Jeopardy*."

That made him laugh. "I don't think so. Not a fan of being in front of an audience, and trust me, under pressure I forget every bit of useless knowledge I've ever picked up."

"What happened to your dad?" As soon as she asked the question, Darcy's cheeks flamed and she waved her had. "Never mind. I take that back. Not my business."

"No, it's fine." He liked that she wanted to know more about him. "He took off when I was young enough not to remember him. I was in high school before my mom got married again, and he's a good guy. They're in Vermont, where my stepdad teaches, and I try to visit them a couple times a year. My mom and I have always been pretty close."

She smiled and warmth rippled through him. Damn, she had a great smile. "My parents live in a small town about forty minutes from Concord. I wanted a little more excitement, or at least the ability to see a movie in an actual theater, so I moved to the city after school. I see them at least once or twice a month."

"What do they think of you being up here for a month?"

"They're excited for me. Proud that Kevin thought enough of me to ask me to do it. They weren't quite as thrilled about me living with a stranger. I should probably warn you I have pepper spray."

He laughed and scribbled on his pad of paper. "Making a note of that."

"They like Kevin, so they decided to trust his judgment and not lock me in my old bedroom."

"Do you think they'll come up for the opening?"

"Oh. I don't know. Maybe?"

"You should invite them to the big Valentine's Day shindig."

She pointed the pen at him. "I've heard you call it a shebang and a shindig and a *thing.* What, exactly, are you planning for the Valentine's Day opening?"

"It's a secret."

"So, in other words, you have no idea."

"You don't think I have a plan?"

She smirked, which wasn't quite as attractive as her smile, but was still cute. "Is it as good as your plan to serve up burned frozen pizza so I'll take over the cooking?"

Busted. "I'm pleading the Fifth."

"And I'm pleading exhaustion. We can work on the menus more tomorrow and we also need to talk about placing an ad. I think it might be good to get one or two really experienced servers in here before opening, and I think we're going to be buried in applications."

"I'll be wrapped up most of the day with Peterson and the fire inspector and a few other things. I'll try to sneak in some menu planning so we can talk about it over dinner. Which, by the way, is your turn tomorrow."

"Whatever. Just throw the silverware in the sink and I'll wash the dishes in the morning."

While she was in the bathroom, he tossed the paper plates and dropped anything washable into the sink. As long as the day had been, he wasn't ready to turn in yet, so he flipped on the television and tried to get comfortable on the couch. Thirty seconds later he turned the TV back off and made a mental note to call the cable company. Or a satellite dish company. Any company that could offer him a distraction.

"Good night," Darcy said as she made the quick trip from the bathroom to her bedroom.

"Night."

And then there was silence. It was late enough so there weren't any cars driving by to make road noise that was just enough to drown out the slight creak of Darcy's mattress as she climbed into bed. The rustle of covers. The small sigh as her head hit the pillow.

He knew she slept on her left side, with her arm tucked under her pillow, because he'd been lucky enough to wake up curled around her, and the memory was slowly killing him.

And it was only the second night.

DARCY AVOIDED JAKE AGAIN in the morning by staying in bed until he'd left the apartment. The idea of having their morning coffee together, all sleepy-eyed and messy-haired, seemed intimate to her and she wanted no part of that. It was hard enough keeping their arrangement focused on the business.

She'd just finished washing the few dishes they'd dirtied when the phone rang. Kevin had arranged for a landline to be put in before Jake had even arrived, from what he'd said, because cell coverage was so spotty. Spotty being practically nonexistent, of course.

After drying her hands, she picked it up on the third ring. "Hello?"

"Hey, it's Kevin." She was hoping to be a little more settled in—both literally and emotionally—before reporting in to the boss. "How are things going?"

"Good." That was the truth, more or less. The

number of hours she spent tossing and turning, trying not to think about having sex with his business-partner-slash-old-friend Jake, weren't really Kevin's business. "We've made a lot of notes on the front end and we're working on the menu."

"You've got the Jasper Burger, right?"

"Number one on the list. Number two being Jasper's Big-Ass Steak."

A couple of seconds and then he laughed in her ear. "That'll sell out every weekend."

"That's pretty much what Jake said."

"I guess I should have told you he prefers Jake." That would have been nice, she thought. "Nobody but me calls him J.P. and he hates it."

"So I heard."

"Any problems? You guys getting along okay?"

"We've got a handle on it. Other than his genius plan to coerce me into cooking every night by feeding me burnt frozen pizza."

"Not much for takeout up there."

She snorted. "To say the least. The gas station was having a sale on microwave burritos, though, and just in time for my night to cook."

"Ouch. Is he around, by any chance?"

"He left about an hour ago."

"He was supposed to call me half an hour ago."

"Must have slipped his mind." Seemed to be a problem with Jake Holland.

"I'll leave a message on his cell so if he passes

through a signal, it'll remind him. Let me know if you have any problems, okay?"

"Yeah. Tell Paulie I said hi."

"She misses you. Says the new girl can only carry one plate at a time and doesn't know scotch from chocolate milk."

Darcy laughed. "It's nice to be missed."

They hung up and she debated on whether or not to go downstairs. The menu was her top priority because they needed to have ingredients on hand before they started hiring cooks. Once they'd narrowed the list down to a few choices, she intended to put them through their paces in the kitchen. They had to be able to master the Jasper Burger recipe, and they couldn't hire anybody who couldn't cook a perfect big-ass steak.

She worked on it for several hours, playing with and discarding meal ideas. Playing with the pricing. It was tough to balance the two demographics—hungry sledders with a little money to throw around versus families looking for an affordable night out—without a big disparity on the menu. And, as Jake had pointed out, they didn't want to be overstocked on a wide variety of ingredients right off the bat.

After a peanut butter and jelly sandwich for lunch, she set aside the pub's menu and started a grocery list. They needed real food in the apartment, even if she had to cook it herself, because being limited to things available at the gas station's convenience store was not only killing her appetite, but wasn't going to do her waistband any favors, either.

The trip to the grocery store took up most of the afternoon since it wasn't a short drive, and she was happy to see Jake walking down the apartment stairs as she parked her car. She'd been so focused on stocking their kitchen so she wouldn't have to make the drive again any time soon that she forgot she had to carry all the groceries up the stairs.

She was barely out of the car before he was looming over her. "Where have you been?"

"Not being a huge fan of peanut butter and jelly sandwiches, I went to the store and did some shopping. Actually, I like a PBJ sandwich now and then, but not with grape jelly. I like strawberry preserves."

"It didn't occur to you to maybe leave a note?"

"No, actually it didn't." Maybe she should have, just as a courtesy, but he needed to back off. "Are you going to help me carry these bags up?"

"Dammit, I was worried about you!"

"When I'm doing work for the pub, that's your business. When I'm not, it's not." She couldn't make it any more plain that he was overstepping. And because knowing he'd been worried about her made her feel all warm and gooey inside, she needed to nip it in the bud.

"We also happen to be sharing a living space, and no matter how platonic it might be, if you're going to disappear for hours, it's polite to leave a damn note."

"Fine." She could be just as loud as him. "Next time I'll leave a damn note. Hopefully it won't get wet."

When she tried to go around him to get to the trunk, he stopped her with a hand on her arm. "What's that supposed to mean?"

"Nothing. Forget it."

"I'm not lying about your number, Darcy. It was pouring and I was on a dirt road and a car was in the ditch. By the time I pushed her out, I was soaked and so was the paper. The ink ran and I couldn't read it."

"I said forget it. It doesn't matter."

He cupped her chin in his hand, gently but firmly lifting it so she had to look at him. "It does matter. You think I blew you off and I didn't. I wanted to see you again and because I was a nice guy and helped a woman get her car out of a ditch, you think I'm an asshole."

Her opinion of him wasn't anywhere near that low, but before she could tell him that, he bent his head and kissed her. There was nothing tentative or shy about it this time and it brought back every minute of that amazing—almost freaking magical—night. It also brought back the teenager-like giddiness as she waited for his call. And how hurt she was when the phone never rang. How stupid she felt.

How much worse it would be to add professional humiliation on top of it if she had to go running home before the pub was open, nursing a broken heart. She broke off the kiss, turning her face away from his.

"Darcy." His voice was rough.

"Technically, while I'm here I work for you. You're my boss and if you do that again, I'll quit."

She pushed past him and grabbed a few bags out of the trunk to carry upstairs. He could lug the rest. After dropping the load in the kitchen, she went into her room and closed the door. Dropping her head back against the wood, she tried not to cry.

He probably hadn't deserved that, but it was the only way she could think of to make him stop touching her.

Jake wasn't the first guy not to call when he said he would, but he was the first she'd invested that much hope in. It was the first time she'd cried into her pillow instead of muttering disparaging comments about the nature of men and moving on with her life. And that scared her.

CHAPTER FOUR

JAKE BURNED OFF some of his anger making trip after trip up and down the stairs with groceries, but by the time he'd brought up the last bag, he still had a low simmer going on.

She was full of shit. Their working together—and him technically being her boss—had nothing to do with her pushing him away. She was pissed he hadn't called her and she wouldn't allow herself to believe him no matter how many times he told her he'd tried. That wasn't on him and she was grasping at straws trying make it otherwise.

"I carried them up, you put them away," he called to her door. "I'm going to make sure they locked up downstairs."

He didn't say it out of courtesy but so, if she was in a snit, she'd know it was safe to come out and put the groceries away without running into him. The last thing he wanted to do after the day he'd had was sort canned goods from boxed and try to figure out how to fit everything in the fridge.

It didn't take as long as he'd thought to do a walk-through of the restaurant, so she was still at it when he returned. She looked calm enough, but he'd spent enough time watching her to see the tension in her shoulders.

Jake wasn't one to let things fester, so he grabbed a bag to unload. "I shouldn't have kissed you. You made it clear to me you weren't interested in anything but working with me, and I should have respected that. But the boss card?"

"That was uncalled for," she said before he could, which surprised him. "I just needed some space, and that was an excuse."

"And you're still mad at me. Admit it."

"Fine. I'm still mad at you. And before you say it, maybe you tried to find me, but I didn't know that, so I was hurt and I was mad."

And that's where the lashing out had come from. Not anger. Hurt. "How many freaking boxes of macaroni and cheese did you buy?"

"It's my favorite food."

"And you gave me shit about frozen pizza?"

"No comparison."

He lined up the boxes in the cabinet and peeked in another bag. "So, if you were hurt when I didn't call, I guess that means you cared if you ever saw me again or not?"

When she got really still, studying the label on a can of green beans, he forced himself to be patient and wait for the answer. "Yes, I cared. I wanted to see you again."

"And now?"

She set the can in the cupboard and turned to face him. "Throwing that whole boss and employee thing at you outside was wrong because of why and how I did it, but the truth is, I do work for you. More importantly, I work for Kevin and this is important to him. I don't know how much money you have to throw away, but he doesn't have a lot, so we have to make a success of this place."

"I promised Kevin I wouldn't touch you." Saying it out loud somehow seemed to make the guilt better and worse at the same time.

"Why did he think you would? I swear, if you told him—"

"I didn't. He didn't mean *you* specifically. He just didn't want me getting involved with whoever he sent."

"Is that a problem you have often?"

"No, which is why it pissed me off when he said it. And when you said it."

"I like you, Jake." The words would have had him singing and dancing on the inside except he heard a *but* coming. "But after one night, I liked you enough to be hurt when you didn't call. If we start something and then we have a problem, I won't be able to stay. I'll let Kevin down and I'll let myself down."

He was pretty sure if he backed her up against the counter and kissed her again, she wouldn't slap his face for it. But she was vulnerable right now, so that would make him a jerk. And she was right about Kevin. If the pub suffered or, God forbid, failed because things went south between him and Darcy, Jake would lose her *and* one of his best friends.

"I'm not giving up," he told her. "Once you're back at the bar, you might see more of me than you think."

"Sure. You'll call me, right?"

"Hey!" She laughed at him, then turned back to the last couple of bags of groceries. "Stop buying cheap pens, woman. We'd probably be married already if you'd used a damn Sharpie."

"You're a real funny guy, Jake Holland."

So damn funny he tossed and turned half the night, wondering how much truth was in his words and imagining what might have been if she'd just used indelible ink.

DARCY NEEDED CHOCOLATE. With alcohol. Alcohol-infused chocolate with a bag of potato chips on the side. She was going to strangle Jake Holland with her bare hands, even if she had to sneak up behind him and knock him unconscious first.

Her car was nothing more than a car-shaped mound of more snow than she'd ever seen fall at one time. The windchill could freeze a person's eyes closed if she took too long blinking. She felt caged in the building, and Jake was going out of his way to be as sexy as possible.

He had to be doing it deliberately. There was no way a man could be like that naturally. In the three weeks since they'd talked and come to an understanding there would be no sex, he'd gone out of his way to make her want him. She was sure of it.

Half the time the man didn't have a shirt on. January in northern New Hampshire and she'd find him painting the stall doors in the men's bathroom, dripping paint down his naked chest in a way that encouraged a woman's gaze to follow the eggshell path south. He must have switched shampoo or soap or something because she was constantly aware of how delicious he smelled. And half the time when she glanced at him, he was watching her with that same look in his eye he'd had the night they met, just before he'd kissed her.

She needed a distraction, so she picked up the phone and punched in the number for Jasper's Bar & Grille. And, just as she'd hoped, it was Paulie who answered.

"Hey, Paulie, it's Darcy. Can you spare a few minutes?"

"Of course. Let me pick it up in the office. Hold on." Darcy heard her yell to somebody she was taking a break and to hang up the phone after she picked it up in the office. Kevin had yet to invest in a real phone system. "Okay, that's better. So, hey, hear you guys are getting a hell of a snow up there."

"Yeah. It's making Jake twitchy because the sledders will be out in hordes this weekend and every engine he hears is lost dollar signs."

"Plenty of riding time left after the Valentine's Day thing. What *is* the thing, anyway?"

"He says he has a plan. He's yet to tell me the plan, but he says he has one."

"How are you two getting along?"

Now, that was a loaded question. On the surface they got along fine and worked together well. Under the surface? They were both a little ticked off they'd talked themselves out of having sex. But she couldn't say that. She and Paulie were friends, but Paulie and Kevin were best friends.

"We work together well" was what she settled for. "We were supposed to start interviewing wait staff today, but I think we're having a snow day instead."

"Oh, I should tell you Kevin wore his T-shirt to dinner at his parents' and now all the kids want one, too."

Darcy groaned. "I can't believe Jake had those made."

He'd special-ordered three T-shirts, one for each of them. Emblazoned on the front were the words *Jasper's Big-Ass Steak House.* She had to admit, she'd laughed pretty hard when he gave her hers.

They talked a few more minutes, mostly about what Darcy should be looking for in wait staff, but then Paulie had to go mediate a situation and promised to call later, when she had more time.

Sick of the beige walls, Darcy pulled on her parka, boots, hat and gloves, then wrapped a scarf around her face for the trek down the flight of stairs to the back door. It was that cold. Once she was in the kitchen, she reversed the process and piled it all up for the one-minute walk home later.

She heard Jake's laugh before she went through the swinging doors and she stopped, peering through the small window. She could only see him over the pile of stuff sitting on the coffee counter, waiting to be put away, but everything about his demeanor said he was talking to a woman. Whoever she was, she either had a sled dog team or drove the plow truck.

Darcy pushed through the doors and went around the counter to the table Jake was sitting at with a fortyish-looking woman with very short blond hair and a bright smile.

"Oh, here she is. Karen, this is Darcy Vaughn. She's more or less in charge of everything on this side of the swinging doors. Darcy, this is Karen Sikes. She's here to interview."

"Wow. I didn't think anybody would make it in."

Karen actually scoffed. "Let a little snow keep you from doing your business up here and it won't be long before you don't have any business to keep."

"Good advice," Jake said. "I know my four-wheel-drive's been getting a workout."

Darcy rolled her eyes. She didn't even want to think about how long it was going to take to shovel her car out. Not that she was going anywhere. After pulling out a chair, she took Karen's application from Jake to refresh her memory.

"Waited tables until I had my kids," Karen said. "Waited on them until they went to school, then went back to waiting tables until the restaurant closed down. You can't compensate for slow business by charging nine dollars for a cheeseburger. You have a menu yet?"

"It's still tentative." Jake pulled his copy out of one of the folders in front of him and handed it to her.

Karen's laugh echoed through the dining room, and she tapped a finger on the page. "Not a man I know who'll pass up a big-ass steak."

Darcy had done everything but beg Jake not to put that on the menu. The cut and the ounces were enough. But he was determined to prove her wrong, and so far, everybody seemed to love it. "I'm a little concerned customers won't want to say it out loud, which makes it hard to order."

"Honey," Karen said, "if you can't say big-ass steak, order the grilled chicken and some cottage cheese, because it's too much beef for you, anyway."

Jake tried to cover his amusement with a fake cough, but failed miserably and she kicked his ankle under the table.

"Little high on the children's menu." Karen marked the spot with her finger. "You want a couple of two-ninety-nine things, like a hot dog or PBJ with fries, and a couple of four-ninety-nine things, like chicken tenders or fish, but you want most to be about three ninety-nine. Grilled cheese sandwiches, mac and cheese, cheeseburgers. Basically you need to cut everything by at least a buck."

She must have caught the look that passed between Darcy and Jake, because she shrugged. "I was born and raised in this area and I've been taking food orders around here since I was fifteen. You can do what you want, of course."

They talked about almost every item on the menu. Then she gave them a list of names to beware of in the stack of applications. So-and-so had a drug problem and would steal from them. Another so-and-so was a sweetheart, but clumsy as an ox with a special knack for spilling coffee. They couldn't tell her if those people had applied or not, but Jake took careful note of them on his legal pad.

It was almost an hour before Karen left, and Darcy's head was spinning from the conversation. She not only knew everybody, but knew what they did and didn't want to eat.

"She's definitely got the knowledge," Jake said after Darcy grabbed them each a bottle of water from the kitchen. "Competent and definitely comfortable with the job."

She wasn't so sure. "Sometimes people like her don't take managing well. And when somebody's that firmly entrenched in the community, being *too* friendly can be a problem, to say nothing of the backlash if there was a problem."

"She's at the top of my short list."

"Mine, too. I just think we need to give her a lot of thought before we jump at making her an offer. But at least we know weather won't keep her from coming in."

He looked at his watch and winced. "We have to finalize that menu tonight, so you hold on to the copy with her comments on it and we can talk about it over dinner. I have to go call Kevin before his head explodes. I blew him off yesterday, so next time my phone picks up reception, I'll probably have a dozen messages from him."

"When's he coming up? Next Tuesday, right?"

"Yeah. He's going to come up Tuesday and look around. Have an on-site meeting. Then Wednesday we're going to hit the trails and he'll drive home Wednesday night. You want to go out with us?"

"Snowmobiling?" She laughed. "Absolutely not."

Shaking his head, he gathered his files and papers. "You don't know what you're missing."

"I'll live." She watched him walk away, loving the way his legs looked in worn denim, and he caught her looking when he spun around.

He winked. "By the way, your turn to make dinner."

JAKE WASN'T SURE HOW he managed to get through every day with Darcy. She would talk and he would try to listen. And on some level he retained the information because he always remembered the conversations later, but every time he was near her, all he could think about was sex.

If they were in the apartment, he'd imagine taking her on the kitchen table. Or bending her over the arm of the couch. The shower. The colorful braid rug she'd bought to cheer the place up. Sometimes he even imagined taking her to bed.

Downstairs, the possibilities were endless, though at least some of them were probably code violations.

"Hey, it's your turn. Unless you're ready to forfeit."

"Never." He took his iPad from her and looked it over. They were playing Trivial Pursuit and she'd just blown an Arts & Literature question. Which was good because she had one more piece of the pie than he did and he didn't intend to lose.

When he landed on the correct space to get the orange Sports & Leisure wedge he needed and knew the answer right away, Darcy made an annoyed sound and leaned back against the couch.

"I think you're cheating."

He laughed. "How would I be cheating?"

"I bet you hide under your covers and play this all night so you can memorize all the answers."

That's not at all what he played with under the covers, but he'd be keeping his nocturnal activities to himself. "You know, you're not a very good sport."

A few minutes later, when she'd added a pink wedge to her collection, he rolled his eyes. "It's the Entertainment category. You're just getting the easy ones first so your pie looks better than mine."

"Now who's a poor sport?"

Inevitably, it became a race for the last wedge each needed, and the game got really intense. And when he blew his Geography question, the words he muttered were pretty intense, too.

Darcy grabbed for the iPad. “My turn.”

He held it out of her reach. “Don’t be grabby.”

“It’s my turn.”

“It’s my iPad.”

She made a mock pouty face at him. “Oh, are you going to take your toys and go home now?”

When she made another grab for it, he held it up over his head because he was tall and she was short, and she *hated* when he did that.

What he didn’t anticipate was Darcy losing her balance and ending up straddling his lap or her hands bracing themselves on his chest. Or the way, to keep her from falling backward and knocking herself out on the monster coffee table, his hand slid under her ass.

His body reacted immediately to the weight of her on his lap and he looked into her wide eyes. He wanted to say something flip, like “now who’s cheating?” but he was pretty sure nothing would come out but a hoarse whisper.

When her weight shifted, which he was afraid might cause things to explode, he thought she was moving back to her own side of the couch. Instead, she settled herself more comfortably on his lap, her knees on either side of his hips.

"This is a bad idea," she said.

"Very bad," he agreed.

"I don't care anymore. Every single day I'm practically out of my mind, wanting you to touch me. I need you and screw the consequences."

Jake dropped the iPad. Maybe on the arm of the couch or maybe on the floor. Didn't care. All he cared about was sliding his hands up under Darcy's shirt and feeling the heat of her soft skin.

All that mattered was touching her.

CHAPTER FIVE

DARCY DIDN'T CARE if it was a bad idea. She didn't care if everything blew up in her face tomorrow. All she cared about was getting Jake naked. Now.

The shirt was easy and she practically purred running her hands over his bare chest. Then she leaned forward and ran her tongue up his breastbone to his Adam's apple. He moaned, one hand clenching in her hair while the other pushed down on her hip, grinding her against him.

"I've missed you," she said before yanking off her shirt.

"I've been right here."

"I've missed *this.* Us." She undid the button on his jeans, loving the way his stomach muscles tensed when she brushed them with her knuckles.

Very slowly, she worked his zipper down and then she rose onto her knees to give him room to shove his jeans and boxer briefs down past his hips.

When she took him in hand, stroking him with the same slow deliberation he'd teased her with, he groaned and dropped his head back against the couch cushion.

"Don't do that too long if you have plans that include you," he warned.

"I've waited too long to let you have all the fun."

She had to stand to step out of her clothes while Jake fished a condom out from under the couch cushion.

"Do you have those hidden around the apartment?"

He grinned and tore open the foil. "Yes, I do. Strategically placed for almost any opportunity."

She laughed and straddled him again, this time relishing the heat of naked flesh. With her hands on his shoulders and their gazes locked, she lowered herself onto him. As she rocked her hips, slowly taking him all in, he fisted his hand in her hair and pulled her mouth to his.

His kiss was savage, devouring her as he cupped her breast, pinching her nipple between his thumb and forefinger. She squirmed, her hips circling, and he groaned.

"No more games," he said in a low, rough voice. "From now on, I'll touch you when I damn well feel like touching you."

She threw back her head as he gripped her hips and forced her to ride him faster and harder. Her fingertips dug into his biceps as his hips jerked to meet her thrusts.

"Come for me, Darcy."

The orgasm hit her hard, and when it was over, she collapsed against Jake. His chest heaved with every ragged breath and he tightened his arms around her.

"I needed that," she whispered when she could talk again.

"Give me a couple of minutes. I'm not done with you yet."

"I think the hideous fabric on this couch wore half the skin off my knees."

His chuckle reverberated through her body. "How do you think my ass feels?"

"It was worth it."

"Yes." His hand stroked up and down her back, making her shiver. "But bed next."

"My bed's closer."

It was another five minutes before they'd recovered enough to make it there and quite a bit longer before either of them slept.

KEVIN DIDN'T ARRIVE until almost noon. Usually Jake would be annoyed at having half the day blown waiting for him, but since he and Darcy didn't roll out of bed and into the shower until ten o'clock, it was probably for the best. And they didn't get out of the shower until the water started running cold.

That wasn't the way Jake wanted Kevin to find out he'd done the one thing he'd specifically told him not to do.

"Everything looks great," Kevin said after Jake and Darcy had given him the grand tour. "I knew you two would be good together."

Jack managed to keep a straight face, but through the corner of his eye he saw Darcy take a deep and sudden interest in her shoelaces. "Everything's right on track."

"How about the Valentine's Day thing?"

"I've got a rough draft of the ad upstairs," Jake said. "We can look it over later."

"There's an ad?" Darcy jabbed him with her elbow. "You haven't even told me what the thing is yet."

"You'll find out."

"She'll be back at the bar by then," Kevin said. "Once the doors open, the front end will be the wait staff's responsibility and Darcy can come home where she belongs. God knows, we need her. Courtney, the temp girl we hired to cover for you, is driving Paulie nuts. She flirts to drive up the tips, but guys start vying for attention and it goes downhill from there."

Jake laughed with the other two, but he wasn't feeling the humor. He didn't want to think about

Darcy leaving. He couldn't imagine wandering around their ugly brown apartment alone. Not seeing her every day. He didn't *want* to imagine it. "Unless she decides to move up here and manage the pub. She's got a lot invested in it."

"Yeah, right." The two words were like a blade through his heart. "I couldn't wait to move to the city after school, and this is even smaller than the town I grew up in."

Jake wasn't stupid. He'd known the time both of them were doing the same thing and working toward the same goal was limited. Eventually they'd have some decisions to make about how their relationship would go forward after Jasper's Pub opened for business.

He hadn't realized how closed she was to the possibility of staying where they were, and that was a problem. He really liked it. He liked the quiet and the snow and the people and he really liked the restaurant they'd built. A three-hour drive each way didn't preclude them seeing each other, but it was enough to put a crimp in a relationship.

Kevin and Darcy were chatting about the wait staff applications and how she felt about Karen Sikes, who was probably going to be their senior server and manage the other wait staff.

Jake didn't care. And he didn't care about the menu and he tuned out the dinner conversation about why Darcy had chosen one coffee supplier over another. And he was aware Kevin kept shooting him questioning glances, but he didn't care about that, either.

He cared about whether or not he and the woman he was pretty sure he was in love with had a future together.

The next morning Jake was up early, disentangling himself from Darcy's arms and leaving her bedroom as quietly as he could. He dressed in layers and downed a cup of coffee before driving up the road to the motel to meet Kevin. Since the motel had a small café that served breakfast, they ate there before donning their snowmobile gear.

Kevin was pretty quiet, Jake thought as he pulled on the bibs and coat that belonged to Kevin's brother, Joe. He'd be riding Joe's snowmobile, too, since Jake's was still in Connecticut. Maybe the motel mattress had sucked and he'd had a rough night. Maybe the stress was getting to him. Or maybe he was just missing his wife and daughter.

They'd put on almost fifty miles before Kevin parked on the side of the trail and took his helmet off. Jake did the same, then rummaged through the tank bag for one of the candy bars he'd stashed there.

"I asked you not to get involved with whoever

I sent up here," Kevin said without introduction. "That was the only thing I asked of you."

There was no sense in denying it. One, he wouldn't lie about it and, two, if Kevin picked up on it, they weren't doing a very good job of hiding it. "Remember the pretty, fun and wicked-smart woman I spent the night with before I came up here?"

"Yeah."

"That was Darcy."

"No." Kevin threw up his hands. "Why the hell didn't you tell me that?"

"We didn't know. Her number got wet and I couldn't read it to call her. I tried everything I could think of to get her number and couldn't. Drove around and couldn't find her place. And you always call me J.P., so…I don't know. And we'd talked about you sending somebody up to help, but you weren't sure who and you must never have told me her name because all of a sudden, there she was."

"How serious is it? She's supposed to come home soon."

"And it sounds like she's not only going to, but she's looking forward to it, so don't worry about it." Jake heard the edge in his voice, but it was too late to temper it.

"You don't want her to leave."

"No, I don't."

"Then make her want to stay."

Jake laughed, his breath hanging in the cold air. "That easy, huh?"

"No, it's not easy. It took me a year to convince Beth I was the guy for her. A damn year. It's not easy at all."

"Maybe we can do the long-distance thing until the pub's in the black enough to hire a manager."

Kevin shook his head. "I hate to say it, but that might be a while."

"I know. And I *want* to run it myself. And I want to wake up with Darcy every day. I want it all."

"If it's meant to be, you'll find a way." When Jake looked sideways at him, Kevin winced. "Yeah, that might have been stitched on my grandmother's pillow."

"Or in a fortune cookie."

"Just don't screw things up with her before the pub opens or I'll have to kill you."

"You're a good friend, Kevin. Really."

"You know it, J.P. Let's rack up some miles."

THREE DAYS LATER, Darcy was curled up on the couch, going over the final menu proofs, when the phone rang. Because they didn't have internet, she'd had to drive forty minutes to the "local" printer they'd chosen and back in the snow to get the PDF files, and she was tempted to let the answering machine pick up. She'd just started to relax.

But odds were it was Jake, Kevin or a contractor calling, so she threw back the lap blanket and went to answer it.

"Hey, Darcy."

It was Jake, and as always, her heart did a little happy dance at the sound of his voice. She purposely kept her voice all-business, though. "What's up?"

"I'm at the supply house and I need the number for the guys who installed the walk-in freezer. The business card is....somewhere in the apartment. Can you find it and call me right back? It's urgent."

"You're sure it's not in your wallet? Or in your truck?" He liked to tuck business cards in the strap on the back of the sun visor.

"I double-checked both before I called. It's probably on the counter. Or the coffee table. Probably. It's there somewhere."

"I'll call you right back." Maybe. *Somewhere* wasn't a lot to go on.

There was no business card on the counter. Nor on the coffee table. It wasn't in the spot he usually threw his keys or near the coffee mug where he tossed the coins he accumulated in his pockets. Maybe it was on his nightstand or dresser.

She hadn't been in his bedroom. Maybe it was

a subconscious effort at separation, but they'd always kept their doors closed. He'd been in hers, of course, but she still hadn't been in his.

He'd said it was urgent, though, so she turned the handle and poked her head in.

The room was pretty much identical to hers. Beige. Brown. Blah. His bed was bigger and there was a straight-back chair next to his dresser, but that was it. He was surprisingly neat for a guy, and she didn't have to wade through balled-up socks to get to the pile of scrap paper she saw on his dresser.

He might not throw his dirty socks on the floor, but the man would jot a note on just about anything. A reminder to check sprinkler system laws on the back of a gas receipt. A guy's name and a number on the corner of a napkin. The deeper in the debris pile she sifted, the further back in renovations the notes referred to.

One crumpled piece of paper had the intriguing title of "Google searches." Under that, in his slanted chicken scratch: *trivia Concord, NH; bars trivia Concord, NH; Concord Tuesday trivia.* In the margins were bar names and phone numbers. All had a line scratched through them. The next sheet of paper had the name of an auto garage. Then the Concord library's number. And at the bottom of the pile was a small piece of paper that had obviously gotten very, very wet. She could make out the pattern across the top as that of her fridge memo pad, but her name and number were just a black smudge bleeding out into nothing.

He hadn't been playing her, after all. He'd tried to call her. The evidence that he'd invested a lot of time and energy into trying to get in touch with her was spread across the dresser, and she felt the sting of tears in her eyes. Why hadn't she listened to her heart instead of her stupid head and believed him when he told her that? Repeatedly.

It didn't matter now. They'd moved past that, but seeing how hard he'd tried to find her after just one night together squeezed her heart.

She loved him. Maybe it had been love at first sight or maybe it had crept up on her, but she knew it was real and she knew it was twisting her up inside. She couldn't imagine what life would be like without him—other than painful—but it was almost time to go home.

She *had* a home. And she missed Jasper's Bar & Grille and Paulie and everybody else. Her friends. Movie theaters. Takeout.

Jake loved the life he was making here. She could see it in him. He thrived on it and there was more than pride in his eyes when he stood in the pub and looked at what they'd done together. There was affection. He'd made this his home.

His home and her home were three hours apart as the highway rolled, but worlds apart in reality. And she wasn't quite sure how he felt about her. She knew he cared about her and enjoyed the sex and her company, but it would take the forever kind of love to work through the obstacles in their path. Anything less would crumble under the weight of logistics and distance and absences.

A WEEK LATER, Jake looked over the dining room of Jasper's Pub and felt the warm glow of satisfaction. It was finally opening night and they weren't packed, but there had been a steady enough stream of diners to call it good.

They'd done the advertising and radio spots. Kevin had handled getting the website and Facebook page up. Now it was up to word of mouth and, judging by the comments he'd overheard here and there over the course of the night, it would all be good.

Karen kept the wait staff on their toes while keeping a perfect balance with the customers. Her natural warmth and friendliness was a draw, but she didn't cross over into too casual and chummy with them. Every dish was coming through the window perfectly cooked to order, and there was nothing for him to do but soak it in.

He spotted Darcy, who was acting as an unofficial hostess, coming toward him and smiled. She was wearing the same mulberry-colored Jasper's Pub polo as the wait staff, which he thought was a lot nicer than the ones they wore at Jasper's Bar & Grille.

"It's going even better than I'd hoped," she said a little breathlessly, keeping her voice low.

"And every single table has ordered at least one Jasper's Big-Ass Steak."

She rolled her eyes. "I've not giving you a hundred dollars."

"I'm sure we can come to some other kind of arrangement."

"Stop it. We're working." But she gave him a look that assured him they'd come to terms. "I'm really proud of this place."

"You should be." He hooked his pinky finger with hers, keeping their hands behind her hip to hide the contact from the dining room. "It was a lot of work and a lot of decision-making and you pulled it off."

"*We* pulled it off."

He liked the sound of that. Hopefully that *we* would be long term. "I think we'll be ready for Valentine's Day."

They were running meal specials for couples, with packages that included dessert and a bottle of champagne. All the lodging establishments in the area had coupons on display, offering discounts at the pub. Kevin had launched an advertising blitz that ensured that practically every guy in

New England who had a snowmobile knew Jasper's Pub was the place to be on Valentine's Day.

There would be flowers and a few special treats not available on the regular menu. They'd considered having a live band, but not only was space an issue, but sometimes people felt awkward having conversations while a band was playing, and that wasn't the atmosphere they were going for.

He also had a diamond ring in his sock drawer. He'd bought it two days ago, when Darcy thought he'd had to go down to the city to handle a fictional problem with their liquor license.

"I hope I'll be able to get back for that," Darcy said, snapping him out of his happy thoughts.

"You have to come back. It's what you've been working for."

"No, tonight's what I was working for. Everything's set. Everybody knows their jobs. From here on out, it's you and Karen."

The glow dissipated and he stepped around her. "Come out back with me."

She followed him through the kitchen and into his office. He took a deep breath as he closed the door, trying to figure out what he needed to say not to ruin everything.

"What's the matter with you?"

He turned to face her, leaning back against the door. "That's not the first time you've made reference to maybe not being here for Valentine's Day.

I don't get it. Why would you work so hard and then not be here with me?"

"I have to go home. I've been gone over a month and I have a life there. I have a job and I have bills that need to be paid and plants to water. I have no idea how crazy it's going to be."

"What about us?" He kept his voice low, but the words were a deafening shout in his head. "Is there going to be time for me anywhere in there?"

He saw the temper rising in her face. "What is it you want from me? I've been here over a month and when I got home I'll barely be unpacked before I have to leave everything again and come back. I'll try. That's all I can do."

It wasn't enough. He straightened up and opened the door. "All right. Maybe I'll see you then. Maybe not."

"What did you expect?"

"I expected you to come spend Valentine's Day with me. Then I expected to take a trip south to see you. I expected we'd figure it out as we went along. And I expected to be more of a priority than watering your fucking flowers."

"Jake."

"It's been a pleasure working with you. Thanks for the help."

CHAPTER SIX

AND, JUST LIKE THAT, they were done. Darcy watched him walk away, her heart breaking and her mind spinning, scrambling to come up with anything to say that might bring him back.

There was nothing. Maybe because she couldn't quite figure out how it went so horribly wrong so fast.

Afraid she was going to come undone in front of the kitchen staff, she grabbed her coat off the hook and went up to the apartment, replaying the conversation over and over in her mind.

Maybe she hadn't expressed herself well. Maybe he'd overreacted. Maybe it was a little of both, but there was no maybe about the fact that they were over. He'd been so cold at the end, his body language totally unforgiving.

She cried for an hour, drenching her pillow in her effort to be quiet in case Jake came upstairs. She never heard him, so either he was very quiet or he stayed downstairs until after she'd cried herself to sleep.

He was gone before she woke up, and she spent the morning packing her car. When the cooks and Karen showed up to start prepping and there was still no sign of Jake's truck, she said her goodbyes, wished them all luck and hit the road.

It felt as if she were leaving her heart behind. The drive seemed endless as she fought to keep her emotions under control. She'd been right all along. The pain *was* too much to bear and she should have walked away the day she got there.

She gave herself twenty-four hours to wallow in heartbreak and then she showered, dressed and drove to Jasper's Bar & Grille.

"Darcy!" Paulie was so glad to see her she gave everybody a round on the house.

The other woman had barely gotten her arms around Darcy for a welcome-home hug before she started sobbing on her shoulder.

"Shit. Office. Let's go."

She let Paulie lead her there like a little kid and push her into a chair. Once the door was closed, Paulie got comfortable in Kevin's chair. "Okay, spill."

So she spilled. The entire story, from meeting at trivia night to finding out Jake and J.P. were one and the same to the horrible end of the story the night Jasper's Pub opened. By the time she was finished, she was pretty much cried out, which was good because she'd decimated the box of tissues Kevin kept on his desk.

"You know I love you," Paulie said. "You also know I'm not good at the whole girl-talk thing, so I'm going to be straight with you. You're both idiots."

That surprised a laugh out of Darcy, and she knew she'd come to the right shoulder to cry on. "How did we screw it up so badly?"

"He's a man and you're a woman. Trust me, that comes naturally." Paulie grabbed a bottle of water out of the mini fridge and handed it to her. "Obviously Valentine's Day's a big deal for him."

"It's a big deal for the pub, yes."

"And he wanted you to be there with him and you told him you'd see if you could fit it in?"

"He wanted me to be there for the pub. That's work."

"Are you sure? It's the most romantic holiday of the year, and you guys are supposed to be doing the falling-in-love thing, so what do you think it says to him that you don't really care one way or the other if you spend it with him?"

Darcy picked at the label on the water bottle. "He kept saying I'd worked too hard to miss being there. Why didn't he tell me he loves me and he wants me to be there with him?"

"I don't know. Because he's a guy?"

"Then tell me, Dr. Paulie, why *wasn't* it more

important to me to spend the most romantic night of the year with him?"

"I don't know. The female mind is a screwed-up thing. Men are easier."

"Great." She drank some of the water just because Paulie had gotten it for her. "We were in work mode and Valentine's Day has been a work thing. If he'd asked me while we were cuddling on the couch or in bed or something if I'd go back to spend the evening with *him,* it would have been different, I think."

"So tell him that."

Darcy shook her head, blinking back a new wave of tears. "When he walked away, it was like he flipped a switch. It was over."

"Doesn't work like that. There is no switch when it's the right guy. It can be years and then you see him and—*bam*—you can't even breathe."

That's how it had worked for Paulie and her husband. It had been years since she jilted Sam at the altar, but he'd walked into Jasper's one day and, as she said, *bam.*

"I'll tell you one thing," Paulie continued. "If you love him and you think there's even the slimmest chance you might still work it out, you have to be there on Valentine's Day."

"Even if he won't speak to me?"

"He will. Like I said, there's no switch."

"It'll hurt if it's not enough."

"It hurts now, right? The important thing is that you let him know he *is* more important than whatever else you have going on. If it's not enough for him, we'll put his picture over the dartboard and have a tournament. But I'm thinking I won't fire Courtney just yet."

JAKE HAD HEARD THAT absence made the heart grow fonder. Now he knew it also gave a guy time to think and realize he'd acted like a total jerk.

On the first day, when he came home to find her car gone and a note on the counter that said nothing but *good luck* and her name, he'd stayed good and pissed off. The second day the heartache and the missing her kicked in. Day three had brought the first inklings of clarity. And today came the realization he'd totally blown it.

Darcy didn't know the Valentine's Day thing was about more than two-for-one Big-Ass Steaks and putting Jasper's Pub on the map. She didn't know he'd been working on the right words to say to make her want to stay with him. She didn't know about the ring. She didn't know he was going to tell her he loved her and ask her to be his wife.

He'd basically told her she'd worked too hard not to be there to watch happy couples eat their half-price steaks and then totally overreacted when she pointed out she had a life that had been on hold for over a month and might need some of her attention.

And to really top things off, he still didn't have her freaking cell phone number. Wasn't that just a kick in the ass?

There was nothing he could do but call the Bar & Grille and hope Kevin would give him the number without verbally taking his pound of flesh first. He'd screwed up, he knew it, and he wasn't in the mood for a lecture.

"Jasper's Bar & Grille, Paulie speaking."

"Hey, it's Jake Holland. Is Kevin around, by any chance?"

He was beginning to wonder if she'd hung up on him before she finally answered, "He's not, actually. Something I can help you with?"

"I need Darcy's number."

"I'm sorry. We don't give out our employees' personal information."

He knew she wouldn't make it easy for him. "Technically, she's been an employee of Kevin *and me* and I need to contact her, which is entirely different."

"Really? That's the way you want to play it?"

He sighed. "I love her and I fucked up and I need to make it right."

"You got a pen?"

Screw pens. He had a fat-tipped permanent marker and a big beige wall. "I'm ready.

"Thanks, Paulie," he said when he'd read it back to her just to make sure he didn't screw that up, too. "I hope she'll listen to me."

"I'll tell you the same thing I told her. There's no off switch. Stop being idiots and work it out."

He took a few minutes to gather his courage and give some profound speech time to pop into his head. Nothing came, so he took a slug of beer and dialed Darcy's number.

And got sent straight to voice mail.

When it beeped, signaling it was his turn to talk, he still didn't know what to say. "Hi, it's Jake. I…uh. I'm sorry. That's the most important thing. I'm sorry. I really want you to spend Valentine's Day with me. There's this great place called Jasper's Pub and they're having a special dinner. I'd like you to be here because…dammit, I'm not telling you I love you on your voice mail. I want you to be my date because it's Valentine's Day and it won't be special without you. That's it, I guess. I'm sorry and I hope you'll come back."

He hung up and rested his forehead against the kitchen cabinet. All he could do now was wait. And plan. It was going to be a Valentine's Day she'd never forget.

If she came.

DARCY COULDN'T BELIEVE how many snowmobiles were parked up and down the road in front of Jasper's Pub. There were some in the parking lot, too, along with a respectable number of cars and trucks. Jake and Kevin had pulled it off. With her help, of course.

Thankfully nobody had parked in the two spaces marked as reserved for the apartment, so she parked next to Jake's truck, even though she technically shouldn't. But she was wearing heels instead of boots and there was a limit to how far she could walk in the damn things. Especially in the cold.

She went around to the front door and stood inside, taking it all in. There were couples and laughter and roses and trays of chocolates and little candy hearts set around the dining room, as well as down the bar.

Nerves danced in her stomach and it took all of her self-control not to reach over and snatch a glass of champagne from the nearest table. She'd listened to his voice mail message a hundred times just to hear him say he wouldn't tell her loved her on her voice mail, but she was still anxious about seeing him. She probably should have called him back, but she was afraid talking things through over the phone could go wrong so easily.

Smoothing the front of the red dress she'd bought just for the occasion, she looked around the restaurant again, this time looking for Jake. She was expecting him to be moving around the room, checking on customers and helping the staff, so she almost missed him sitting at the bar, an empty stool next to him.

Then Karen spotted her. "Look, everybody, Darcy's here!"

And everybody turned to look before a cheer went up. She froze, not sure what the hell was going on. Then Jake turned to face her, and nothing else mattered anymore. Paulie was right. There was no off switch.

He walked over to take her hand. "My partner's here, so let's play!"

She let him lead her to the stool. "What's going on?"

"It's the Valentine's Day thing. Shindig. Shebang. Whatever you want to call it."

She'd anticipated a quiet table in the corner where they could talk. Instead, all eyes were on them and Karen, for some reason, had a microphone. *God, please don't let it be karaoke,* she thought.

"Okay, everybody, let's play Valentine's Day trivia! Remember, the winning couple doesn't pay for dinner." From what Darcy could tell, half the room had signed up to play. But Karen looked at her. "Jake and Darcy, you're up first. Which day of the week is said to be named in honor of the Norse god of combat and victory?"

Jake rested his arm across the back of her stool

and leaned over to brush his lips against her ear. "Tuesday."

The night they met, which was funny. "Tuesday," she repeated to be official.

"That's correct!" Karen went around the room, asking each couple a Valentine's Day-themed trivia question. Darcy wasn't sure how Tuesday fit in, but it was fun, anyway.

When their turn came around again, Darcy didn't miss the wink Karen sent Jake's way. "Which permanent marker was introduced by the Sanford Ink Company in 1964?"

Again, Jake brushed his lips across her ear. She really couldn't think when he did that. "Sharpie."

It wasn't until Jake answered a question about a popular stove-top dish introduced by Kraft Foods in 1937 that Darcy realized the questions had very little to do with the holiday at hand and a lot to do with her.

This time she did the leaning over and whispering in his ear. "What are you doing?"

"I asked myself what kind of gift I could give you for Valentine's Day that would be uniquely you."

"Uniquely *us,*" she corrected.

His expression grew serious and he laced his fingers through hers. "Is there still an us?"

The diners around them applauded and cheered for another couple, and Darcy sighed. "Is there someplace more quiet we could talk? Maybe come back to this later?"

Without letting go of her hand, he signaled to Karen that they'd be back and led her into the kitchen. She was surprised when he took her out the back door and up the stairs. Luckily there was no wind, so she wasn't too numb by the time he closed the apartment door behind them.

The first thing she saw was her telephone number scrawled on the wall in black marker. "What did you do?"

"Didn't want to lose it again." When he shoved his hands in his pockets and hunched his shoulders, she could tell he was nervous. "I know this isn't the most exciting place to live. And I know you like your job at the bar and have your own place. And I'm not going to lie to you. I like it here. Even if I hadn't given my word to Kevin that I'd stick it out until it ran in the black long enough to hire a manager, I'd drag my feet about leaving. But I want you in my life, Darcy, even if it's only for one weekend a month and a week here or there. I'll take it, if you still want me."

"I'll always want you."

"And I'm sorry I was a jerk that night. I was excited about Valentine's Day because that's when I was going to tell you I love you. It's all I could think about, and when you said you might not come… I know it's stupid because you didn't know what was in my head, but I felt like you'd rejected me." He had to stop and clear his throat. "I got so wrapped up in the life I was making here I lost sight of the fact that you already had one waiting for you to go back to."

"You know what my life there doesn't have that this one does? You. And I love Jasper's Bar & Grille. I always will. But when I was there, I realized that's Kevin and Paulie's place. They built it together and it's special. I feel that here. This is ours and it's special."

"I love you, Darcy." He pulled his hands out of his pockets, and in one hand he had a small box. "I bought this before you left."

He opened the lid, and Darcy's breath caught in her throat. The diamond caught the light from overhead and winked at her. "It's beautiful."

"I want to marry you. I love you and I want you to be my wife."

"I love you, too. And I want you to know I'd made up my mind to come tonight before you called. No matter what I was going to be here."

"So, will you marry me?"

"Yes. Did I forget that part? Yes, I want to be your wife."

He barely got the ring over her knuckle before she threw her arms around his neck and kissed him. As he held her close and their breath mingled, she realized she'd get these kisses for the rest of her life, and everything else—logistics and moving and work—faded into the background.

"I shouldn't have told Karen we'd be back," he muttered against her neck as his hands roamed down to her ass.

She laughed and pushed him away. "It's our big night. And we have a trivia tournament to win."

"Just so you know, we're not actually eligible to win. Technically, you know all the answers."

"*We* know all the answers," she corrected.

"I'm going to love being a *we* with you. Let's go celebrate."

* * * * *

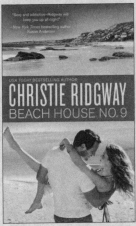

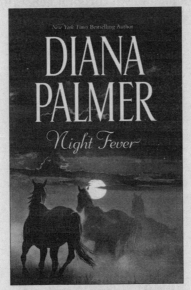

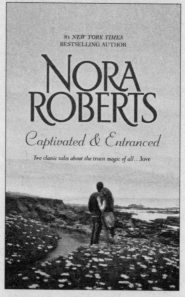

New York Times Bestselling Author

CARLA NEGGERS

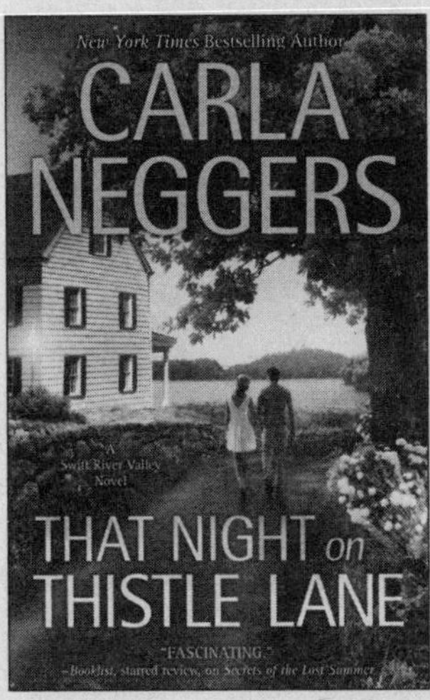

Librarian Phoebe O'Dunn deals in stories, but she knows that happy endings are rare. Her life in Knights Bridge, Massachusetts, is safe and uneventful...until she discovers the hidden room.

Among its secrets is a cache of vintage clothing, including a spectacular gown—perfect for the gala masquerade. In the guise of a princess, Phoebe is captivated by a handsome swashbuckler who's also adopted a more daring persona. Noah Kendrick's wealth has made him wary, especially of women: everybody wants something.

When Noah and Phoebe meet again in Knights Bridge, at first neither recognizes the other. And neither one is sure they can trust the magic of the night they shared—until an unexpected threat prompts them to unmask their truest selves.

Available wherever books are sold.

MCN1420